Praise for
The Woman Who Lied

"Her best yet. It's gripping, atmospheric, and so original."
—Gillian McAllister, author of *Wrong Place, Wrong Time*

"Thrilling, twisty, and impossible to put down. Claire Douglas at her very best." —Tim Weaver

"A gripping read, so cleverly plotted and brimming with tension."
—Gilly Macmillan, author of *The Long Weekend*

"An intriguing, twisty mystery combined with first-rate suspense—hard to put down."
—Shari Lapena, author of *Not a Happy Family*

"A tightly plotted, dazzling thriller, filled with Claire Douglas's trademark suspense. An up-all-night read."
—Lucy Clarke, author of *One of the Girls*

"So many ingenious twists, so many gasp moments. I absolutely loved it." —B. P. Walter, author of *The Dinner Guest*

Praise for
The Girls Who Disappeared

"Thrillingly tense and twisty."
—B. A. Paris, author of *The Therapist*

"Clever and terrifically compelling, I think *The Girls Who Disappeared* might be my new favorite Claire Douglas novel!"
—Sarah Pearse, author of *The Retreat*

"Claire is a mistress at weaving the reader into a web of domestic deceit." —Jane Corry, author of *The Dead Ex*

Praise for
Just Like the Other Girls

"*Just Like the Other Girls* is just the sort of distraction I need at the moment: an immersive page-turner with numerous red herrings and a twist I didn't see coming."
—Sarah Vaughan, bestselling author of *Anatomy of a Scandal*

"A wickedly clever page-turner of a psychothriller."
—Emma Curtis, bestselling author of *One Little Mistake*

Praise for
Last Seen Alive

"Fast-paced and chock-full of twists, *Last Seen Alive* is both absorbing and gripping. After reading it you'll never dream of a house swap again."
—Paula Daly, author of *The Mistake I Made*

THE WOMAN WHO LIED

ALSO BY CLAIRE DOUGLAS

The Sisters

Local Girl Missing

Last Seen Alive

Do Not Disturb

Then She Vanishes

Just Like the Other Girls

The Couple at Number 9

The Girls Who Disappeared

THE
WOMAN
WHO
LIED

A Novel

CLAIRE DOUGLAS

HARPER

NEW YORK · LONDON · TORONTO · SYDNEY

HARPER

Originally published in 2023 in Great Britain by Penguin Random House UK.

FIRST U.S. EDITION

Library of Congress Cataloging-in-Publication Data has been applied for.

ISBN 978-0-06-327746-5 (pbk.)
ISBN 978-0-06-338263-3 (library edtion)

24 25 26 27 28 LBC 5 4 3 2 1

For Ty – here's to the next twenty years!

THE WOMAN WHO LIED

Prologue

May 2022

There is a film of sweat on DC Anthony Haddock's top lip and his fringe is stuck to his forehead, his tie askew. He has purple smudges under his eyes and his shirt is creased. Emilia must look as exhausted as he does – she had no sleep last night. She can't even remember if she brushed her hair this morning (definitely not her teeth) and she's still in yesterday's clothes.

'I want to say again how sorry I am for your loss,' he says sincerely. He has a large Adam's apple that bulges in his skinny neck as he swallows. She can't stop looking at it. She digs her nails into her palms to prevent herself from crying. She can't really blame him, this man in his rumpled short-sleeved shirt that makes him look like a sixth-former. She should have made more fuss when she was first introduced to him last month, and then maybe they wouldn't be here now, in this stifling, claustrophobic room on the hottest day of the year so far.

She shifts in her seat, her skirt sticking to the backs of her legs. The notebook – the one she started using on the advice of another police officer, back when all this began – sits between them on the table. Her fifteen-year-old daughter, Jasmine, had given it to her for her birthday in January to plot out her new novel idea, her first stand-alone. It has colourful butterflies in descending sizes on the front and Emilia always felt it represented renewal, a change. Growth. Yet it never fulfilled its purpose. Instead, it contains all the warped events that have taken place over the last few months. The macabre echoes of stories already written. And now a murder. Someone she loved.

'We're doing everything we can to catch whoever is behind this.' He's silent for a few moments, his pale eyes never leaving hers, then says, 'And you're sure this is someone you know?' DC Haddock glances down at the list of names she's just given him.

'Yes. I'm sure of it.' She wishes she was wrong but she knows she's not. 'Only my close friends and family have read *Her Last Chapter*, apart from my editor, of course. It hasn't been published yet. And some of what's happened, especially in the last few weeks, well, it's come from that manuscript.'

He nods sagely, his thin lips set. He doesn't say anything. He doesn't have to. His silence speaks volumes and the implication is clear. Because she, Emilia Ward, best-selling crime writer of the popular Detective Inspector Moody series, is running out of time. At the end of *Her Last Chapter* she kills off her beloved main character, DI Miranda Moody. If the pattern continues, if whoever is doing this is keeping to the plot of the book, it means there's only one main event left in the manuscript.

DI Moody's death.

And, therefore, hers.

PART ONE

I

March 2022

Emilia is on the bus home, staring out of the window at the overcast sky and thinking she'd eaten too much for lunch, when it happens.

A blur of flashing lights and the blare of sirens as a police car whizzes by, followed in quick succession by two more.

She doesn't think much of it. Another accident. She's used to them. This is London after all and it's 4.45 p.m. on a Friday, the beginning of the weekend rush hour. She leans back against the seat, wondering if she can find a way to loosen the waistband on her skirt. She shouldn't have said yes to that apple crumble and custard. *Grazia* magazine pokes out of the bag at her feet. She'd bought it before catching the bus from High Street Kensington, but the journey has taken so long and she feels so confined that she hasn't picked it up for fear of travel sickness.

An elderly woman wearing a patterned orange headscarf sits next to her hugging a long-haired sausage dog on her lap. As the bus chugs to a halt, belching fumes that blow in through the open window, she tuts impatiently. She turns to Emilia with an exasperated expression. 'Rigsby's going to need a wee in a minute.'

The dog looks up at Emilia with sorrowful brown eyes. She smiles reassuringly at the woman, but bends down and moves her bag so it's between her thigh and the window, just in case Rigsby decides to release his bladder on her beloved Mulberry tote.

They are on the Kew Road. Soon they'll be passing Kew Gardens, but due to the tube strikes the roads are busier than usual. So here she is, stuck on a bus with the aroma of the Cornish pasty that a young guy is devouring in the seat in front of her, and the threat of a urinating dog. She can't wait to tell Elliot about her meeting with her editor when she gets home. She'd rung him briefly as she left the restaurant, mainly to remind him to collect Wilfie from school, but hadn't had the chance to tell him everything.

She'd been so anxious this morning: she couldn't find her favourite leopard-print scarf, then forgot where she'd put her house keys.

'You'll be fine,' Elliot had said when she was finally ready to leave. He kissed her cheek so as not to mess up her lipstick. 'Just be honest. She'll understand. It's your career, after all.'

So, honest she had been – to an extent anyway. Her editor, Hannah, had paled beneath her make-up when Emilia admitted she wanted to kill off the main character in the book she was writing, her tenth in the series.

Hannah is nearly eight months pregnant and Emilia was worried she'd send her into early labour. Her elegant fingers curled around her glass of lemonade as though frozen while Emilia explained that with book eleven she wanted to write a standalone thriller and that she felt DI Miranda Moody's story was over. She didn't admit that this book had been one of the hardest to write and, at one point, had doubted she'd ever be able to come up with a good enough plot.

It had taken Hannah a few moments to respond. Eventually, in a strained voice, she said, 'The Moody series has sold over two million copies in the UK alone. It's a huge risk.'

Emilia knew that, of course she did. And it terrified her. But she felt it was the right time. Ten books in ten years, and writing *Her Last Chapter* had been a struggle.

The lunch ended on a kind of truce: Emilia would send over the first draft of *Her Last Chapter*, which included DI Moody's death, and Hannah would see if it worked. If not, Emilia would change the ending, take a break and write something else but keep it open for a DI Moody return in the future.

The bus still hasn't moved and all Emilia can see is the queue of traffic ahead. She wonders if she should continue her journey on foot, it's only twenty minutes from here, but if the bus driver refuses to let her off she'll have to do the walk of shame back to her seat in front of all these people.

The double doors at the front of the bus ping open with a sucking sound and a police officer boards. Instantly the passengers fall silent, glancing at each other questioningly. The woman next to her leans to the right so she has a view down the aisle, then turns to Emilia and barks, 'What's he doing on here?' as if Emilia's going to know.

'Maybe he's telling the bus driver there's been an accident,' she replies politely. 'Or that the road's blocked.'

The policeman exits the bus and the driver stands up to address them.

'I'm sorry, everyone,' he says, his face ruddy and his jacket straining across his large belly. 'But I'm afraid there's been a serious incident further along this road. Unfortunately you'll have to disembark here.'

People start groaning and cursing. The man in front stuffs the remnants of his pastry back into its paper bag. The woman beside her tuts loudly and mutters about the inconvenience. At least Rigsby can pee now, Emilia thinks as she watches her place the dog on the floor of the bus, as though he's made of glass. Emilia can't wait to get off, but she sits patiently as everyone else gets up and shuffles towards the front. Her phone rings as she's stepping onto the pavement.

'Hey, Jas.' The wind picks up and she has to pull her leather jacket around herself, wishing she'd worn a warmer coat. A crowd from the bus has congregated in front of her and she can't get past. Rigsby has cocked his leg against the nearest lamppost.

'Where are you? Wilf's being, like, a *brat* and Elliot isn't doing anything to stop him, and Dad is supposed to be picking me up, but he's late and I can't find my high-waisted jeans.'

She takes a deep breath and moves her phone to the other ear. 'They should be in the tumble-drier . . . I'm on my way home. I think there's been some kind of accident.'

'Accident?' Emilia can hear the fear in her daughter's voice. Despite being touchy and hormonal, underneath it all she's sensitive and a worrier.

'It's okay,' Emilia reassures her. 'It's not involving me. But I've had to get off the bus.'

'Can't Elliot pick you up?'

Emilia glances at the road. Vehicles are lined up almost bumper to bumper in both directions. Someone is tooting their horn, which instantly sets her teeth on edge. Why do people do that? It's not going to make the traffic move any quicker. She manoeuvres around the hovering group and begins to walk quickly, her heels clipping the pavement. 'No, it's not far and the roads are jammed. It's quicker for me to walk.' She hesitates. 'I thought your dad was collecting you from school.'

Jasmine huffs down the phone. 'Something came up apparently so I caught the school bus. He said he'll pick me up at six instead.'

Emilia imagines her daughter rolling her eyes as she speaks. She knows Jasmine has a complicated relationship with Jonas. 'Okay, I'll be as quick as I can. And your jeans –'

'I know, I know. Tumble-drier you said.' There's lightness in her voice now, which lifts Emilia. She worries about Jasmine. The lockdowns have had a negative impact on her mental health, although Elliot has been great with her, giving her advice after suffering with anxiety himself as a teenager. Jasmine always was a little socially awkward, but returning to school for year ten had been particularly challenging for her and she'd struggled initially to settle back in.

'If you're gone before I'm back, have a lovely time at your dad's and see you Sunday. Love you.'

'You too,' Jasmine says, and hangs up.

Emilia slides the phone into her pocket and picks up her pace. She'd like to be home before Jasmine leaves. She thinks of her ex-husband, Jonas, and his wife, Kristin – her one-time friend – playing happy families with her daughter. Somehow she's managed to stay close with Jonas for the sake of Jasmine, but it hasn't always been easy. She finds it harder to forgive Kristin.

Emilia hoists her handbag over her shoulder, wishing she'd worn her flat boots. As she's about to turn down a side-street she notices a police officer in a fluorescent yellow coat directing traffic, two fire engines and a number of police cars blocking the road. She wonders what's happened.

2

'I don't know what was going on but there were police everywhere,' Emilia says to Elliot later, as they make dinner in their large open-plan kitchen. It's her favourite room in the house, with its pale wood parquet floor, marble work surfaces and navy blue cabinets. It's the hub of their family, a place they all congregate. It was a pipe dream when they moved in four years ago, but after five months of building work to extend and refurbish, it was ready last year in time for Christmas.

'Couldn't you ask your copper friend, what's-her-face?' Her husband is dreadful with names. Everyone is either what's-her-face or what's-his-name.

'Louise. I could, although she's in CID, so I doubt she'd know.' She reaches down, gets four plates automatically from the cupboard and places them on the worktop, then remembers Jasmine is at her dad's and puts one back. She hates it when Jasmine is away. The house feels too large, too empty without her. Elliot said Kristin had come to pick her up as Jonas wasn't sure when he'd be able to get away from the office. That had instantly annoyed Emilia. He only sees Jasmine every other weekend – the least he can do is make sure he leaves work on time.

She turns to assess Elliot as he stands at the stove, his soft cashmere jumper straining across his broad shoulders, accentuating his slim waist and his tanned skin. She has often wondered over the years whether, if Kristin had set her sights on Elliot, he would have succumbed as easily as Jonas. He's so different from her ex, not only in looks – dark and stocky while Jonas is wiry and blond – but in personality. Jonas always was a bit of a flirt: he likes to think other women find him attractive and charming, wanting everyone to like him, always the life and soul of the party, the last to leave the pub, always out with different mates. Elliot is honest, sometimes brutally so (he once told her she looked like Morticia Addams when she dyed her hair a few shades darker) and would quite often shy away from social situations, but at least she knows where she stands with her second husband.

Elliot wanders towards the TV at the family-room end of the kitchen; a mirror image reflects back at them from the bifold doors that lead onto the garden. He picks up the remote from where Wilfie had thrown it onto the grey linen sofa. 'It might be on the news.' He turns to smile at her as he aims the remote at the TV and her heart explodes with a sudden burst of love for him. He's a good man. A solid man. He's not vain. As an author, she earns more than he does and it doesn't bother him at all. It's because of her money that they can afford this five-bedroom detached whitewashed Victorian villa on one of Richmond Hill's premier streets. Jonas had sworn under his breath when he'd first seen it.

She stirs the wok, satisfied to see the chicken and peppers sizzling away nicely, the smell making her stomach rumble despite her huge lunch.

'Dad! Can I watch *Adventure Time*?' Their eight-year-old son, Wilfie, bursts into the room from the den, clutching his PlayStation controller and hopping from one foot to the other, a ball of energy with wavy dark hair like his dad's.

'Hold on, little man,' says Elliot. 'Just need to check the news – Mum saw something interesting on her way home and we just want to . . .' But Wilfie's already left. Elliot raises his eyebrows at Emilia and she laughs. It's a long-standing joke between them that their son is never still for long enough to do anything, apart from eat and sleep. When it comes to food he takes after her.

'Dinner's nearly ready!' she calls after him, although there's no answer. She's only allowing him on the PlayStation because it's Friday night. He's certainly taking advantage of it – he's barely surfaced from it since she got home.

'Hold on . . . I think this must be it,' says Elliot, backing towards her, his eyes trained on the TV.

She turns off the wok and goes to stand beside him.

He wraps one arm around her shoulders. She feels tiny at just over five two compared to his nearly six feet. They watch as BREAKING NEWS flashes onscreen and then a well-dressed news presenter with an immaculate blonde bob is talking over a series of photos that show the entrance to Kew Gardens and the police outside.

'There has been a serious incident today at Kew Gardens in London. Police had to evacuate visitors and clear Kew Road directly outside the popular tourist attraction over fears of a terrorist attack. Personnel at Kew Gardens received an anonymous tip-off, at approximately four twenty-five p.m., claiming a bomb had been left in the grounds. A duffel bag was located by specialist police but we've since been informed that it was a hoax, and the bag contained an old transistor radio.'

The presenter moves on to another story and Elliot switches off the TV, placing the remote on the coffee-table. He moves over to the stove and she follows, her mind mulling over the news item.

It's very familiar.

'Probably teenagers thinking they're funny,' he says as he dishes out the stir-fry. 'It's serious, though. If they got caught . . .' He looks up and must see the expression on her face because he asks her what's wrong.

She shakes her head. 'Nothing. It's just . . . I dunno. A bit weird.'

'What?'

'In my first book – you know, *The Fire Starter* . . .'

'How can I forget?' he says, his eyes softening. They'd met in a café while she was writing it, nearly eleven years ago. She was going through the divorce and renting a little flat with Jasmine after Jonas had bought her out of their marital home in Twickenham. She'd always wanted to write a novel but after university she'd taken a job on a local newspaper. She'd just landed a role as a staff features writer for one of the Sunday supplements when she found out she was pregnant with Jasmine. She'd been twenty-three, broke and living with Jonas, whom she'd met in her first year at university in Brighton, and the pregnancy hadn't been planned. As soon as she'd broken the news to Jonas he'd proposed and they'd married a few months later: a small, somewhat rushed affair at the local register office.

After Jasmine was born she couldn't afford to go back to work full time: the nursery fees would have eaten up her modest salary and her parents lived too far away to help – not that they would have done even if they'd lived in the same town – so she freelanced when she could. When Jonas left her she used the time while Jasmine was at school to write a book about a female detective with a no-nonsense attitude. Someone strong and ballsy because at that time she'd felt so weak and impotent.

Elliot had wandered into the riverside café on his lunch break from visiting a client. Her first impression of him was that he had warm brown eyes. Kind eyes. They'd got chatting after she'd asked if he could watch her laptop while she went to the loo.

'How did you know I wouldn't run off with it?' he'd asked later.

'Because you have a trustworthy face,' she'd replied.

He still uses that against her now when she accuses him of taking the last bag of crisps or using up the remainder of the coffee. *What – me? But I have a trustworthy face!*

'What about it?' he asks now, rooting in the cutlery drawer.

'Well,' she says, as she carries the plates to the oak-topped dining table. 'I wrote about this happening. A hoax call. A duffel bag with a transistor radio inside, left at Kew Gardens, remember?'

He dumps the knives and forks on the table with a clatter. 'These things happen. It's London. It's just a coincidence, that's all. You wrote that book years ago.'

Of course it's a coincidence. That's just the kind of rational thinking she loves about her husband. She always goes from zero to a hundred. But he's right, it's just one of those things. It will be kids mucking around, she suspects.

Like in her book.

Elliot turns back to the island. She watches him, trying to push away the niggling feeling that this is *too much* of a coincidence. It's been eleven years since she wrote her debut, and it's not like she can remember it word for word. But it's coming back to her now.

When the bomb scare happened at Kew Gardens, her main character, DI Miranda Moody, was travelling along Kew Road on a bus that had to be evacuated.

Just like she had been.

3

'Ma'am. It's this way. She's up there . . .'

DS Saunders is pointing to the wind-battered building overlooking the sea front. It's late afternoon, the sky is a thick white and Saunders stamps his feet against the cold. Either that or he's running out of patience. It's hard to tell with him. I'm his boss so he can't very well tell me to hurry the fuck up, although I'm sure that's what he's thinking. I don't tell him I busted a gut to get here, or that when I received his call I was trying to persuade my elderly father that the wife he doted on – my mother – really would be better off in a nursing home. Or that my ex-husband has just announced he's getting married again.

In the five years we've worked together I haven't told him a thing about my private life. It's better that way. Although, because he never stops talking, I know all about his. Not that there's much to know except a lot of drinking in pubs with his mates after work, and the women he falls for hard and fast but never seem to return his feelings.

We flash our badges at the two uniformed officers who are guarding the property and stop to put on shoe covers. Police tape is already erected around the site. They step aside *to make way for us. We duck under the tape, careful not to touch the front door as we head into the hallway and up the stairs. The brown carpet is threadbare, the walls a salmon-painted woodchip.*

The smell hits me as soon as we reach the top of the stairs. The door to the bedsit is open and the scenes-of-crime officer is already in the small bedroom just off the hallway. Saunders and I stand at the threshold of the bedroom, careful not to touch anything, waiting to be allowed into the room. From where we stand we can see the victim is lying on the bed on her back, her hands and feet tied. She's wearing a teal satin nightdress, the front soaked with blood.

The SOCO looks up. It's Celia Winters. Mid-fifties and fierce. We know better than to walk into the room while she's doing her job. Her whole demeanour is serious, professional. You wouldn't know that we're friends, or that we regularly go out drinking, more often than not ending the night singing tunelessly at the karaoke bar in Plymouth town centre.

'Stabbed,' she clarifies. 'Multiple times. Time of death to be determined but I'm thinking she's been dead at least twelve hours. And there's something else.' She walks over to the victim's leg. 'Here on the ankle . . .'

I turn to Saunders knowing that his expression and the adrenaline rush will be mirroring mine. We hold our breath expectantly. Waiting. Already knowing what she's going to say.

'. . . a marking. Like a recent tattoo but made with a

kind of penknife. It's fresh and I think it was done just before she died or maybe just after. You probably can't see it from there but it's small and quite intricate. Triangular with these weird eyes and antennae. I've never seen anything like it before. But it looks like an insect's head.'

I exchange glances with Saunders. We know exactly what it is even though we haven't seen it in years and Saunders only from police photographs.

A praying mantis.

And then Celia seems to twig. We've talked about it before even though she hadn't been working with us the last time he struck.

Her mouth falls open. 'Shit,' she mutters, her eyes locking with mine.

My voice sounds grim even to my own ears. 'It looks like he's back.'

4

The front door is open, light spilling onto the frost-coated pavement. Jonas has his back to her so doesn't notice as she gets out of her Nissan Leaf and makes her way carefully down the path, trying not to slip. That's one of the many things she doesn't miss about her ex-husband: how impractical he is. Not like Elliot, who has already dusted their driveway with rock salt. It's unusually cold for the beginning of March.

'Hurry up! Your mum will be here in a minute,' he calls up the stairs. He must hear or sense her at the threshold as he spins around and smiles through his strained expression. 'Oh, hi, Em. Sorry she's not ready. I've been telling her for the past fifteen minutes to get her stuff together.' He shrugs to give the illusion of nonchalance but she can sense the stress coming off him like steam. Has Jasmine been playing up? Jonas doesn't always know the best way to handle their daughter's moods.

'How has she been?' she asks in a low voice.

He grimaces. 'Not too bad. Spent most of yesterday up in her bedroom although Kristin did take her shopping this morning. Come in, you'll get cold standing on the doorstep. Do you fancy a cup of tea while you're waiting for Her Highness to get her act together?'

She steps over the threshold into the hallway. It's been decorated a few times since she lived here and now has a warm stone colour on the walls, brass wall lights and a huge mirror that makes the small space look much bigger. Apparently, according to Jasmine, Kristin is going through an 'interior design phase'.

Emilia contemplates the offer of tea. On the odd occasion, when Kristin isn't around, she's agreed. But she'd noticed Kristin's Mini convertible outside. 'Thanks, but I'd better be getting back,' she says, closing the door behind her but just so that it rests on the latch.

'Sure.' His smile wavers and she's reminded of that time, a year or so after they split up, when, after dropping Jasmine back to hers, he'd surprised her by admitting he missed her. She'd just started dating Elliot and she'd put it down to him suddenly wanting something another man had. Which was typical of him. He's never mentioned anything since but the knowledge is like a secret jewel she occasionally holds in her palm to marvel at before tucking it away again in the folds of her memory. 'How's the book going? Finished yet?'

'Just. Sent to my editor today.'

'What's DI Miranda Moody up to in this one?'

'It's my darkest yet, I think. A serial killer who brands his victims with an insect's head. Women stabbed to death. Nice and light!' She lets out a self-deprecating laugh. 'Oh, and Miranda dies at the end.'

'What?' Jonas stares at her with wide, shocked eyes. 'Why would you do that? You know I love the old boot!'

'She's had ten books. She's had her day.'

He stares at her, like she's grown an extra head. 'But why?'

'I want to write something different.'

'I bet your publishers aren't too happy.'

'We've come to a compromise.' She tells him about her lunch with her editor on Friday.

'So Hannah's reading the finished version now?'

'Well, I doubt right now. It's Sunday. But hopefully she'll get back to me soon because if she really doesn't think it works she'll ask me to keep the ending open. Maybe have DI Moody severely injured but not actually dead . . . I don't know yet. Maybe that's the best thing to do.'

'I personally think you should keep it open. But, then, I'm a fan.'

'You have to say that, as the father of my child!'

'Have to say what?'

They turn as Kristin appears in the hallway. All five foot ten inches of her – and most of it legs, her dark hair gathered in a messy but somehow elegant knot atop her head. A sliver of fake-tanned flesh shows through the cut-outs at the shoulders of her jumper. Nearly forty and still as gorgeous as when Emilia had first met her back at university. Instantly Emilia feels dumpy and she pulls her thick wool coat further around herself as though for protection.

'We were just talking about Em's new book.'

'Ooh, yes. I'm intrigued. Loved the last.'

That's one thing she has to give Kristin and Jonas credit for. They've always been supportive of her writing. Fascinated, even. Maybe they're terrified they'll appear in one of her books. The pen mightier than the sword and all that. She has been tempted.

'Thanks.' Emilia's cheeks grow hot. She never knows how to take Kristin. Even when they were friends Kristin could swing from charming to acerbic in the blink of an eye. But she'd admired her go-getting nature and her wicked sense of humour. Nobody has ever made her laugh like Kristin used to back when they were friends. And, even though she was gorgeous, she never took herself too seriously – on nights out, she would goof around on the dance floor, not caring how she looked. Even now, all these years later, part of Emilia misses their friendship.

Kristin leans into Jonas, and he drapes an arm over her shoulders, smiling contentedly. It's been eleven years but it still gives Emilia a surreal jolt to see them so loved up, like she's tumbled into an alternative universe.

'We have some news,' Kristin pipes up.

'Oh, yes?' Is Kristin pregnant? She's surprised that it hasn't happened yet. Kristin used to say she'd love kids one day. She glances at her former friend's stomach, which is still as flat as it was when they were twenty-two.

'We're moving! At last!'

She feels a surge of relief that there will be no baby yet. Jasmine was still so young, just four, when Emilia met Elliot and then, three years later, had Wilfie. But the disruption and emotional upheaval of a new baby in their lives might not be the best thing for her daughter right now.

'That's great news. Where?' *Please don't say Richmond. Please don't say Richmond.*

'Teddington. By the lock. A gorgeous house. So much more space, isn't it, darling?'

Jonas nods and smiles tightly, but Emilia isn't fooled. She can sense the panic behind his eyes.

'I'm really pleased for you.' She knows it's been hard financially on Jonas since they'd split and he'd had to find the money to buy her out of their house. He'd never wanted to move, which he's always said was down to his parents living a five-minute walk away, but she suspects it's because he's lazy and can't be bothered with the disruption. Although she remembers the flicker of envy in his face when she and Elliot bought their Victorian villa four years ago. She gets the feeling Kristin isn't much help on the money front, swapping one venture for the next.

'Thank you.' Kristin's bright blue eyes gleam. 'I'm really excited about getting my hands on the decor. I'm thinking white walls and pale floors. The light is particularly special. Can't wait for you to see it. It's lovely to be able to choose my own home, at last. This one . . .' she says and glances around the narrow hallway '. . . it's not what I would have picked.'

Jonas raises an eyebrow at Emilia but doesn't say anything, although she's tempted to ask Kristin what she'd have chosen if she'd been working on a local newspaper for a meagre salary at the age of twenty-three and pregnant. Emilia had always thought she and Jonas had done okay for themselves, buying an actual house when they were so young. But Kristin hadn't had to worry about all that. She'd been swanning around Australia at the time with some rich boyfriend whom everyone thought she'd marry.

'Anyway,' says Emilia, glancing pointedly at her watch – although without her glasses on she can't actually read it, 'where's Jas?'

Jonas turns away from her to bellow up the stairs and Jasmine thunders down, rucksack over her shoulder and her mobile attached to her ear. 'Yeah, yeah, I said I was coming.' And then into the phone, 'I'll ring you back, Nance.' She pockets her mobile and brushes her blonde hair off her face. When she reaches the bottom of the stairs, she thrusts her feet into a pair of chunky white trainers that Emilia has always hated.

'Come on, then, sweets. Let's go,' says Emilia, placing an arm around Jasmine's shoulders.

'Is Aunty Ottilie still coming over?'

She can't help the small flicker of pleasure as Kristin squirms at the sound of their once mutual friend's name. Not that Ottilie has spoken to Kristin for the last eleven years. The three might have been inseparable in their late teens and the first half of their twenties, after Emilia had introduced Kristin to Ottilie, but Emilia has known Ottilie since they'd joined their cold, uptight boarding school at the age of eleven and their bond runs deep. Ottilie has never forgiven Kristin for breaking what she's always called the 'girl code'.

'Yes, she is, along with Grampy Trevor.' Trevor is Elliot's dad so not technically Jasmine's grandfather but she's always adored him and vice versa.

'How is Ottilie?' asks Kristin, trying to look disinterested, even though Emilia knows she's always had a strange fascination with her. Most people who meet her do. She's unlike anyone else Emilia has ever known.

'She's great. Amazing, actually. She's started dating someone although I haven't met him yet. He lives in Germany. She met him when she was visiting her dad in Hamburg.'

'I'm pleased for her.'

'And Elliot is cooking a roast.'

It's childish of her, she knows, but Jonas is a terrible cook.

'Ooh, Elliot does the best roasters,' exclaims Jas, much to Emilia's delight.

'How lovely,' Kristin trills as Emilia opens the door, 'to be able to eat roast potatoes. I haven't eaten carbs since 2008.'

Jasmine gives her dad and Kristin a perfunctory hug goodbye and Emilia ushers her down the path as quickly as is humanly possible in the icy conditions, relieved to get back into the car. God, she can't wait until Jasmine is old enough to drive so that she doesn't have to face her former friend every other week.

5

Jasmine pushes open the unlocked front door, dumps her rucksack in the porch next to the expensive lurid green bicycle that Elliot always promises to ride but never does, races through the glass double doors that lead to their spacious hallway and straight upstairs. Emilia is left to pick up the rucksack. She hasn't the energy to call her back down.

She's about to take it to the utility room when she hears a woman's voice coming from what they call the 'posh front room' because they only really use it when they have guests. It has a teal blue velvet chesterfield-style sofa, floor to ceiling bookshelves and no TV. Ottilie is perched on a gold velvet armchair in the bay window, still in her white fake-fur coat and hat, her hair spilling over her shoulders. She looks like a snow queen. Elliot is on the sofa, a glass of wine in his hand. When Emilia walks in, he excuses himself to check on the dinner, looking relieved to be able to make a hasty exit. She knows Elliot finds small talk difficult, even with Ottilie, who never lets him get a word in anyway.

'Mils,' Ottilie squeals when she sees her – she's the only one who ever calls her that, a hangover from their schooldays when everyone called her Milly. She jumps off the chair and catapults into Emilia's arms. She smells of fresh air and expensive perfume. They haven't seen each other for more than a month, but even if they'd met yesterday this is how Ottilie would greet her.

Emilia laughs. 'How was Hamburg and when do I get to meet the new boyfriend?'

'Fabulous as always, and soon. I promise. His name's Stefan and I'm so excited about this one.' Emilia doesn't point out that she always is. She doesn't really understand why Ottilie's relationships never work out, except that her friend admits she's fiercely independent and refuses to adjust any part of her lifestyle to accommodate someone else.

'The spare room is all made up if you want to stay,' she says, taking Ottilie's coat and hat. They hang over her arm like an Arctic fox.

'Thanks, but I'll get an Uber home later.' Even though her dad, Charles, lives in Germany he was savvy enough to buy a flat in South Kensington back in the late 1970s, which Ottilie now rents from him for a pittance on the proviso he stays with her when he's back in the UK. 'My dad's basking in the Indonesian sunshine at the moment with his latest squeeze.' She rolls her eyes but Emilia knows it hurts her. Her mother died when Ottilie was young and she has always looked around for a mother figure, but never found one in her father's succession of younger women. 'When does Trev get here?'

Ottilie is the only person allowed to call Elliot's father 'Trev', probably because Trevor's a little in love with Ottilie. Elliot's mother died eight years ago, and even though she and Elliot suspect Trevor has had girlfriends, he's not met anyone serious. He likes to come to dinner at least once a month, but always on his own.

Emilia checks her watch. 'He'll be here in about half an hour. I'd better get changed.' Ottilie is wearing an emerald-green 1930s dress with a diamanté clasp around the waist. She looks like a film star and suddenly Emilia feels very underdressed in her boyfriend jeans and baggy jumper, even if she did put on extra makeup to go and pick up Jasmine.

Elliot returns with a glass of wine for her. 'Hi, beauty, how's Jas doing?' He hands her the glass.

'She's rushed straight into her room to gas away with Nancy,' she replies, taking the wine and sipping it.

'Just like us at school,' says Ottilie. 'Do you remember the time Mrs Maynard sent us out of the classroom because we couldn't shut up?'

Elliot raises an eyebrow. 'Now why doesn't that surprise me?'

'It was a regular occurrence.' Emilia laughs. 'Right, I need to get changed.' She slugs back more of her wine, then gives the glass to Elliot. Before heading upstairs she checks on Wilfie. He's sitting on the sofa in the kitchen watching a cartoon while simultaneously leafing through a comic.

'Grampy will be here soon,' she says, ruffling his hair.

Wilfie groans. 'It's going to be boring grown-up talk.'

'You know Grampy used to be in the police force a long time ago when your dad was a boy. You could ask him about it.' This week Wilfie has decided he wants to be a detective when he grows up, like Toby's mum, Louise. Last month it was a fireman.

'I wanted to ask Toby's mum about it the other day but she wasn't there.'

'Toby's mum isn't around that often. You know that.' Louise has become a good friend to Emilia since her son joined the school in year two and has been invaluable in helping her with her latest Miranda book. But Louise works long hours so it's usually Frances, her mother-in-law, who is at school pickups and playdates.

He sighs heavily. 'Fine. I'll ask Grampy then. But he's old now. What if he can't remember?'

Trevor is sixty-two. Hardly old. And he's fitter than she is, regularly running half-marathons. She laughs. 'I think he'll remember just fine.' She kisses the top of his head and tells him she's going to get dressed.

She runs upstairs to her bedroom and throws open her wardrobe, taking out a selection of clothes and tossing them onto the bed. She settles on a pair of taupe trousers that suck in her tummy, a black silk top that is flattering around her large chest, and gives her dark-blonde hair a quick comb through.

As she's coming down the stairs she sees Trevor

standing in the porch, trying not to knock into Elliot's bike as he turns the handle on the internal glass doors. There is a dusting of frost on the shoulders of his navy blue trench coat and his nose is red. He grins at her as he hands her a parcel. 'This was in your porch,' he says as she takes it from him. 'I've told you before you should really keep this front door locked.'

'I lock the glass inner doors.'

'Well, they aren't locked now. I could walk straight in. And glass can be smashed.'

She rolls her eyes in mock frustration. 'Typical security-guard talk.'

He shifts his weight from one foot to the other. 'There have been burglaries in this area. The shop got broken into last month.'

Trevor is a security guard for Currys, a job he loves because, as he says, it makes him feel useful.

'The shop is in Brentford.'

'Emilia.' He lets out a puff of exasperation.

'Okay.' She holds up her hands. 'I get what you're saying. And I do lock it at night. It's just during the day . . . you know, with everyone coming in and out. And I figured Elliot's bike is too ugly for anyone to want to nick it.'

She dumps the box on the hallway table next to the white lilies she was sent a few days ago. There had been no note on the card and she'd assumed it was either her publisher or agent – although both said it wasn't.

Trevor shrugs off his coat and hangs it on the stand in the corner. 'I hear the divine Ottilie will be in attendance this evening.'

'Oh, stop it with the sweet talk. You know she's way too young for you!'

'What's twenty-five years?' He winks at her and runs a hand through his thinning white hair. He'd gone completely grey after Elliot's mum, May, died.

'Ah, Trev, you know you're my number-one guy,' says Ottilie, emerging from the living room. She hugs him, then takes his arm and lets him lead her down the Victorian tiled hallway towards the kitchen, as if they're two actors at a premiere. Emilia is about to follow them when Jasmine comes down the stairs – the scent of the roast dinner is clearly pervading the house.

'I'm starving. There's never anything to eat at Dad's, apart from gross rice cakes and salad. Ooh, is that my parcel?' Jasmine breezes past her, smelling of mint chewing gum and her favourite watermelon Body Shop spray. She picks up the package, her face alight. 'I've ordered some new notebooks from Amazon.' She's obsessed with stationery. And then her expression falls. 'Oh, it's for you.' She dumps it back on the table and saunters down the hallway to join the others in the kitchen. She hears the pop of a cork, followed by Ottilie's laugh.

Emilia picks it up. It's not from her publishers because it's typed out to her married name of Rathbone rather than her maiden and pen name of Ward. The last thing she ordered was a new top in the sales, which has long since arrived, been worn once, then discarded because it was an impulse buy. Curiosity gets the better of her and she rips it open. Inside there is another box, royal blue with a crest on the front, as if it's come from a jeweller. Maybe this is a surprise from Elliot. Although she doesn't know why. She suddenly wonders if there's an anniversary she's forgotten about, but no. They met in November and married in June. Carefully she takes the blue box from the cardboard. It feels light in her hand. She lifts the lid, intrigued. There, nestled in the blue tissue, is a ceramic seagull. It's quite ugly and cheap-looking, as if it was found at a charity shop or a bargain-basement sale. Not a jeweller. And definitely not the kind that has a fancy silver crest pressed onto a royal blue box. She stares at it, mystified. Then she picks it up, but just the body comes away in her hands. The head still rests in the blue tissue paper, severed at the neck. She checks inside the box, then the packaging, expecting to see a note. But there is nothing.

DI Miranda Moody has a phobia about seagulls. It's a running theme throughout all ten books. She checks the packaging again and her heart beats faster. There is no postage stamp. It looks like it's been hand delivered.

And, despite the large old-school radiator pumping out heat, she shivers.

6

I watch, repulsed, as a seagull by the shoreline necks a fish in one fell swoop. I despise the things. Vermin of the sky, my mother always said. I'm relieved when it flies off into the clouds. I light a cigarette and take a few drags. The sun has gone down, casting dappled ochre light on the grey surface of the water and streaking the sky a nicotine-orange. I'm still haunted by the scene I've just left behind. How can the world be both beautiful and so very ugly?

'Here we are, ma'am,' says Saunders, beside my shoulder, handing me a coffee.

'Thanks.' I take the cup from him. He jumps up to sit beside me on the wall. At thirty-five he's twenty-two years my junior and only a few years older than my son, and most of the time he annoys the fuck out of me, but right now I'm comforted by his presence. I sip the too-weak coffee and stare into the darkening sky. The wind is picking up, swirling around my ankles, and I grip my cup tighter for warmth.

Eventually he says, 'I can't believe he's back.'

'I know.'

'It's been . . . What did you say? Fifteen years?'

'Sixteen. Almost to the day. His last victim was in February 2005.'

The first murder had been twenty-five years ago. I'd been thirty-two and a newly qualified detective sergeant. It had been one of the biggest and most frustrating murder cases I'd ever worked on. He'd killed seven women – that we know of – over an eight-year period without being caught, and then just seemed to vanish into thin air.

'Could it really be him?' Saunders continues. 'After all this time?'

We've been through this. I know Saunders is talking for the sake of it. If there is a silence Saunders will fill it. Although, like I said, this evening I'm grateful for the distraction. Nothing has made me feel more like a failure than my inability to solve this case. Guilt for all the women who have died at the hands of that bastard still keeps me awake at night.

Saunders touches the tips of his dark spiky hair, which looks stiff with gel. He stares perplexedly towards the sea as though that holds the answers.

He's about to open his mouth again when I interrupt: 'If I'm honest I'd hoped he'd died. But this means he could have been in prison. We need to look at anyone who has been released lately. Someone who was incarcerated sixteen or seventeen years ago. After his last victim.'

'Belinda Aberdale,' he recites solemnly, as if I'm not going to know even though I told him about it. He'd still have been a student back in 2005. The names of the seven victims have been etched into my memory. I can still recall Belinda's freckled face as though it was yesterday. Her dark hair, her blue eyes, her slightly crooked smile. She'd been forty-two. A wife, a mother, a sister, a daughter. 'You don't think it could be a copycat killing, do you?'

I'd wondered this myself while we were upstairs and Celia was showing us the etching. It's a crude drawing, intricate but hurried, bloody. Just like the others had been. It looks like the head of an insect – it was my boss at the time, DCI Charles Bentley-Gordon, who dubbed it a praying mantis and it stuck long after he'd left the force.

'We've never released the detail about the insect markings, though,' I say. I stub my cigarette out on the wall and take another swig of coffee. 'That information was never released to the public or the press.' I sigh. 'No, I think this is the same killer. It has to be.' I jump down, crunching over the shingle beach, and head back towards the house where Celia is finishing up. Saunders follows me.

'Stay here,' I instruct him when we've reached the house. 'I won't be a minute.'

He nods and begins talking to the two officers guarding the scene.

As I'm walking up the stairs Celia is coming out of the flat, a grave expression on her face. 'Ah, there you are,' she says, when she sees me. 'Can you come with me? I need to show you something I think is important.'

Emilia is up in her attic office on Tuesday morning. Hannah is calling her at 10 a.m. and she can't relax until she's spoken to her. She's still worried about what her editor might say about her latest book.

She tries to keep herself busy, half-heartedly picking up the stack of papers piled on her keyboard, which includes the birthday cards from six weeks ago, which she likes to keep, and stuffs it into a box under her desk. She really should tidy up in here. The rest of the house is pristine but her office is where she can be her true messy self. Elliot and the kids keep out of it, thank God. Once, when Elliot spotted the mess from the landing he joked that it looked like they'd been burgled. 'I don't understand how you can work in such a pigsty,' he'd said then, and quite often since. Maybe it's a throwback to all the times she'd written in her tiny flat surrounded by Jasmine's paraphernalia before she and Elliot moved in together, but in a lot of ways she finds the mess comforting.

She stands in the middle of the room and surveys it now: her desk overflowing with books, papers and a coffee cup that has started to grow mould in the bottom, the tripod and ring-light shoved into the corner, the exercise bike she'd bought in lockdown but has hardly ever used, except to hang clothes meant for the charity shop over the seat. On the shelf above the desk sits the box with the decapitated seagull inside. She should chuck it away and doesn't understand why she's kept it. She'd been shaken after receiving the parcel on Sunday evening. She hadn't wanted to mention it at dinner in front of the kids, but when Jasmine and Wilfie had run off after they'd wolfed their food, Ottilie had turned to her and said, 'What's wrong, Mils? You've been distracted all evening.' Then she'd told them about the strange 'gift'.

'So it was just left on the porch?' Ottilie had frowned. 'Inside the door?'

When she'd nodded, Trevor had launched into another lecture about safety measures and not letting anyone have access to the porch. Ottilie quaffed more wine, her head to the side as though she was watching a play.

'I bet it's an obsessed fan of the series,' Ottilie said with a wave of her hand, nearly knocking over a wine glass. She always became more animated after she'd had a few. 'Maybe the seagull broke in the post.'

'It just unnerves me that they know where I live,' Emilia said, sitting back in her chair.

'I expect it's easy to find on Companies House.'

'Not my married name, though. I dunno. The use of my married name makes it feel personal somehow.'

'I wouldn't worry about it, sweetheart,' Elliot said, pouring himself another glass. 'Is it because of what happened on Friday?'

And then, of course, Trevor and Ottilie had wanted to know what had happened on Friday, so Emilia had had to explain about the hoax, and how it was similar to a scene from her debut novel.

Trevor had patted her hand reassuringly. 'It's just a coincidence, that's all. There's no way someone could orchestrate a hoax at the exact time you're riding a bus.' He had shaken his head, signalling it was the end of the matter. This man, who only moments before had been chastising her about an unlocked front door. But he was like that, was Trevor. She'd always found him a bit contradictory and hadn't really liked him when she was first introduced to him ten years ago. She'd found him a bit brash, slightly dominant of May, who ran around after him as if he was a king and she a mere subject. Elliot had laughed when she'd told him so. 'My mum loves it,' he had said. 'It makes her feel useful now that I no longer live at home, and they adore each other.'

Elliot was their only child and May had once told her she'd longed for more but kept having miscarriages, until the emotional toll became too much and they gave up. May had died suddenly from an aneurysm at the age of fifty-six, a year after seeing her only son get married and only a few months after holding her first grandchild in her arms. 'I never thought he'd settle down, my lovely,' she'd said, hugging Emilia on their wedding day. 'He's had serious girlfriends but he always insisted he wasn't the marrying kind. And then he met you. You've changed him.'

It was only after May's death that Emilia realized the depth of love Trevor had felt for his wife. He was lost without her and her death diminished him. He spiralled into a depression that lasted nearly a year. Emilia and Elliot had encouraged him to sell the family home in Devon and move nearer to them. It took some convincing but eventually Trevor bought a flat in Isleworth and found a job as a security guard in Brentford. He threw himself into being a good grandfather to Jasmine and Wilfie and, over the years, Emilia had grown very fond of him. It was clear how much he adored his son and grandkids – which was more than she could say for her own parents, whom she saw only occasionally even though they lived just an hour or so away in Guildford. She often wished she had the same bond with her parents as Elliot had had with his.

There was something reassuring about Trevor – and likewise Elliot. Something about their calm, measured personalities that made Emilia feel secure. Even so, after Ottilie and Trevor left that night, she took heed of her father-in-law's words and double-locked all the doors.

Her mobile springs into life on her desk and Emilia's stomach swoops. She snatches up the phone.

'Okay. I admit it. It works,' says Hannah, without any preamble, as is her way.

Emilia exhales with relief as she moves a pile of papers from her chair so that she can sit down, her mobile balancing between chin and shoulder. 'So you're happy for me to keep it in?'

'It's your book. As long as you know there's no coming back from this. Once Miranda is killed off you can't have a resurrection in a later book. That's it for the series. But at least she'll go out with a bang.'

Emilia leans back in her chair and stares out of the dormer window into the garden. From here she can see the shadowy form of Elliot moving around his insulated outside office. Can she really do this? But she's thirty-eight years old: she's been careful with her money and knows she can survive if her career takes a nose dive. 'It feels like the right thing to do,' she admits. 'Time to move on. I want to write about something else. Something different. I'll miss Miranda, but –'

'It's an emotional ending,' interjects Hannah. 'Her death. It affected me.'

'Oh. That's good.' Emilia feels a tug on her heart. She'd cried when she wrote that final chapter with Miranda's death, the first time she'd ever cried at anything she'd written. But Miranda had been everything she wished she was, and when she killed her off she felt like a part of her had died too.

She glances around at her framed book jackets,

adorning the dusky pink walls of her office, feeling a sense of accomplishment even if it is tinged with worry and guilt. She reassures herself that it's done now: the story has taken on a life of its own and there is no going back. She always feels at a loose end when she submits a book, not quite ready to start another, her last story still hanging over her, like a recent dream she can't quite shake off. She already misses Miranda and the doubt sets in. What if she's making a huge mistake?

'I'll get the edits back as soon as I can. There's not much to do, it's already very fully formed. Well done, Emilia. It's very clever. I'm impressed.'

A wave of guilt washes over Emilia. If only Hannah knew the truth.

8

Emilia takes the box with the decapitated seagull inside and closes the door to her office firmly behind her. It's right at the top of the house, in the converted attic and next to the guest bedroom. She watches a pigeon walking across the large skylight window, its feet tapping against the glass. She makes her way down the narrow staircase that leads onto the main landing, and when she's reached the kitchen on the ground floor she throws the seagull into the bin, wondering why she hadn't done so as soon as she'd received it.

She makes Elliot an instant coffee, slips on her coat and shoes and crosses the frost-coated lawn to his garden office. They'd built it in the middle of the first lockdown so that Elliot had somewhere quiet to work (even though he now goes into the central London office three times a week). It always smells of wood and electrical equipment and, unlike her office, is meticulously tidy. There is a photo on his desk of the two of them on their wedding day and another with the four of them on a trip to Land's End when Wilfie was only four. They are all pulling silly faces and pointing at the sign and it always makes her heart lift. When she first started dating Elliot he wasn't put off that she already had a four-year-old daughter, as she'd thought he might be, and treated Jasmine like his own.

As she walks in now, he looks up, handsome in a black ribbed polo-neck jumper. His dark wavy hair needs cutting and stands on end as if he's been raking his hands through it. He has his reading glasses on; they make him look like Patrick Dempsey. 'Thanks, beauty,' he says, smiling, as she hands him the coffee in his favourite Super Dad cup, which Wilfie had given him for Father's Day last year. He takes a long gulp and sets it down. It always amazes her that he can drink liquids when they're still piping hot.

She tells him about her conversation with Hannah and his face lights up. 'So that's it. The end of Miranda?'

'It looks that way. I have no idea what I'm going to write next but I'm excited it will be something different.'

'At least you've got a bit of time off now. When am I allowed to read it?'

'After I get it back from Hannah. So not yet.' Anxiety washes over her every time she thinks back to last year and how hard the book had been to write. She pushes the uneasiness away and changes the subject. 'What are you working on?' She moves so she's standing at his shoulder and peers at his computer screens concertinaed in front of him. He puts his arm around her waist. He has three screens set up with different images on each. He's a brilliant artist, inherited from Trevor, and it's been passed down to Wilf.

'Packaging. Which one do you prefer?'

She looks at all three cereal packets, each varying in colours and fonts. 'This one,' she says, pointing to the left. 'I like the orange.'

He gives her waist a little squeeze. 'That's my favourite too, although it'll be up to the client. Now go. I need to get on. Just because you've got nothing to do now your book's in,' he teases. She bends down to kiss him, then heads back into the house. It feels large and empty: she prefers it when it's full, like it was on Sunday night, with the kids and in-laws and friends. Her parents' house was always so quiet. Her father was in the RAF so they moved around a lot, but when she went home to wherever they were living (and it varied from Scotland to Cornwall) they never seemed to have anyone around, no family or cousins, aunts and uncles. Most of the time she'd hated boarding school, the only light being Ottilie, but it was still preferable to being at home with a mother who always seemed disappointed with her lot, and a father who tried to blend in with the furniture.

Emilia grabs her bag. She's got a few hours before she needs to pick up Wilfie but Jasmine is going to her friend's house after school and won't be home until after dinner. She'll wander into Richmond, have a look around the shops. Wilfie is in need of more school shirts after a recent growth spurt. Even though Elliot is in the garden she locks the front porch for once, remembering Trevor's words. She wraps her coat around herself and pulls up her hood when she feels light rain.

As she's making her way down the hill her phone vibrates in her coat pocket. It's a text from Louise: *Still okay for tomorrow night? It's been ages!*

She taps a message back as she's walking: *Can't wait! Same time and place?*

Louise pings back a reply: *Yes! Soooo looking forward to seeing you.*

Emilia is smiling as she slips the phone back into her pocket. Louise is a few years younger, but as soon as she had sat down next to Emilia, on that first coffee morning, blowing her dark fringe off her heart-shaped face, and joked, 'Fuck, what a first day! Is it too early for a gin and tonic?' she'd known she would like her. In her baggy jeans and oversized sweatshirt with a Scottie on the front, she was a breath of fresh air after some of the Breton-wearing mums she had met: they only talked about problems with their nannies, wearing their entitlement like a favourite scarf. She had never fitted in with them, as if they knew she was an imposter despite the accent she had picked up at school.

As soon as Emilia and Louise got talking they realized they were mutually fascinated by each other's jobs and spent the whole morning ignoring everyone else. Emilia had liked Louise so much she'd suggested they go for a drink, and, over the two years they've been friends, they try to meet up for dinner when Louise's shifts allow, usually once every few months. Emilia had always found it easy to make friends. She tries to be warm, open and sociable (the opposite of her parents), but what had happened with Kristin had shaken her and she is now more wary, preferring to meet up with Louise alone. Even Elliot hasn't met her, although that's mainly because, as a single woman, Louise would rather it was just the two of them. Emilia understands that. After she and Jonas had split up she hadn't wanted to socialize with couples, and Louise's ex, Mike, sounds like a nightmare who – according to Louise – shirks his childcare responsibilities by loading them onto his overbearing mother.

Emilia is still thinking of Louise when she notices a familiar figure coming out of the little French restaurant just off the green. It's Jonas, looking dapper in a long camel coat over a business suit. He's with a very attractive brunette who is at least ten years his junior. She's wearing a figure-hugging dress and heels so high Emilia is surprised she can walk in them. Emilia stops in the shadow of a shop, her heart speeding up. She's never bumped into her ex-husband in Richmond before – his office is in Moorgate – but she's spotted Kristin once or twice and pretended she hadn't. Now she doesn't know what to do, how to act.

She can hear the brunette's laughter, as tinkly and clear as a fork against glass, and watches, mesmerized, as the woman weaves an arm through his and leans in to him. It's an intimate gesture, and, despite everything, she experiences a pang of pity for Kristin: if this isn't an affair it's obviously more than friendship. She watches as they stop at the corner and he leans down to kiss her cheek, then stands back and thrusts his hands into his pockets. The woman laughs again, reaches out and tenderly strokes the side of his face before walking away. Jonas stands for a few seconds staring after her until she's rounded a corner and is out of sight. Emilia decides to step out of the shadows just as Jonas is crossing the road and, as their eyes meet, she's satisfied to see a flush spread up his neck to his face.

'Hi,' she says as he crosses over. 'Who was that?'

'Ah, just a . . . er . . . client,' he says, looking at his feet.

'She's very beautiful.'

His head shoots up and she sees it. The guilt in his eyes.

'Oh, Jonas.'

The guilt has gone, his expression now closed, defensive. 'What?'

'I'm no fan of Kristin but I thought you loved her.'

'I do.'

'You're buying a house together.'

He shuffles his feet. 'Listen.' He takes her arm and steers her out of the path of office workers heading towards the green. He lowers his voice. 'Please don't tell anyone about this. Nothing is going on. It's just a bit of flirty banter, that's all.'

'That was how it started with Kristin. Have you ever cheated on her?'

'Of course not.'

Emilia had always thought he'd been faithful to her until he ran off with Kristin. She'd thought it was Kristin's charm, her magic, that had ensnared him, turned him. But now she wonders if Kristin wasn't the first. Having the love of one gorgeous woman is obviously not enough for him. She thinks of Elliot in his home office, poring over drawings of cereal packets, and is so grateful she wants to cry. She's known it deep down for years, of course, but Jonas did her a favour. If it hadn't been Kristin it would have been someone else.

'I just . . . I just get bored,' he says, so quietly she can barely hear him. He looks at her imploringly. 'I don't mean to hurt anyone.'

She stares at him in shock at his rare moment of honesty. And she briefly glimpses the boy she'd first met as a fresher nearly twenty years ago. In a flash she remembers how she'd felt when he'd asked her out. Her, Emilia Ward, who had never felt as loved, as special, as attractive as anyone else. And she'd been so desperate for love, for affection that she'd ignored the red flags: the late nights, the flirty 'banter' with every attractive female. Ottilie had said she didn't quite trust him but Emilia had refused to listen. She'd been infatuated.

She sighs. 'But you do hurt people. You hurt me and now you're going to do the same to Kristin. Why bother getting married if you feel that way? And the thing is . . .' she says and bites back her anger '. . . not only did you hurt me by cheating on me, but you ruined a friendship.'

'I'm sorry, I really am. If I could take it all back . . .'

He looks lost standing there, the tip of his nose red with cold, and despite it all, she feels sympathy for him. Maybe she can talk some sense into him. Stop him doing to Kristin what he did to her. It starts to rain and she makes a split-second decision.

'Have you got time for a coffee?' she finds herself asking.

They spend nearly an hour holed up in a little café, which smells of wet umbrellas and coffee, where they have, for the first time in years, an honest conversation. He tells her how frustrated he is with Kristin and her constant career changes, how she's not bringing in enough money, and she's demanding. 'I'm happy in the Twickenham house, you know. It was affordable and now we're going to be stretching ourselves.'

Emilia sips her cappuccino while he talks. 'I can understand why she wouldn't want to live in another woman's house.'

'You haven't lived in it for ten years. It's hardly another woman's house anymore.'

'You know what I mean. We chose it together. Listen, you need to be totally honest with her. Like Elliot and I are with each other.'

'Really?' He raises an eyebrow. 'So you'll tell him you had coffee with your ex-husband?'

'Of course. Why wouldn't I? I have nothing to hide.'

He stares at her for a while, then shakes his head slowly. 'You're a good person, Em. And I'm sorry for the way I treated you, I really am.'

She blushes and tells him it's all water under the bridge now.

He pushes away his half-drunk Americano. 'So when am I going to get to read your book? Surely there must be some perks to being the ex-husband of a crime writer.'

She knows Elliot thinks it strange that she allows Jonas to read early copies of her books, but he's always been supportive of her writing, even after they split up. And, despite her faults, so has Kristin. 'Once I've done the edits I'll email it over to you.' She drains the remnants of her cappuccino.

'Great. I can't wait to see how you kill off Miranda.'

They chat some more, then Jonas leaves to go back to the office. After Emilia has bought Wilfie his school shirts she heads back up the hill thinking of Jonas and their conversation. The handle of the plastic bag cuts into her wrist and she's grateful when she reaches her house.

The rain has held off on her walk home but steel-coloured clouds gather ominously. There is a blossom tree on the patch of grass next to their driveway, not yet in bloom. Elliot planted it when they first moved in, and it still hasn't reached its full height. Its branches are stark and naked without their frothy dressing. As she walks past she notices something swinging from one of the upper branches. Her eyesight isn't as good as it was and she squints, but as she gets closer she can see, from the dirty yellow hair standing up in a peak, the hard body and scrunched-up face, exactly what it is. A troll doll. Hanging from the neck by a piece of string. She stands and watches it for a few seconds, gently swinging in the wind, her mind racing. Was it left there at the same time as the package? She hadn't noticed it when she left the house earlier. The glow she had felt from her coffee with Jonas extinguishes as quickly as a wet match.

The troll dolls are from her second Miranda book, *His Calling Card*, about a serial killer who left them hanging from trees.

After he'd murdered his victims.

Elliot.

She sprints around the side of the house, into the garden and straight to Elliot's office. She can't see him through the glass doors but she wrenches them open anyway. He's not there. She stands in the doorway, confused. He wouldn't just go out and leave the office unlocked, not with all his expensive equipment. The mug she'd brought him earlier is lying on its side on the floor. She darts across the lawn to the house, fumbling with her key as she unlocks the bifold doors. 'Elliot!' she yells. 'Elliot!'

But there's no answer.

9

'See here,' says Celia, pointing at the open skylight in the hallway. 'I'm certain this is where the perpetrator got in.'

I look up. It's a big skylight, easy for a slim-ish person to wedge through and not too high for them to jump down from. Although they'd have to be reasonably fit and agile. Was the victim known to him or was it opportunistic? I think back to the other victims. Each one had been killed when they were alone in the house, usually in the early hours of the morning, and the killer had entered the building through either a skylight or a window. The only victim where we'd never understood how he'd broken in was the second, Jennifer Radcliffe. No doors or windows open or smashed. That had been perplexing, but it had been very early in the case, when we were just realizing we had a serial killer on our hands.

We turn at the sound of a heavy tread on the stairs. Saunders is lumbering up them, puffing. 'Ma'am ... just been speaking to the woman in the flat below, Lorraine Butterworth, who raised the alarm. She was away last night but has said the victim is Trisha Banks, aged thirty-nine. Single with no kids. Worked at Poundland.' He consults his notebook. 'Apparently she was quiet, kept herself to herself, and had only been living at this address for six months. Before that she was in London. Lorraine realized something was wrong when she went to give her a parcel this morning and the door was ajar. She pushed it open and saw her lying on the bed. She ran out of the room and contacted the police.'

'Great. Can you go door-to-door, find out if the neighbours saw or heard anything or know her? Where is Lorraine now?'

'She's downstairs, ma'am, being comforted by Michelle . . . DC Doyle.'

'Good.' I like Doyle. She gets the job done with minimal fuss and she'll keep Saunders in line even if he is a rank higher. It's nearly five thirty and it's already started to get dark. I watch as Saunders retreats and is swallowed into the bleak hallway.

Trisha Banks is lying on the bed in her dank bedroom, the wallpaper peeling off. Her body is in shadows now and the powder-white soles of her feet are all I can see. I'll get Doyle and Saunders to inform her next of kin. It's the job I hate most.

As I make my way down the stairs, I see Forensics and the police photographer, Ray, and they stop to let me pass before clustering as one mass into the building.

I stand on the doorstep, watching, as Saunders, his back to me, talks to a group of neighbours who all want to know what's happened. I turn away, light a fag and take a few puffs before stubbing it out against the brick wall. A gull skims the surface of the sea.

Then I head back into the building, which smells of damp and death, to talk to Lorraine Butterworth.

10

'Fuck, that sounds terrifying. And then what happened?'
Louise is staring at her, hazel eyes wide, hand gripping
her wine glass.

'It was horrible. I didn't know what to do. I really
thought . . .' Emilia says and shakes her head. 'I don't
actually know what I thought. That I'd find Elliot in the
house somewhere, stabbed, like in my book. Anyway, I
rang his mobile and, thankfully, he answered straight
away. He'd popped out to get petrol because he knew he
had a long journey today. The relief I felt at hearing his
voice. Shit, I can't even tell you. He was angry with himself for not locking the door.'

'Fuck,' says Louise again, and swigs some wine. They're
sitting in a restaurant they love in Richmond – it's chintzy
with velvet-flock wallpaper, padded pink velvet chairs
and huge chandeliers hanging from the high ceiling.
Louise says it makes her feel glamorous and always follows up with 'Because God knows I need glamour in my
life.'

'It freaked me out,' says Emilia, toying with the stem of
her wine glass, 'especially when I saw his favourite mug on

its side on the floor. He said he must have knocked it when he left. Thank goodness it's not broken.'

'You thought it was a sign of a struggle.' Louise leans towards Emilia with her elbows on the table. 'I'd have thought the same. So that's two things now, the seagull with the broken neck and the troll doll.'

'That it's happening at the house is what's unnerving me most. I mean,' Emilia says and leans back in her chair and sighs deeply, 'whoever is doing this knows where I live.'

'But it's harmless. Nuisance stuff, really. What did Elliot say?'

'The same as you. I think the fact I knew I was meeting you tonight stopped me really losing my shit yesterday. But today leaving the house . . . I was a bit worried about what I'd find.'

'I think you should report it. Just to be on the safe side. Just with your local police station, which is Twick-enham for you.'

Emilia's stomach turns and she pushes away her unfin-ished salmon. 'Really? But you said you don't think it's serious.'

'Don't panic,' says Louise. 'I'm not saying you should be worried. It's some idiot messing with you. Some fan, probably. But I think better to log it. Have you got one of those Ring doorbells? Or cameras or anything?'

She's sure Louise has asked her that before. She's as security conscious as her father-in-law. 'I'm crap at that sort of thing. Elliot's dad is always telling us to have more security around the place.'

'Didn't you say he was once in the police?'

'Years ago. Before your time.'

'Why did he leave?' Louise picks up her knife and fork and continues to eat her steak.

'I don't actually know,' says Emilia, refilling her wine glass, thankful she's getting a taxi back. She's already starting to feel a bit light-headed but she needs this tonight after the stress of the last few days. 'Elliot said not to interrogate him.' She laughs. 'You know what I'm like. Nosy.'

'Interested,' says Louise, kindly.

'Anyway, he said his dad didn't like to talk about it. He implied it had something to do with his mother.'

'Hmm, yes, it probably didn't help my marriage.' She gives a sardonic smile.

'I think he was only in the force a few years, anyway.'

Louise swallows a mouthful of steak. 'Did you say his wife has died?'

'Yes, about eight years ago now – quite a while. He's moved to be nearer to us as well.'

'In-laws on your doorstep.' She laughs bitterly. 'Not always a good thing.'

'He's better than Jonas's parents. His mum was so overbearing at times. Jonas is definitely her little prince. Although his dad's a sweetheart.' She does miss them. They vowed to keep in touch after the divorce, but as

Jasmine got older the need for her to communicate with them became less and less and now she sees them maybe during the Christmas holidays. 'But I don't miss Eliza "popping in" every five minutes.'

'Sounds like Frances.'

'I know Frances isn't that nice to you but at least she's great with Toby.'

Louise nods. 'There is that. And to be fair to the monster-in-law I'd find it hard to do this job without her. And Mike is useless. He's a big kid himself.'

Emilia had met Mike only once. He'd come to pick up Toby from a playdate when Frances couldn't. She'd thought, with a stab of guilt, that he was nice: warm and friendly, and he'd seemed great with Toby, letting him climb onto his back as he carried him to the car. But she didn't know the ins and outs of their marriage and subsequent divorce. Louise was quite private about her past, saying she didn't like to dwell. 'It's the here and now that we need to focus on,' she'd always say. And Emilia agreed. The past could stay where it was as far as she was concerned.

'Anyway . . . I have news.' Louise puts her knife and fork together on her empty plate, and dabs at her lips with a napkin. She's not dressed up for the occasion, wearing her usual outfit of jeans and an oversized jumper, often with an animal on the front. This time it's a llama with a tartan bow-tie. Emilia had put on a silky blouse and curled her hair. 'That was delicious by the way. First proper meal for ages.' Louise always joked that her diet was awful as she mostly ate on the run. That didn't surprise Emilia. Louise was short, like her, but whippet-thin and androgenous with her gamine hairstyle. She looked like a pretty boy.

'Ooh, tell me more.'

'Remember that guy I was seeing early last year?'

'The one who really liked you but you weren't sure?'

Louise looks sheepish. 'Yes. I'm such an idiot sometimes but it felt too soon after Mike. Anyway, it's back on.'

'That's great news. I'm so pleased for you. What was his name again?'

'Marcus. He's also a police officer. Although we work in different forces. I originally met him on a training day. So . . .' she says and gives a self-deprecating laugh '. . . that means we won't see much of each other but I feel more ready this time. I haven't told Toby yet, so I'd appreciate it if you kept it to yourself.'

'Of course.' Emilia downs the rest of her wine.

'Oh, and I've got a cat. I know, I know, I'm going to turn into one of those cat ladies, but Mike is allergic so now he's out of my life I can finally get one.'

'My kids would love a pet but Elliot is too anal.' Emilia laughs. 'The friends he shared a house with at uni called him Mrs Mop because he was always cleaning. Is it a kitten?'

'Yes. A boy. Hamish. He's gorgeous. Black, except for

a white bib and a pink nose. Look at him!' She pushes her phone under Emilia's nose to show her a photo. 'Do you like his tartan collar? Notice a bit of a theme?' She points to her sweatshirt.

'I do. He's very cute,' she says, with a twinge of envy. She'd love a cat. She passes Louise back her phone.

It's getting late now and the restaurant is emptying. They talk some more, and as they're leaving Louise asks about the book.

'So you're calling it *Her Last Chapter*?'

'That's its working title. Although it might get changed. Do you want to read the finished version? I'd appreciate you checking for any inconsistencies. As you know, there's a lot of police procedural in this one. Thanks for all your help on it. You're a lifesaver. You know how difficult I found it.' She feels the familiar swirl of dread in the pit of her stomach when she remembers.

'I was glad to help, and I'd love to read the finished version. Email it to me, if you like.' Louise presses a black beanie onto her head and buttons her coat before heading through the entrance hall.

'And you're coming to my launch party, aren't you? On the seventeenth?' she asks as they step onto the rain-slicked pavement.

'Launch party? But I thought *Her Last Chapter* was being published in October.'

'This is for the paperback of book nine – *The Lost*

Man. I didn't get the chance to have a launch for the hardback because of lockdown.'

'Sure,' she says, linking her arm through Emilia's. 'If I'm not working, I'll be there.' They head towards the green, which looks shadowy and ominous ahead, the light from the lampposts carving out halos in the mist. It's deserted and eerie, the darkness pressing around them, like they're being swaddled. Emilia shudders and Louise notices. 'Are you okay?'

'I am. It's just . . . I keep thinking . . . What if I've got a stalker?'

'You're with me. Anyone gives you any hassle and I'll arrest the prick.'

'How do you know it's a man?'

'Or the prick-ess. Whatever.' Louise collapses into laughter and Emilia can't help but smile.

'I don't think you're in the right state to arrest anyone just now.'

'Good job Toby's with Mike tonight. Although I miss him.'

'I hope you mean Toby.'

'I do. Of course I do. I don't miss that fucker Mike.'

'Talking of fuckers, you'll never guess who I saw yesterday.' Emilia fills Louise in on her meeting with Jonas.

'So he's cheating on Kristin?' she says, horrified, when Emilia has finished.

'I don't think so *yet*. But he's tempted.'

'Well, that's karma for you.'

'I don't know, though. I thought I'd be happy to think of him doing that to her, but I'm not. It just makes me think, What was it all for? Why did he put me and Jasmine through all of that heartache for it not to work out with Kristin?'

But Louise isn't listening. She's stopped suddenly on the dark path, forcing Emilia to stop too as their arms are still linked, and her whole body has gone rigid.

Emilia shivers. 'What is it? What's wrong?' she whispers.

'I think someone's following us,' she whispers back. All the joviality has gone from her voice and she suddenly seems stone-cold sober.

'What?' Emilia spins around but nobody's there, just darkness stretched between shadowy buildings and the green on their left.

'I could sense someone behind us . . . and then I saw a man dart into that alleyway. We need to keep walking. Come on.' She pulls Emilia's arm firmly.

Emilia's heart starts banging so hard that she feels sick. Who the hell is following them and why? Is it the person who is responsible for the seagull and the troll, or someone unrelated to them? She sneaks a glance at Louise, but her expression is serious, focused, her cheeks red. She almost has to run to keep up with her friend's pace. She hears footsteps behind them. Louise is right, someone is following them.

And then, thankfully, they're out on the main high

street where there are people, and cars and lights, and Emilia feels weak with relief.

'Come on,' says Louise, almost dragging her to where a taxi has pulled up and a young couple are getting out. It's nearly ten thirty on a Wednesday but there are still people around, for which Emilia is suddenly grateful. Louise speaks to the driver while Emilia climbs into the back seat, scanning the street to see who was following them. Someone emerges from between two buildings – the way they had come – but turns in the opposite direction, towards Richmond Bridge. They have on a hooded coat and Emilia can't see the face. She squints, trying to see more, but can't, and curses her failing eyesight. She used to have twenty-twenty vision.

The taxi moves away from the kerb and they flop back in the seat.

'They probably weren't following us,' says Louise, turning her head to look at Emilia, the light from the streetlamps sweeping over her fine cheekbones. She doesn't sound convincing.

'Why are we going this way? Your flat's just up there, isn't it?' says Emilia, sitting up to look out of the window.

'I'd rather see you home safely first.'

'So, you do think we were being followed?'

Louise doesn't answer. Instead she purses her lips, as if she's trying to stop herself revealing her true thoughts.

Fifteen minutes later the taxi pulls up in front of

Emilia's house. Elliot must already be in bed. He's left the light on for her, which she can see in the fan of glass above the front door. The rest of the house is in darkness.

Louise instructs the taxi driver to wait until Emilia is inside. 'Promise me you'll report all this to the police tomorrow,' she says, in an urgent whisper. 'And get yourself some security cameras. Pronto.'

11

Daisy,
2005

Daisy was nearly eleven when her mother was murdered.

She remembered the night like it was yesterday rather than eight years ago. She'd been in bed asleep when she'd heard a noise from downstairs: the sound of something smashing, a yelp, and then silence. Their house was small, a two-up-two-down terrace overlooking the sea in a quaint Devonshire village near Plymouth, and most sounds were hard to muffle, like her mum's drunken giggles when she thought Daisy was fast asleep, which meant her boyfriend had turned up. Her mum wasn't aware that Daisy knew about The Boyfriend because he was only ever invited around when Daisy was in bed. But she'd been aware of the evidence left behind the next morning: an extra wineglass, the doodles he made in the margins of the newspaper that was always abandoned on the arm of the chair, the empty cigarette packet that left a lingering smell of manure mixed with something she couldn't quite place.

Sometimes she stayed awake on purpose so she could

see him leaving, kissing her mother on the doorstep, briefly illuminated by the flickering of the porch light-bulb that needed replacing. He had sandy hair that stuck up slightly at the back in a double crown, and a broad neck that reminded her of the ham joint they'd sometimes have at her dad's house.

Now, at the grand old age of eighteen, she wondered if all the secrecy surrounding her mum's relationship was because her boyfriend had been married. Her parents had split up a few years before, so there had been no other reason why her mum had been so cagey.

It went on for months, the secret rendezvous with the mystery man. He came over at least two or three times a week, and she knew that when she spent Friday night and all day Saturday at her dad's, her mum was making the most of it. Something about it unsettled Daisy, maybe that her mum wasn't being honest. Not like Dad and his girlfriend, Shannon, who were all over each other, like a rash, in a way that made Daisy smile, secure that her dad was happy.

When she asked her mum about the mystery man she'd bat away her questions, telling her he was just a friend, someone she worked with, which was doubtful to Daisy as her mum cleaned people's houses while she was at school.

She wished now that she'd been more insistent, more forceful with her mum, made her tell her the truth – tell her his name at any rate.

Because then maybe Daisy could have saved her.

12

The next morning, following Louise's advice, Emilia contacts her local police station and logs the incidents with a bored-sounding constable. She waits until she's dropped the kids at school as she doesn't want to alarm them. Last year, Wilfie went through a spate of night terrors, his screams cutting through the silence of the night, making Emilia sit bolt upright in bed, her heart hammering, sweat clinging to her body. She'd go to his room and lie with him on his top bunk, comforting him until it had subsided. The experience had been frightening but mostly for her, as Wilfie wouldn't remember much about it the next day. Elliot had said their son had taken after her with his vivid imagination. He seems to have grown out of the terrors, but Emilia lives on a knife's edge, worrying that any little thing will cause them to come back.

Elliot is nursing a cup of coffee in the kitchen. He's moved the lilies to the dining table and they fill the room with a sweet, cloying scent. She senses his eyes on her as she paces the length of the kitchen.

'What did they say?' he asks, after she ends the call. She stands opposite where he's sitting at the island.

'Just to let them know if anything else happens, but they couldn't have sounded less interested.' She sighs and lays her mobile on the hard stone surface.

He regards her for a few seconds over the rim of his mug. 'What worries me is that you and Louise thought you were being followed last night. You didn't mention that to them?'

She walks around the island, pulls out the stool next to him and sits down. 'I don't know if that was just a bit of hysteria because we were talking about it and riling each other up. We were both a bit tipsy.'

He frowns, clearly unconvinced, and pulls up the sleeves of his cable-knit jumper. 'You'd think she'd know better, being a detective.' He sounds annoyed.

'What do you mean?'

'She should have stayed calm. Maybe confronted the guy.'

'She wasn't on duty.'

He shrugs. 'I thought detectives were always on duty. That's what my dad used to say.'

She bites back her annoyance. 'Louise wasn't there in her role as a detective but as my friend. And we were tipsy, like I said.'

'I just worry. You and the kids mean everything to me.'

She reaches for his hand and squeezes it in response. 'Anyway, Louise suggested getting Ring Cams. Front and back.'

Elliot withdraws his hand and presses his glasses further onto his nose. 'I was just thinking that while you were on the phone. I'd feel more comfortable about it, with me being in Iceland next week. I wouldn't go but it's an important client. I'll ask Dad's advice.' He downs the rest of his coffee and hops off the stool. He kisses her lips, takes their mugs and puts them into the dishwasher, then heads out to his office.

It's not until he's gone that she remembers she still hasn't told him about seeing Jonas yesterday.

She's grateful that the remainder of the week is uneventful, and as Friday approaches Emilia can breathe again. Now that Elliot has installed the cameras she feels safer. But she vows to keep the porch door locked, just in case. The weekend is busy with a football match for Wilfie and basketball for Jasmine. She's relieved that Jasmine has seemed happier lately, making more effort to go out into the town centre with Nancy. Emilia is pleased that it isn't Jonas's turn to have their daughter this weekend. Even though she doesn't have much time for Kristin she still feels guilty when she remembers her conversation with Jonas and she would rather avoid her.

Last night while lying in bed she'd finally told Elliot about bumping into her ex-husband. She had been putting it off because she knows he doesn't think much of Jonas. 'I'll tolerate him because he's the father of your daughter,' he'd said, early on in their relationship. 'But you can't expect me to respect the guy after what he did to you. And don't get me started on Kristin.'

Deep down she'd been pleased that he felt so strongly about her that her hurts were also his. Elliot took his marriage vows seriously. He was very black and white about betrayal and had told her on more than one occasion that he would never be able to forgive her if she ever cheated on him. She felt the same. She couldn't go through it again, so she was relieved about his strong moral stance. It had been one of the reasons she'd allowed herself to fall in love with him. He had such high expectations but sometimes that made it hard for her to be honest with him.

They'd turned to face each other, the crisp white duvet pulled up to their chins, holding hands beneath the covers. She loved their bedroom, recently redecorated in varying shades of grey with a splash of purple threaded through the checked throw at the end of their bed. He'd reached over and tucked a strand of hair behind her ear. 'He's a fool,' he said, a slant of moonlight cutting across the cheekbones of his face. 'Why remarry if he knows he's going to cheat again?'

'I don't understand him either,' she murmured. 'I didn't want to say anything to you about it in front of Jas. She adores him. And she likes Kristin – she was too young to remember all the heartbreak. I've tried to keep from her what they did.'

'You're a lot nicer about it than I could be. As long as he doesn't come sniffing around you again.' Even though he tried to sound lighthearted she could hear the jealousy in his tone.

She laughed and snuggled closer to him. 'As if. I never thought I'd feel sorry for Kristin, but I do.'

Elliot leaves for his work trip on Monday morning. He hates flying, and she can sense his nervousness as he clutters the kitchen, getting in the way as she tries to make breakfast. He'd told her once, not long after they first met, that he'd had a 'bit of a breakdown' when he was a teenager and had had to go on anti-anxiety medication and anti-depressants for a few years after his GCSEs. He'd stopped taking them long before he met her. Most of the time she wouldn't know that he'd ever suffered from mental-health issues, but every now and again it shows, like wood grain through paint. She remembers a similar thing happening to Ottilie at school and she'd had to take some time off, as did a few others around the same age. She'd put it down to being at a high-pressured establishment where exam results mattered more than the pupils' welfare. Elliot had gone somewhere similar, although it was two hundred miles away and a day school.

Jasmine is sitting at the dining table shovelling porridge into her mouth with one hand while tapping out a text with the other. Wilfie bounds into the room with his shirt hanging out and no jumper on.

'Go and sit down,' Emilia instructs her son as she hands him his Shreddies. 'Remember you've got PE today.'

'Can we get a dog?' he asks, taking the bowl and plonking himself next to Jasmine at the table.

'Not at the moment.' She shoves his trainers into his PE bag.

'Why? All my friends have pets. It's not fair. You keep saying we'll get one and then you change your mind.'

'Will you be the one to feed it? To walk it? To clear up its poo?' she says mildly, pouring herself a cup of tea. She can see Elliot in her peripheral vision, searching through one of the kitchen drawers, his face grey.

'Yes. I'll do all those things! I promise.'

'Like you did with the hamster? That all fell to me in the end.'

'I was too young then. I was only five.'

'I'd rather get a cat,' says Jasmine, without looking up from her phone.

'Cats are boring,' says Wilfie. 'If we got a dog –'

'For Christ's sake, Wilf,' snaps Elliot. 'Put a sock in it. Your mother's said no!'

They all turn to Elliot in shock. He's staring at his son with fury on his normally good-natured face. In his hand is his passport. Emilia notices that his hand is trembling.

Wilfie's chin wobbles and Jasmine rolls her eyes as if this domestic scene is way beneath her, then turns back to her phone.

Emilia pats Wilfie's shoulder in reassurance, then goes over to her husband. 'Hey, are you okay?'

He runs a hand over his jaw. 'I'm sorry. Sorry, bud,' he says, going over to Wilfie and ruffling his curly hair. 'Dad's just got out of bed the wrong side this morning.'

Jasmine looks as if she wants to make some quip but Emilia shakes her head in warning and Jasmine lowers her eyes.

''S okay,' says Wilfie, but Emilia's heart aches to see how subdued he is.

She rubs Elliot's back. 'It'll be fine,' she says.

'I know. I'll be okay once I'm at the airport,' he replies in a low voice. 'I'm just a bit jittery, that's all.' He tries to hide his fear of flying from the kids, doesn't want it imprinted on them.

A beep from outside alerts them to the taxi and he pulls her into a hug. 'I'll miss you,' he says into her hair.

'I'll miss you too. It's not long. You'll be back on Thursday.'

'In time for your launch.' He pulls away. 'I just hate leaving at the moment after . . . you know.'

'Nothing else has happened and your dad isn't far. And Louise is just a few streets away. If the worst comes to the worst, I can even call Jonas.'

His expression darkens. 'That's a last resort.'

'It is, don't worry.'

Elliot hugs the kids, apologizes again to Wilfie, and

Emilia follows him into the hallway. He picks up his suitcase. 'I'm sorry I've been grumpy this morning.'

'Hey, don't beat yourself up. It's fine. I'll see you on Thursday. Give me a call when you land.'

She kisses him again, then watches from the open doorway as he walks down the steps and to the waiting taxi at the end of the driveway.

It's not until the car pulls away that she sees it: a wreath propped up against the brick wall to the left of the front door, behind the pillar. She checks to make sure the kids can't see, then bends down to look at it. There is a card, which simply says *In Sympathy*, and her insides turn to ice.

Miranda received a wreath in the third book of the series, *No Stone Unturned*, to warn her off a serial-killer case on which she was working.

But who would be warning her? And why?

13

Lorraine Butterworth is a tall, thin woman who exudes nervous energy as she constantly uses her hands, either to tuck a lock of dyed black hair behind her ear or light numerous cigarettes. She must be in her early sixties at least. Her hand trembles as she passes me a chipped mug full of too-milky tea. She's standing with her back against the sink in the small kitchen with the window open, dragging deeply on her cigarette. The striplight above us buzzes, a fly's corpse stuck behind the plastic. The poor woman looks utterly traumatized. I still remember the first time I saw a dead body. Nothing could have prepared me for it. It had haunted me for weeks.

'What can you tell me about Trisha Banks?' I ask, from where I'm sitting at the tiny Formica table. 'How long has she been living in the flat above?'

'Not long. I've lived here years. Seen lots of people come and go. She moved in five or six months back. Kept herself to herself mostly. I always got the sense she was running away from something or someone. She only went out to her job at Poundland, came home and then stayed upstairs. Very rarely saw her go out otherwise.'

'Did you ever see any men coming or going? Boyfriends?'

'Like I told the other copper, I've seen a guy hanging around in the distance. Although I'm not sure if he was her boyfriend. I never saw him come into the building, so I don't think he ever went up to her place. But he was a tall fella.'

I sip my tea and regret it. The milk tastes sour. I put my mug down. 'When you say "hanging around", what do you mean exactly?'

Lorraine takes a deep drag of her cigarette, her veins sticking up through the thin skin on her hands. She exhales a puff of smoke that fills the small space. On the fridge I notice a child's painting of a house, held on with a fluffy-sheep magnet. 'I dunno, really. Lurking outside, I suppose you'd say. Once I saw her talking to him right on the street out there.' She waves her cigarette vaguely in the direction of the front of the house. 'But mostly I'd just notice him a little way off, outside on the pavement. Like he was waiting for her. I called to him once, asked him what he wanted, but he didn't reply, just walked off towards the beach.'

My heart picks up speed. This could be the man. The killer. This could be the person we've been searching for all these years. There have never been any witnesses before apart from once . . . a long time ago. And that was unreliable at best. 'What did he look like?'

She scrunches up her face and sucks at her fag. 'Well-built. Fit-looking. Difficult to say. I didn't see his face. He always wore a hood.'

'And did he have any distinguishing features? Anything that stood out about him?'

She shakes her head. 'Not that I can remember. He had on dark clothing, and it was always at night and, as I said, he always had on a hooded coat. I never saw him during the day.'

'Hair colour? Eyes?'

'Like I said, too dark to see and he was too far away.'

'Height, roughly?'

'I reckon a good six foot at least. I'm five nine and he looked taller than me.'

I swallow my disappointment. I don't know what I expected her to say. He might have been off the scene for sixteen years but he's far from stupid. I was hoping he was rusty. That he'd finally slip up, make a mistake, as he was out of practice.

I get up and tuck my notebook into the pocket of my coat. 'Well, thank you so much, Lorraine. I know this is a shock.'

She stubs out her cigarette in the overflowing ashtray and immediately lights another. 'Am I in danger here? What if he comes back for me this time?'

I couldn't rule it out. Who knows what attracted this man to his victims? They ranged in age from thirty to forty-five. He never sexually abuses them, just stabs them and marks them with his sinister praying-mantis etchings. One thing is for certain, he's a misogynistic psychopath.

'Is there anywhere you can stay for a few days?'

She sniffs. 'Yes. My daughter lives in Paignton. I can stay there.'

'I think that would be a good idea,' I say, moving towards the hallway. She follows me out. 'I'll get one of my officers to sit with you until you're ready to leave.'

She opens the door to her flat and we step out into the main hallway. The front door is still open, the crime-scene tape still surrounding the garden. I'd like her to be out of here before the body of Trisha Banks is taken away.

The wind whips at the hem of my smart wool coat. I can see Saunders and Doyle standing in the doorway of one of the neighbours opposite. Michelle Doyle is making notes – a good sign. Hopefully they've seen something. I'm about to go over when Lorraine suddenly pipes up: 'Wait,' she says. 'I know it's not much, but he smokes. The man I saw. He was a smoker.'

'Okay.' It's not much but it might help. We've had sod-all else over the years.

'But not regular cigarettes,' she continues from the doorway. 'Those menthol ones. They have a very distinctive smell. I know because my granddad used to smoke them, and my dad and brother.'

Menthol cigarettes have recently been banned due to a higher risk of cardiovascular disease, so I wonder where he's getting them from. I thank her, then hold up the crime-scene tape so I can walk underneath it. A tall man who smokes recently banned menthol cigarettes. It's more than we've ever had before.

Maybe he's making mistakes after all.

14

Emilia stares at her phone, swallowing her panic as she tries to work out the doorbell-camera app that Elliot had installed before he went away. She'd had to hide the wreath in the garage at the end of the garden, so the kids wouldn't see it, then make an effort to act normally until she'd dropped them off at school. She didn't want to ring Elliot and worry him while he's away.

Now she's alone in the house, standing at the island in the echoey kitchen that suddenly seems too big. One of the lilies' petals has dropped onto the marble worktop. Elliot would have scooped that up in a flash, frantically bleaching the area it touched just in case the pollen stained the expensive stone. But she leaves it where it is. Eventually she works out how to see the camera footage and her heart beats faster as she brings it up on screen. She rewinds. It must have been put there this morning when they were still getting ready. And, yes, there at 7.45 a.m. is a figure walking down their driveway holding the wreath. Emilia presses her reading glasses further onto her nose. The figure comes into focus and she can see that it's a man, and now he's bending down to place the wreath on the brickwork to the left of the front door. That was why Elliot didn't notice it when he rushed out this morning.

The man doesn't ring the bell but takes a few steps back to look up at the windows. Who is it? Does she know him? His face is now in view in the fish-eye lens. He's bearded, in his fifties perhaps. And then she notices the familiar brown uniform. It's a delivery guy, for fuck's sake. She closes the app with a frustrated sigh. And then her eye goes to the card that she'd pulled from the wreath, now lying on the dining table. She snatches it up. The *In Sympathy* is scribbled in black ink and was probably written by the florist at the request of whoever ordered it. She holds the card up to the light so she can see the address better. It's written in a small font in the corner of the card but she can just make out that the florist is local. Twickenham. Does that mean whoever sent it lives around here? Or did they just choose a florist that was close to her home?

Her mobile is still in her hand, so she dials the number. A woman answers cheerfully.

'Hi,' says Emilia, swallowing, her throat suddenly dry. 'I have a wreath here that was sent to me this morning but there is no name or address and I wanted to check who it's from.'

'Oh, okay,' the woman says brightly. 'Hold on a sec, I'll just look.' She hears the sound of typing and then, 'There's no address or telephone number . . .'

Emilia takes a deep breath. 'Okay. What about pay-ment details?'

'Well, it was paid for in cash. Hold on . . .' More typ-ing. 'Yes, that's all we have. Someone called us and later they came into the shop to pay.'

Her stomach lurches. Does this mean they're local? 'Can you remember what the person looked like?'

'It was a man I think . . . in his thirties, maybe. Mid-brown hair cut short. He said – I remember now – he said he was ordering them on behalf of his wife, Miranda Moody.'

The room spins. *What the fuck?* 'And that's all you have?'

'Yes.'

'And he didn't give his name?'

'No, I'm afraid not.'

'Okay, thanks.' She's just about to end the call when she has a thought. 'Would it be okay to check whether this Miranda Moody has sent me anything before? A bouquet of flowers arrived a week or so ago, with no card attached.'

'Let me just have a look,' the woman says, in her over-enthusiastic voice, which seems at odds with the situation Emilia is finding herself in. She stares out into the gar-den. It's overcast and gloomy, a mist hanging over the trees. From here she can see the edge of Elliot's office and she feels a sense of unease that he's not in there.

There is a rustling sound and then the woman is

back on the line. 'Hi, yes. Miranda Moody also ordered you a bouquet of lilies on the first of March, again over the phone. I wasn't in that day but my colleague was here. I'll ask him if he remembers anything about the order and whether it was the same gentleman who came in to pay.'

'Thank you. That would be really helpful.' She gives the woman her name and telephone number. 'Would it be possible to let me know if this Miranda Moody makes another order before you send anything? I don't want to receive anything else from this person.'

The woman's voice is more subdued now. 'Oh, I'm very sorry. Of course. We'll make a note.'

Emilia ends the call, her mind reeling. A man. She clicks the kettle on, then runs up the two flights of stairs to her office, still in her coat. She'll fetch the notebook Jasmine gave her for her birthday and start writing down everything that happens, like the policeman she spoke to advised. She'll also call Louise and tell her about this latest development, just to be on the safe side. She refuses to let whoever is doing this freak her out. She's not the little mouse she was when she was married to Jonas. She can handle this.

She's panting slightly when she gets to the second floor. She should really use the exercise bike she spent a fortune on, but it's like a form of torture. She's never liked exercise, despite trying her hand at most forms of it, hoping that maybe, this time, she'd have found her 'thing'.

She pulls out the drawer to her desk, finds the notebook and gazes at the first lined page with a sinking feeling. This was supposed to contain her plans for her standalone novel, not that she has any ideas yet. It had been bad enough trying to think of a plot for *Her Last Chapter*. Grabbing a pen she sits at her desk and lists everything that's happened so far, however minor.

By midday Emilia feels like she's going mad, alone in the house, unnerved by every strange sound, every bang of the old-fashioned radiators, the creak of the floorboards. She's thankful she's arranged to meet Ottilie for lunch in Richmond.

The day has brightened up, a weak sun struggling to come out from behind the clouds even though there is dampness in the air.

When Emilia arrives, Ottilie is already seated at an outside table wearing a floor-length powder-blue coat with a fake-fur collar and a matching fluffy hat pressed down over her blonde hair. She waves a gloved hand as Emilia approaches, then gets up to air-kiss her. They hardly sit indoors when they come here; a habit formed during the pandemic, she supposes, but she prefers to be out in the fresh air.

'I've already ordered you a cappuccino,' Ottilie says as they sit down.

'Are you saying I'm predictable?'

'Not at all, darling.' Ottilie grins at her. 'I nearly

ordered you a glass of wine but remembered you need to pick up the kids later.'

Emilia takes off her gloves. 'Only Wilfie. Jasmine makes her own way home now, with Nancy.'

'And so she should. She *is* fifteen.'

Emilia knows she's a bit protective of Jasmine. But her daughter has always been a sensitive child, and then there was the divorce, her remarrying Elliot and them having a baby so soon.

'So,' says Ottilie, leaning back in her chair. 'I've only got an hour unfortunately. I'm seeing a new client this afternoon over in Hampton.' Ottilie has her own interior-design business that she set up back in 2010. It was doing well until it took a hit in the pandemic, and now she's having to work longer hours to get it back up and running. 'But we've got lots to talk about. Not least what happened the other weekend.'

'What do you mean?'

'At dinner, when you received that broken seagull, you seemed a bit on edge afterwards, that's all.'

'Oh, Lordy. Where to start.' Emilia's just about to launch into it all when the waitress arrives with their coffees and to take their lunch order. They opt for the quiche and salad. When she's gone, Emilia says, 'I had a wreath delivered today with a sympathy card attached.'

Ottilie leans forwards, her clear green eyes widening, and Emilia fills her in on everything that's happened since she last saw her.

'Fuck,' she says in response. 'That's quite a campaign.'

'I know.' She tells her friend about the information she'd received from the florist.

'It sounds like you've got yourself a stalker, Mils. You'd better be careful.' She stares at Emilia with concern. 'Have you reported it?'

'Yes. And I told Louise. My detective friend,' she clarifies when Ottilie looks blank. 'You haven't met her yet, but she'll be at my book launch hopefully. She told me to install cameras and one of those Ring doorbells.' Emilia weaves her fingers around her warm mug. 'The fact it's the same as my plotlines freaks me out a bit.'

'Not surprised. It's harassment. At least you've reported it now. Some people are just weird.' Ottilie sighs and glances towards the river as a family of swans swim by. She turns her attention back to Emilia. 'They get a kick out of this kind of thing.'

'It worries me that they know where I live. And what my married name is.'

'You only use Rathbone at school, don't you? Could it be someone from Jasmine's or Wilfie's place?'

She thinks back to all the parents she knows from her children's year groups. She can't think of anyone who would have a grudge against her. 'No. Not at all. They seem like decent people. Some have even become friends.' She thinks of Louise and Marcie, Nancy's mum, whom Emilia has known since their girls started in preschool. 'I can't believe it would be one of them.'

'Maybe it's a crazed fan. You've read *Misery*, haven't you?'

'Cheers, thanks, Ottilie. You really know how to make me feel better.' Emilia tries to keep her tone light but something dark has settled over her.

Ottilie pats her hand. 'I'm sorry. That wasn't helpful. You've reported it now, and you've installed cameras and stuff. There's not much else you can do.' She sighs again, and Emilia realizes her friend has something on her mind.

'What is it? What's wrong?'

The waitress appears again with their quiche but, unusually, Emilia finds she's lost her appetite. When she's gone, Ottilie says, 'It's Stefan. It's not going to work out.'

This doesn't surprise Emilia. Ottilie's relationships never last longer than a year. 'Oh, no. Is it the distance thing?'

'Partly. He's just not for me, though. Too immature.' She digs into her quiche. 'You're lucky with Elliot, you know. To find someone you really gel with. I'm nearly forty and I still feel like I haven't got my shit together.'

'You're still three years away from forty. And you're a successful independent woman. I admire you,' Emilia replies sincerely, picking up her knife and fork and making an effort to eat.

Ottilie scoffs. 'Why would you admire me? You've got it all. A successful marriage, a brilliant career, two wonderful children, that stunning house . . .' She pats her stomach. 'At this rate I'll have to use a sperm donor. And I would if I could afford it.'

'Look at me ten years ago, though. Jonas had walked out – run off with one of my closest friends . . .'

'Glad you didn't say best friend.' Ottilie winks, spearing a tomato with her fork and causing juice to fly onto the table.

'You have been and always will be my only best friend,' Emilia says seriously, dabbing at the tomato juice with a napkin. 'And, anyway, you don't need a man to make your life whole.'

'You know I have trust issues, thanks to my darling daddy.' She rolls her eyes self-mockingly and grins, waving her fork in the air.

Ottilie's jokey tone doesn't fool Emilia. She remembers how devastated Ottilie had been when her parents split up, blaming her father for her mother's unhappiness.

'Not all men are the same. If I'd let what Jonas did to me fuck me up, I'd never have met Elliot. Talking of Jonas, I think he might be on the verge of cheating on Kristin.'

Ottilie nearly chokes on her quiche. '*What?* How do you know? Although I don't see why I'm surprised.'

She tells her about bumping into him with a young woman and their conversation in the café.

'Do you know I actually heard from Kristin this week?' says Ottilie, when Emilia has finished. 'For the first time since she did the dirty on you. Can you believe it?'

'What? Really?'

'It was all a bit weird. I wasn't quite sure whether to tell you.'

The quiche feels heavy in Emilia's stomach. 'Of course you should tell me. We don't keep things from each other. What did she want?'

'Well,' Ottilie says and glances at her, and Emilia knows she's wondering how honest she can be, 'she said she was worried about you.'

'Worried about me? In what way?'

'She said you've been working too hard, arguing with Elliot, and secretly meeting up with Jonas. She implied that there might be something going on between the two of you. Did he tell her you bumped into him and then went for a coffee?'

Emilia's mind reels. 'I don't know, but there's nothing going on with me and Jonas. She must know that. And Elliot and I aren't arguing. And if we were – *which we're not* – how would she know?' She shakes her head. 'I don't get it. And why would Kristin tell you all this anyway when you haven't spoken to her in years?'

'I don't know. To garner my sympathy, perhaps? You know what Kristin can be like. It was a strange conversation and . . . well, she started crying on the phone. She said she missed me, missed our friendship and that she was sorry for everything that had happened.'

'Unbelievable!' Emilia spits. 'She's not once said sorry to me in all these years.'

Ottilie puts down her knife and fork. 'She must know there's another woman on the scene, thinks it's you, and wants info out of me, not that I'd ever tell her anything. I hope you know that.'

Emilia pats Ottilie's arm. 'Of course.' Ottilie has always been fiercely loyal to her, right back to when they were in their first year at boarding school and Emilia was being picked on by an older girl.

'She sounded a bit pissed on the phone. She also wanted interior-design tips and asked how I had started my business. I bet she was mortified the next day.'

Emilia pushes her plate away. She doesn't know how she'd feel if Ottilie decided to be friends with Kristin again. The betrayal still runs too deep. She was the one who had brought them together – these two separate but, at the time, most important people in her life. She and Kristin had been on the same English literature course and had bonded over their love of alternative guitar bands, regularly going to gigs together. Ottilie, finding it hard to settle to anything, as is her way, would come to Brighton whenever she could to hang out with them.

'I'll never forgive her, don't worry, Mils,' says Ottilie, as though reading her mind. She finishes her coffee. 'Do you want another?'

Emilia says she does, but she can't really concentrate after that.

As soon as she steps into her house she feels it. The chill in the air. She walks into the kitchen, and freezes when she sees the skylight windows. They are wide open, like three gaping mouths, mocking her. The praying-mantis killer in her latest Miranda Moody thriller, *Her Last Chapter*, accesses his victims' homes by their skylights. Yet nobody, apart from her editor, has read that book yet. So this, she hopes, is at least a coincidence.

A floorboard creaks overhead and her blood runs cold. Someone is in the house.

15

Daisy,
1998

Daisy remembers waking up early on the morning she found her mother dead. It was Sunday, 15 February 1998, and it was still dark. She doesn't know what it was that filled her with a sense of dread as soon as she opened her eyes. It was as though something had shifted in the universe, alerting her to the horror she would soon face. For a few moments she lay there, still, her heart beating beneath her pink gingham duvet, as she remembered the noises she'd heard in the night, the muffled voices, knowing that once she got out of bed everything would change.

The first sign that something was off was the light that still glowed in the hallway. Her mum always turned the lights off before she went to bed but sometimes she would fall asleep in front of the television, and Daisy would hear her in the early hours making her way up the stairs. The second was the unmade bed in her mum's room, the feeling that it hadn't been occupied all night, the air too clean and not filled with sleep. In trepidation

Daisy descended the stairs, hoping her mum had fallen asleep in front of the TV again, that she'd hear the reassuring sound of the early-morning presenters. Instead, she was met with an eerie silence. The hallway light might have been on, but the rest of downstairs was in darkness.

'Mum?' she said. Her voice sounded small. 'Mum?' she said again, louder this time. She pushed open the first door on the left, her eyes sweeping over the living room and adjusting to the gloom. It was unusually tidy: no cups or plates left out on the coffee table, no empty crisps tubes rolling around on the floor, no biscuit wrappers or newspapers littering the surfaces or shoved down the sides of the chairs. For someone who cleaned other people's houses, her mother wasn't that bothered about their own. The heavy floral curtains were drawn, the television off. But lying on the sofa, on her side, fully dressed, her eyes closed, was her mum.

An overwhelming feeling of relief swept over Daisy. She'd just fallen asleep in front of the telly, that was all. She looked peaceful as Daisy approached her, a curl of her dark hair falling over one eye. Daisy was tempted to move it away and tuck it behind her ear, like her mum always did for her. Daisy pulled at her nightie so she could bend her knees to squat down, and gently shook her mother's shoulder. 'Mum. You fell asleep. Wake up.'

As soon as Daisy touched her mother, she knew. She was so cold, her skin a strange bluish-white that made her look like the pierrot doll she had. And then she saw it.

The circle of dark red that had stained her mum's favourite pale pink blouse. 'Mum!' Daisy screamed then, and began shaking her vigorously even though she knew it would be fruitless. 'Mum! Wake up! Wake up! Please . . . Please . . .' She sobbed, bending over her mother's cold, still body. She didn't know how long she stayed like that but eventually daylight was seeping in around the curtains.

There was only one person she could call. Her dad. He was there within ten minutes, prising her off her mother's dead body and calling the police.

'Yes,' she heard him say into the phone, panic and fear in his voice. 'It's my ex-partner. Her name is Jennifer Radcliffe. She's . . . ah . . .' She heard the catch in his voice as he turned to his daughter, his eyes red. 'There's no pulse.'

It was all hectic after that, the cosy two-up-two-down she'd shared with her mother invaded by officials roaming around the house like rats. One lady with a kind face and a swishy ponytail tried to steer her out of the living room and away from her mother. She remembers kicking up a fuss – which was unlike her as she was always polite, unassuming, too shy even to put up her hand in class – as the kind-faced lady coaxed her away.

But not before she'd spotted it. A drawing of an insect's head on her mum's ankle that was definitely not a tattoo.

Her mother's mysterious boyfriend flashed through her mind, with his double crown, his wide, ham-like neck and his penchant for doodling in the margins of newspapers.

And she knew – she just knew – that he was responsible for this. The Doodle Man, as she came to think of him, had killed her mother, and she vowed, right there at the age of ten, standing in that living room surrounded by police, that she wouldn't rest until she had found him.

16

With a scream in her throat Emilia darts out of the front door, slamming it behind her, and calls the only person she knows who might be able to help.

'Hello,' says a familiar voice at the other end.

'Trevor. I'm sorry to bother you at work but . . .' Emilia hesitates. She's standing in her driveway looking up at the house. Those windows didn't open by themselves. 'I'm worried someone is in the house.' She explains about the skylights.

'Don't go back in. I'm coming straight over,' he barks, ending the call before she's even had the chance to reply.

She stares up at the windows. It begins to rain, light drizzle that settles on her coat and darkens the path. She feels impotent standing there, afraid to go into her own house. Her home has always been her sanctuary. The first place she and Elliot had owned together after a succession of rented flats. And now it's tainted. Tainted by the unwanted packages turning up at her door, by the troll doll hanging from her tree. This invasion of her personal space, her life. The life she makes such an effort to keep separate, refusing to go on social media, not least because she has a phobia about anything she deems too technically complicated but mainly because she's very private and always has been. And now her fiction is blending into her reality.

While she's waiting for Trevor, she assesses her Ring-Cam app to see if it's picked up anyone. Her heart is racing as she rewinds the footage on the cameras at the front and the back. But there is nothing. Could someone have got in by circumventing the cameras? She looks up at the roof. It's high, with its two dormer windows and the sky-light at the side. It would be easier to access the kitchen, with a single-storey roof at the back, but the culprit would have to climb over her neighbour's wall to do so without being seen by the cameras.

By the time Trevor pulls up in his Honda Civic the rain has stopped, leaving behind the familiar earthy smell she's recently learned from Jasmine's science lessons is called petrichor. She breathes it in, feeling instantly calmer now she can see Trevor hurrying towards her, still in his security-guard uniform, fit and lithe at sixty-two. He'd been young, just twenty-three, when he had Elliot. His face is serious, but he gives a reassuring smile when he sees her. 'You okay?' he asks, patting her shoulder in a fatherly way (Not that her own father ever did that. Physical affection seems to terrify Hugh Ward).

She nods. 'Thanks for coming, Trevor. I've not been back inside.'

'Good. Stay here. If I'm not out within ten minutes call the police.'

Her insides fold over. 'What?'

He raises his bushy eyebrows. 'I'm sure it won't come to that.' He takes her front-door key and marches purposefully towards the house. She remembers all the times she'd left the porch door unlocked, feeling completely safe in this neighbourhood. A false sense of security in middle-class suburbia. What a fool she'd been.

'Everything okay?'

Emilia turns to the sound of her next-door neighbour Madge's voice. She's walking her beagle and pauses at the entrance to the driveway. Madge is mid-sixties, fit and robust, with rosy cheeks and a variety of different-colour quilted gilets. Today she's in pink with a navy blue waterproof slung over the top and looks spring-like and bouncy. 'Have you locked yourself out?'

'No. My father-in-law's inside. Just checking the house for me.' She explains about the windows, and a kaleidoscope of emotions passes over Madge's face. 'Did you see anyone?'

'Sorry, I didn't, but you can't be too careful. Apparently there have been a few burglaries around here lately.' She lowers her voice and glances fearfully over her shoulder as though said burglar is listening. 'We don't even have security cameras. Truth be told, the house is way too big for myself and Philip now the kids have flown the nest, but . . .' She sighs and consults her watch. 'Better get on. I'm meeting my daughter for coffee.' She waves at Emilia as she makes her way down the hill and Emilia feels a pang for what will never be. She can't remember the last time she met up with her mother. It's hard to entice her from the depths of her detached mock-Tudor house in Middle England.

Her toes have turned numb and she stamps her feet. What is Trevor doing? It's a big house, granted, but he's been ages. She looks at her watch. What if the intruder has hurt him? Just as she's contemplating calling the police, Trevor appears at the front door. He beckons her over. 'It's okay. I've looked in every room, behind every door, in every wardrobe. No one's in the house.' He sounds officious standing there, reminding her of the cop he once was. She's so grateful she wants to hug him.

'Thanks so much. I just don't understand why the skylights were open. Was the one outside my office open too?'

'No, they were all closed when I went in, but I think they shut automatically when it rains. Maybe a dodgy switch had opened them. Have you got them on a timer?'

'That's the weird thing. They haven't been opened in months.'

Trevor moves aside. She squeezes past him and Elliot's bike, the handlebars almost poking her in the ribs, into the hallway and then the kitchen. Trevor follows. She calls to Alexa to turn on the kitchen lights.

'You've got her well trained.' Trevor laughs and folds his arms. He looks like he's put on a bit of weight. It suits him. She wonders again if he's met someone.

'Blame your son. I'd love to use a light switch now and again, but he's got everything hooked up to Alexa, even the radio.' She clicks the kettle on. Trevor pulls out one of the wooden barstools at the island and sits. The whole kitchen is awash with a bluish hue now that what little is left of the afternoon sun is at the front of the house. 'I have to pick up Wilfie soon but I've got time for a quick coffee. What would you like?'

'Tea would be great, thanks.'

'I'm sorry I wasted your time.' She turns to face him while the kettle boils noisily. 'What excuse did you give to leave work so urgently?'

'Oh, just that I had to pop out because there was a family emergency. It's okay, it's a quiet day. Elliot says you've now got cameras front and back. That's reassuring. And you didn't waste my time. It's better to be safe than sorry, Emilia.' He frowns and she knows the open skylights are still troubling him. Her too, but she doesn't know what else to do. Trevor has assured her that nobody is in the house and the cameras haven't shown anyone breaking in.

Trevor picks up the lily petal that sits on the counter from this morning and starts rolling it between his fingers, getting yellow stains on his thumb. 'The person sending you this stuff is obviously a coward and doesn't want to show their face,' he continues. 'It's like those trolls you get behind keyboards, writing insulting twits online.'

'They're called tweets, Trevor.' She laughs. He knows

what they're really called and she suspects he's just trying to lighten the mood.

'Ah, tweets, twits, whatever.'

She makes him some tea, builders', just as he likes it, and joins him at the island. They chat a bit more, about his job, about Elliot's business trip to Iceland, about Wilfie and his newfound love of classic cars, which have always fascinated Trevor.

Half an hour later he's left and she's standing outside the school gates waiting for Wilfie. She finds herself evaluating the other parents, wondering if they could be behind everything that's happened. She feels suspicious of everyone. Even Frances, Louise's monster-in-law, who comes barrelling out of the main school doors clutching Toby's hand as he's wriggling to get away. Toby must be in trouble again. She knows from Louise that he can be mischievous, lacks attention, can sometimes be disruptive in class. Frances acknowledges her with a nod. She's a big woman, large feet clad in sensible walking shoes, and is brisk, a bit abrupt, but her love for her grandson shines from her. Emilia can see why she'd bug Louise, though. Frances isn't a woman who likes hearing the word 'no'.

Wilfie is waltzing out behind them, shirt hanging out, hair standing on end, so like Elliot's. She ruffles it when he approaches, and he tries to dodge her. 'Too late,' she says, laughing. He grins, conker-brown eyes shining, and hands her his backpack. 'Please, Mum,' he wails when she refuses to take it. 'It's heavy.' She rolls her eyes inmock-irritation and slings it over her shoulder. As they walk the ten minutes home he chatters on about his day, what he had for lunch, who got told off for talking in class (Toby, inevitably) and how he doesn't like his new art teacher.

She tries to concentrate on what Wilfie is saying, but all she can think about is what might await them when they return home.

17

'Your dad, thankfully, came over and there was nobody in the house,' she's telling Elliot in hushed tones on the phone later that evening. Jasmine and Wilfie are watching *Ghosts* for the tenth time, and she's just thrown a garlic-and-herb chicken in the oven. Of the two of them, Elliot is the one who loves cooking.

It's started to rain again and it drums on the skylights. She doesn't like the thought of spending the night alone in the house. Thank goodness for the cameras.

'So all three skylights were open?' Elliot sounds shocked. 'But Dad didn't find anybody in the house?'

'Nobody. I checked the app, too, and couldn't see anyone on the cameras.'

'I don't like the thought of this going on at home when I'm not there. Can't you ring someone to stay the night?'

'It's fine.' She hadn't wanted him to know about the skylights but she was worried that Trevor might ring to tell him.

'Do you think this is the work of another writer?' he asks. She imagines him sitting on the edge of a pristinely made bed in some minimalist hotel in Reykjavik. She wishes he was here, with her. Or, rather, that she was there with him. 'An enemy you've made perhaps?'

She isn't in the habit of making enemies, and all the writers she's met, mostly at festivals or through events, have been lovely. Supportive. She can't imagine any of them doing something like this. This, she realizes, with a stab of fear, is the work of some sociopath. She suspects she doesn't even know the person, that it's just someone who has read her books and become a bit fixated. 'I've reported it to the same policeman I spoke to before. A PC Clayton.'

'And what is he going to do about it?'

'I don't know . . . he didn't say. What can he do? This is the thing . . .' She takes a deep breath. She can feel her voice rising and she doesn't want to get hysterical. She notices Jasmine turn to look at her from where she's sitting on the sofa. Emilia lowers her voice and turns away. 'He said we've done the right thing by putting cameras up. But there isn't much they can do yet.'

Elliot makes a sound of frustration at the other end of the line. 'I could kill whoever is doing this.'

'It's just silly stuff,' she says, trying to reassure him. And herself.

'Can't you ask Louise to help? Surely there must be some perks to having a copper friend.'

'She's in the Major Crime unit and covers homicide. Not this kind of thing.'

'But she might know someone who can help.'

She glances towards her children. Wilfie is watching the telly, Jasmine sitting against the armrest, her knees pulled up to her chest, engrossed in her phone, but Emilia knows her daughter has ears like a bat. She suddenly feels a surge of protectiveness towards them. 'I'll call her and ask. You're right, there have to be some perks.'

And she'd do anything to keep her family safe.

Emilia has just put Wilfie to bed and is talking to Jasmine in the kitchen about Jake, a boy Nancy fancies, when there is a knock at the front door. Her heart quickens and she instructs her daughter to stay where she is.

'Why are you being weird?' Jasmine says, cupping her mug of hot chocolate. She's in pyjamas that are slightly too big for her and fat, fluffy socks, reminding Emilia of the little girl she used to be.

'I'm not,' she replies, flashing her daughter what she hopes is a reassuring smile.

'You look mad.'

Emilia's heart is in her mouth as she opens the glass double doors and peers through the spyhole. She exhales in relief when she sees Ottilie's blonde hair and fur-collared coat.

She opens the door and is hit by the cold, dank air. 'What are you doing here?'

Ottilie shoves a bottle of wine at her and brushes past Elliot's bike to hang her coat on the stand at the bottom of the stairs. 'I always forget how huge this hallway is,' she says. 'To answer your question, yes, Elliot rang. He was worried. So I'm staying the night. No.' She holds up a hand. 'Don't even try to stop me.'

Emilia wouldn't dare. And she's relieved that Ottilie is here. If she had her way the house would be filled with people, life and laughter every night of the week. Elliot is more reserved: he'd prefer it to be just the four of them.

'Hi, Aunty Ottilie,' trills Jasmine, coming into the hallway, still nursing her mug of hot chocolate. 'What are you doing here?'

'Ssh.' Emilia ushers them into the kitchen and closes the doors so as not to wake Wilfie. She opens the bottle of wine and fetches two glasses.

'I fancied a sleepover,' says Ottilie to Jasmine, taking the glass from Emilia.

Jasmine rolls her eyes. 'I know something's going on,' she says, directing this at her mum.

'It's nothing.' Emilia takes a sip of wine to hide her lie. 'Just some pranks have been played on me, that's all.'

'Like what?'

'Oh, silly things. Receiving lilies with no note, a seagull –'

'A seagull?' Jasmine shrieks.

'A ceramic one,' clarifies Emilia, noticing her daughter's horrified expression. She doesn't mention the skylights, the troll doll, or the wreath.

'But that's not why I'm here, sweetheart,' says Ottilie

with a wave of her hand. 'Your dad's away so we thought we'd have a girly night.'

Disbelief is etched on her daughter's perfect face. Near her eyebrow there is a tiny mark left from the chicken pox she caught at the age of four but otherwise her face is blemish-free, skin Emilia can only dream of. She's suffered with hormonal spots since she was in her teens. 'I'm going to bed, then,' Jasmine says. 'I don't want to hear you both reminisce about boarding school for the millionth time.'

'Rude,' quips Emilia. She pulls Jasmine in for a kiss. She smells of chocolate, and apple shampoo. 'Goodnight. Love you.'

'Goodnight, darling,' calls Ottilie as Jasmine wanders out of the kitchen, closing the kitchen door pointedly behind her. Emilia is thankful that the doors are glass so she can see into the hallway and watch as Jasmine goes up the stairs. She's checked the attic skylight ten times since she got home and it's firmly closed. She has even considered fastening some kind of rope or tie around the latch to stop anyone getting in, but that would involve the ladder, which is in the garage.

'So,' says Ottilie, walking over to the squashy sofas at the family-room end of the kitchen, 'what else has been happening since I saw you at lunchtime? Elliot sounded quite rattled on the phone.'

'I haven't told him all of it.' Emilia sighs, flopping onto the opposite end of the sofa and facing her friend. Then she has a thought. 'You didn't mention the wreath, did you?'

Ottilie frowns. 'I did. I thought you had.'

Emilia pulls her feet up underneath her. No wonder Elliot freaked out and insisted Ottilie come over. 'I was going to tell him, but I didn't want to worry him while he's away. I didn't want to tell him about the skylights either.'

'I'm so sorry, I didn't know. Anyway, I'm here now, and when I find out what piece of shit is doing this, I'll . . . I'll . . .' She plays with the stem of her wine glass.

'You'll what?'

'Give them a piece of my mind.' They burst out laughing. It's what their house mistress used to say to them. 'Anyway . . .' Ottilie flicks her hair back from her face. Her fingernails are painted bright pink '. . . it's probably some geeky nerd who has a crush on you and wants your attention.'

'A crush! I'm an overweight, middle-aged mum of two.'

'You are not overweight! Don't be so ridiculous. You have a great figure. And you're not even forty. I'm sorry, but middle-aged is definitely over fifty, maybe even fifty-five, these days!'

'If you say so.'

'I do. So there. God . . .' She shakes her head while studying Emilia.

'What? You're unnerving me now.'

'You! Jonas and Kristin really did a number on you, didn't they?'

'What do you mean?'

'You're gorgeous, kind . . . and yet, I don't know, you have such low self-esteem.'

Emilia feels tears prick her eyes and sips her wine to hide her feelings. 'We can't all be superconfident like you,' she says, trying to sound light. 'It's easy to be confident when you're five foot nine and look like Claudia Schiffer.'

'I wish! I don't look like Claudia Schiffer. And I have my insecurities as you well know. Maybe I made a mistake finishing with Stefan.' She sips her wine. 'I'd love to have what you have. Obviously not your current situation with this creeper.'

Emilia laughs despite herself. With Ottilie here things don't seem quite as foreboding. She has a way of making Emilia feel lighter.

Ottilie sighs. 'I'm a bit worried about my business, to be honest. Dad, thankfully, has lent me some money but I don't know how much longer I can prop it up.'

'Have things still not picked up?'

'A bit. The woman in Hampton I saw this afternoon has a huge house and wants help with every room, so that will tide me over for a while. Maybe I'm just tiring of it, I dunno.' She sits back against the cushions.

'It would seem a shame if you stopped. You've been doing it now for nearly twelve years. I'm proud of you for sticking at it as long as you have,' says Emilia.

Ottilie doesn't have a great track record for sticking at things. She took a few years out before deciding to go to university, but then managed just one term before realizing a degree wasn't for her. A myriad of dead-end jobs followed before she opted to do an interior-design course in her late twenties. There's always been something restless about her friend. At school they'd bonded over their similar childhoods with parents who were physically and emotionally distant, Emilia's because of her father's job in the RAF and Ottilie's due to her mum's early death and a father who decided to move to Germany. Although they are the same age, Ottilie always seemed older to Emilia back then. More worldly and knowing, almost like a big sister, but she sensed that Ottilie was never really fulfilled, that she was always looking for some unobtainable thing to complete her.

They go to bed too late – Ottilie always was a night owl – and Emilia has only just dropped off to sleep when she's woken by loud music blasting through the house. She sits up in bed, disoriented for a few seconds, and then her heart is banging, adrenaline pumping through her. What the hell?

The music sounds like it's filtering through all the speakers that Elliot has set up around the house. Talking Heads' 'Psycho Killer' of all things. She jumps out of bed and rushes onto the landing. Jasmine and Wilfie wander out of their respective bedrooms with bed hair and puzzled expressions, and the three stand in mutual shock until Ottilie darts down the stairs, resplendent in a long silk nightdress. 'What the fuck – Oops, sorry.' She claps a hand over her mouth and looks at Wilfie.

Emilia has to shout over the music to instruct Alexa to stop playing and the house falls mercifully silent.

'Why has the music gone off in the middle of the night?' Wilfie cries, staring up at Emilia with his big brown eyes.

She hugs him to her and kisses the top of his head. 'She must have got confused. It's okay.'

'Perhaps it's on the blink,' says Ottilie, glancing at her with concern over the top of Wilfie's head.

'Is there a way to disconnect the speakers?' asks Jasmine. 'And why is it so cold?'

Emilia turns towards the staircase that leads to the attic and the back of her neck prickles. 'Stay here,' she instructs the kids. She can hear Ottilie close behind her as she runs up to the second floor. Just as she feared, the skylight is wide open.

Emilia wants to cry. 'But I checked it so many times. I . . .' She can feel the blood draining from her face.

Ottilie places a reassuring hand on her arm. 'There's got to be an explanation.'

They head back to the children, who are still hovering on the landing. Even Jasmine looks worried and has her arm around Wilfie's shoulders.

Emilia tries to keep the panic from her voice. 'It's okay. It's sorted now. You both go back to bed.'

Once she's settled an anxious Wilfie in his top bunk, reassured Jasmine and closed the skylight on the attic landing, she and Ottilie head down to the kitchen.

'Your skylights? They're connected to Alexa too, right?' says Ottilie, bending down and examining the white Echo on the kitchen shelf above the sink.

'Yes. Elliot set it all up through the app.'

Ottilie stands back, her hands on her hips, her eyes still on Alexa. 'Hmm. It sounds to me like it's been hacked and someone's instructing your Echo to do these things.'

Of course. Why didn't she think of that? After all, she wrote it in book four, *Who Lies Beneath*. The killer in that book was living in the basement of a family's house and terrorizing them through their digital home assistants.

'Thank goodness you don't have a basement,' says Ottilie, ominously, as though reading her mind.

18

Daisy,
2005

So now here Daisy was, eighteen years old and living with her dad and stepmother, Shannon, in a town far away from where she'd spent her first ten years. Happy, she supposed, although she'd lived nearly half of her life without her lovely mum. She'd tried to find out everything she could about her mother's murder, but there was surprisingly little information. Her dad had shielded her from all of it, orchestrating a move away from their little seaside town in Devon to Pocklington in Yorkshire.

At first she'd been too young to fully understand what had happened to her mother, but from snatches of hushed conversations, police visits and phone calls, she knew she'd been murdered. And the marking on her ankle, she was sure, had been made by the secret boyfriend. She'd shown her father the newspaper with the doodles in the margin, had told him her suspicions about her mother's secret boyfriend. Her dad had listened and had taken her observations seriously. He'd even set up an interview with a grave-faced female detective who, it had been obvious, found it hard to know exactly how to talk to ten-year-old girls. She'd heard whispers bandied about between the grown-ups of a 'cereal killer', which always made her imagine the murderer eating lots of cornflakes. Finding him had consumed her throughout her teenage years.

'He's killed other women,' her dad admitted one day, when she was about fifteen, and had begged him to tell her more about her mother's murder. 'One woman before your mother and several after. The police will catch him eventually.'

It baffled her that this man was getting away with it. Killing in plain sight, and all in Devon. It hadn't been a coincidence that she'd chosen Exeter University. She knew she had to be around the south-west again – she couldn't do anything from North Yorkshire.

The day her father had driven her to university he had turned the radio down and said, in his most serious voice, 'I hope you don't have any silly ideas about trying to find the man you think killed your mother. You leave anything like that to the police, do you hear, Daise? It's not safe.'

'Of course I will,' she had scoffed in reply. And what could she really do, except on occasion take the bus from the university to her old seaside town on the outskirts of Plymouth to scan the streets, the shops, the arcades, the seafront for any sightings of the Doodle Man. Because she had something the police, and nobody else, had ever had. She had *seen* him. She had watched her mother sneak him into the house and sneak him out again. She had seen the doodles in the newspapers he'd left behind. And, okay, she hadn't had a good glimpse of his face, but she'd told the police about his fair sticky-out hair that was caused by his two crowns, his ham-like neck. They'd told her they would try to find out the identity of her mother's mystery lover, if for no other reason than to eliminate him from their enquiries. But as far as she knew, he had never been found.

And then, during her first term at university, everything changed when she met Ash.

19

Over the next few days, Emilia has no choice but to try to put the recent events to the recesses of her mind. She's busy preparing for her paperback launch of *The Lost Man*, and has received the edits on *Her Last Chapter*. She wants to work on them as quickly as possible so that she can send them to Hannah before her editor goes off on maternity leave. She buries herself in her book, grateful for the distraction, working long hours to get it finished.

Elliot arrives just two hours before they need to leave for her launch. She hasn't long been home after picking up the kids from school and there is clutter everywhere, last night's dinner plates still stacked in the sink, the kitchen table covered with Jasmine's coursework, and half-cut card left over from Wilfie's English project. She feels a flicker of guilt, then remembers how busy she's been. Still, she goes about stacking the dishwasher as soon as she hears his key in the lock.

He looks tired but relieved to be home when he walks into the kitchen. He wraps his arms around her waist as she bends over the dishwasher rack and rests his cheek against her shoulder.

'Can't tell you how good it is to be home.'

She turns to hug him. 'It's great to have you back.' All the anxiety she's been feeling the last few days ebbs away and she relaxes into him, inhaling his familiar warm scent. He kisses her, then pulls away, asking where the kids are.

'In the den. I've said they can come to the launch tonight.'

He frowns as he casts his eye around the room but he doesn't say anything. 'Great. I'll just go and say hi to them.' He leaves the kitchen and she continues stacking the dishwasher. When Elliot returns five minutes later he has both kids in tow. He must have told them to tidy up because they wordlessly, if reluctantly, begin packing away their things. Wilfie sighs at least five times as he gathers up the card. She bites back her irritation, wishing Elliot would relax for once and tell them about his trip rather than fixating on any mess.

'Be ready for six,' she calls to them after they've finished and made a hasty retreat. She's greeted with two grunts in response.

'You could have made more fuss of the kids,' she says as soon as they've left the room. 'Especially Wilf. He missed you when you were away.'

Elliot's face falls. 'Sorry ... I wasn't thinking. I've brought them gifts.' He reaches into his bag and extracts two fluffy moose. He holds them up and makes them talk to each other in silly voices until she laughs. 'I'll go and give them to the kids.'

While he's gone, she finishes clearing up. When he returns he looks more relaxed. He takes her hand. 'Come on, let's have five minutes to catch up before we have to leave.' They head to the sofa and sit down. 'So? What else happened while I was away?'

She crosses her ankles and tells him about the night Ottilie stayed over.

He runs a hand through his hair and pulls at his tie as though it's strangling him. 'I think we need some more security. You've changed the password for Alexa?'

'Of course. I did that straight away. Made it more secure.'

'Could someone have got hold of the original one?'

'I don't know. I can't see how. I keep it, with others, on my phone and the kids don't know it, but . . .' She shrugs.

'I'll ask Dad about getting this place some proper security alarms,' he says, reaching over and taking her hand. 'Just to be on the safe side.'

The book launch is only for her close family and friends in a small, narrow independent bookshop called the Shop on the Corner in Richmond. They aren't really her thing – she hates being the centre of attention and both her weddings had been small, intimate affairs – although with Jonas that had been because she was pregnant. Her friends have always encouraged her to do a book launch – although she knows that's because it's a good excuse for a get-together and a booze-up. She knows Elliot doesn't really enjoy them, and he finds it difficult being in too close proximity to Jonas. He's said before he doesn't really understand why she always invites him and Kristin or why they come. But they are Jasmine's family so, therefore, still part of hers. And it's been years since she's done a book launch.

'Did you invite your mum and dad?' asks Elliot as he pours prosecco into glasses while they wait for people to begin arriving. Wilfie and Jasmine are slouched on the bookshop's only sofa, already looking bored.

'I did, but who knows if they'll come?' They've only made one launch, for her debut.

Elliot squeezes her arm in sympathy and she moves away when she sees her editor with her publicist, Ava, walk in. Hannah looks like she's about to give birth at any minute and places a hand on her back as she greets Emilia. Ava, who is mid-twenties at the most, with waist-length dark hair and a ready smile, rearranges the stock of *The Lost Man* on the table.

It's not long before the small bookshop is packed. Drummond, her agent, arrives with his very glamorous wife. Now both in their late sixties they were childhood sweethearts and still look very much in love. Ottilie is in the corner chatting to one of Emilia's crime-writer friends, Rob. He's handsome, single and seems to be enjoying his chat with Ottilie, who has him almost pinned up against one of the bookcases. She looks fabulous in a low-cut red dress and matching lipstick, her long blonde hair gleaming. Emilia wishes she felt as confident in her new dress.

She glances around for Louise. She'd said she was going to pop in on her way back from work but she can't spot her among the sea of faces. There are a few people she doesn't recognize – maybe plus-ones of her friends – but her heart stutters at the sight of them. What if her stalker is here tonight? She remembers what the woman at the florist said about a man in his mid-thirties coming into the shop to place the order for the wreath. Emilia had called her back yesterday to ask if her colleague thought it was the same man who had placed the lilies order and it was. Is there anyone here matching that description? Her eyes roam the room and she almost jumps out of her skin when a hand clamps onto her shoulder.

It's Elliot. She's hardly seen him all evening. She knows he's been with Wilfie. Nancy is here with her mum, Marcie, so at least Jasmine is occupied.

'Are you all right?' he asks her, his face full of concern.

She nods. 'It's just . . . I keep thinking, What if he's here?' She assumes it's a he based on what the florist has told her.

'Don't let this ruin your night –' He stops mid-flow as Kristin and Jonas walk in arm in arm and head straight for where Pam, the bookshop owner, is handing out drinks.

'Be nice,' Emilia warns her husband.

'When am I ever not nice?' He grins.

Emilia surveys the room. Despite the wet weather it's warm in the shop, and people are packed quite closely together. The hum of a dozen conversations wafts over to her. 'I was hoping Louise was here so I could introduce you. I hope she can make it. Shit. Look who's just arrived.'

Elliot's eyes are round as he follows her gaze. Her parents have just walked in. Her mother is in a heavy shearling coat, darkened at the shoulders by the rain, and her father is stiff and soldier-like in his Barbour and tweed cap. She can't believe they've ventured here in this weather. They stand at the door, looking bewildered, and Elliot steps forwards to go over to them, then stops when he sees they've been intercepted by Jonas.

He turns to Emilia with an air of disappointment. She made the mistake once of telling him how much her mum had loved Jonas, and she knows he worries that he's not as close to them. But it's hard to be close to her parents. 'I'll check on Wilfie,' says Elliot. 'Go and mingle. This is your launch.'

She watches him weave his way through the crowd to where their son is sitting in the children's area of the bookshop. Jasmine and Nancy are giggling together, huddled on the yolk-yellow sofa, both peering at Jasmine's phone. Emilia smiles to herself, remembering Ottilie and herself at that age. She's glad Elliot is keeping an eye on them all. She still can't shake the feeling that the person behind everything that has happened to her lately could be in this room or, at the very least, watching her from outside.

She heads towards her parents and Jonas, wondering where Kristin has gone.

Her father steps forwards when he sees her, his eyes bright. 'Hello, love.'

'Darling,' her mother says, air-kissing her. 'This is a great turnout.'

'Thank you so much for coming,' Emilia says. She hasn't seen them since Christmas.

'I loved the book,' says her father, in his quiet voice. 'I read it in hardback.'

'He bought it,' says her mother, 'despite the price. I told him he shouldn't have to pay for it, considering his daughter had written it. I hope we get an early copy of the next one.'

Jonas turns to her for the first time and raises an eyebrow. She tries not to smile. 'I'm sure that can be arranged,' she says.

'You do know what she's doing in the next one, don't you?' says Jonas. 'She's killing off Miranda Moody!'

Her father gasps. 'You're not!'

'Jonas,' hisses Emilia, 'don't ruin it.'

Jonas's hand flies to his mouth. 'Sorry.'

Her mother shuffles out of her coat and folds it over her arm. 'Well, I've never read them. I don't like crime novels. Enough depressing stuff in the news as it is. I don't know why you can't write something a bit more uplifting, darling. Something funny.'

'Maybe because Em doesn't have a sense of humour,'

Jonas quips, and she digs him in the side with her elbow.

'I must have had one to marry you,' she retaliates.

'Ouch.' He laughs, a lock of blond hair falling over his eye.

Her mother purses her lips in disapproval at their easy manner, as though she'd rather they were fighting and sniping at each other. 'Where's your *current* wife, Jonas?' she asks icily, like he's been married a dozen times.

Jonas inclines his head to where Kristin is talking to Marcie. They are very close to where Ottilie is chatting up Rob, and she notices Kristin glancing at her every now and again. Emilia wonders if she will try to talk to Ottilie.

She turns her attention back to her parents and Jonas. 'Your grandkids are at the back of the shop with Elliot if you want to say hi.' It annoys her how hands-off they are as grandparents. They hardly ever ask after Wilfie and Jasmine.

'Of course we do. Come on, Hugh,' her mother says, grabbing her dad's arm and leading him through the throng.

Emilia exhales in relief when they've gone.

'Same as ever,' laughs Jonas. 'I'm surprised they spoke to me.'

'They were fond of you. You could always make my mum laugh.'

'Not anymore,' he says. He digs his hands into the

pockets of his wool blazer. 'Elliot is avoiding me too, I see.'

'He finds it hard. It's awkward.'

'The only people who should feel awkward are us, and we don't, do we? It's all water under the bridge.'

That's the problem with her ex. He just wants everything to be brushed under the carpet, for there to be no consequences to his behaviour. That everyone just forgets and moves on. But some people's memories are long, and her mother loves to hold on to a grudge. She needs little reason to dislike someone. 'You know what my mum's like. She loves any excuse to feel aggrieved. She was gutted when we split up. You were the son she never had.'

His cheeks redden and he sips his prosecco. 'Anyway, most importantly, are you having a good night?'

'I am, actually.' Even though my stalker might be in this very room, she thinks, but doesn't voice it to Jonas. She hasn't told him any of it yet and she certainly doesn't want to get into it here.

'You sound surprised.'

'You know this isn't my type of thing.'

He smiles sympathetically. 'I do but, Em, this is such an achievement. I'm proud of you, I hope you know that. I remember how much you wanted this. How you talked about your dream of being a novelist. And you made it happen.' His eyes lock with hers and the room seems to shrink a little as she's taken back to when they first met, to how she'd felt about him. To when things were good.

She lowers her eyes. 'Thanks, Jonas. That means a lot.'

They smile shyly at each other, as Ottilie wanders over to them 'Long time no see,' she says to Jonas.

'Hi, Ottilie.' He twists his glass between his fingers.

Emilia immediately tenses, remembering that she'd told Ottilie about Jonas's flirtation with his co-worker. *Please don't say anything*, she silently wills.

'So, how's things going, Boner?' Ottilie asks.

Emilia winces at her old nickname for him. Jonas's blue eyes widen a little but he ignores the jibe. 'All good. You?'

'Nice of you and your *wife* to come tonight.' She opens her mouth to say more but Emilia throws her a warning look and she shuts it again. Her heart sinks when Kristin decides this is the moment to join them.

'All the old gang together again,' Ottilie says acidly.

'Lovely to see you.' Kristin's smile is warm, needy almost, and Emilia can't forget what Ottilie told her about the phone call.

Ottilie doesn't respond, just sips her drink.

Kristin clears her throat and Emilia can see that she's nervous. 'I wanted to say sorry about the other night,' she begins. She turns her attention to Emilia. 'I rang Ottilie. It was a stupid, drunken thing to do. I just wanted some advice about interior design and . . . well . . . I – I'm sure she's told you.'

'She has,' says Emilia, trying to inject coolness into her

tone. It doesn't work. She's rubbish at confrontation. Another reason why she loves writing fiction: she can be bold and daring on the page in a way she never can in real life.

'I'm sorry,' Kristin says to Emilia. And Emilia wonders what she's saying sorry for: the phone call to Ottilie, or what she did more than a decade ago. She doesn't have much time to wonder as, before she can respond, Ava appears and whisks her away to introduce her to a journalist.

The next hour is a whirlwind of speeches, industry talk and catching up with some author friends. She can't see Kristin anywhere and wonders if she's gone home. She hopes Ottilie hasn't said anything controversial to either of them.

She's just about to go and speak to Marcie when her eye catches something at the window. A face is pressed to the glass, features distorted by the lights and condensation. Her heart is in her throat. It's her stalker, she knows it is. She pushes her way desperately through the throng, but it takes her a good five minutes to get to the door as she tries to extract herself from first Marcie and then Hannah.

When she finally reaches the entrance it's with a sinking feeling, knowing that whoever was there has probably gone. Or, even worse, slipped inside and is somewhere in the crowd. She wrenches the door open, letting in a blast of cold night air. The light from the shop casts a rectangular amber shimmer onto the wet pavement, illuminating two people having what sounds like a heated discussion. They fall silent when they notice Emilia, and the taller of the two, a woman in a skimpy dress, tilts the umbrella away from her face, and Emilia is surprised to see that it's Kristin. She has a cigarette in her hand. She thought she'd given up a long time ago. The other figure turns to face her. It's Louise.

'Lou. You came. Is ...' She glances from her to Kristin. 'Is everything okay?' She steps onto the pavement.

Kristin blows out a puff of smoke. 'Sorry, it was hot in there so I came out for a ciggie and bumped into your friend.'

Louise looks uneasy and shifts from foot to foot. She has her mobile in her hand and is wearing a long raincoat with the hood up. Was it her face she'd noticed in the window?

'I'm so glad you could make it. Come in,' she says to Louise.

'I'm so sorry, I was just about to but I've noticed a text.' She holds up her phone. 'I've been called in to work.'

'Oh, no, that's such a shame. Elliot would love to meet you.'

'So sorry. I've got to dash. But ...' She pushes her hood back, not caring that her hair is getting wet. She looks concerned.

'What is it?'

'It's just ... when I arrived, before Kristin came out –'

'She apparently saw someone,' Kristin butts in,

dropping her cigarette and grinding it into the pavement with her heel. 'A lurker.' She shrugs, unconcerned. 'Anyway, he's gone now. I'm going back in – it's freezing. Nice to meet you, Louise.'

Louise doesn't say anything, and they watch as Kristin folds down her umbrella and pulls open the door, releasing a waft of laughter and the smell of salted peanuts. It closes softly behind her, leaving the street silent.

Emilia wraps her arms around herself. Her hair is turning to frizz out here. 'Is everything okay?'

'I didn't want to say much about it in front of Kristin. I wasn't quite sure what she knew. She's a weird one . . . She seems to have a thing about you.'

Emilia steps closer. 'What do you mean?'

'As soon as she realized I was a friend of yours she started questioning me – honestly, she'd make a great cop.'

'About what?'

'About you and Elliot. How happy you are and if you ever talk to me about Jonas. It was weird. She was a bit pissed, I think, but anyway, that's not what I wanted to say . . .' She hesitates, her face serious. 'I saw someone, Em. A man. Standing here at the glass, looking in. I called out and he ran off when I approached.'

Emilia feels sick. It was him. She knows it. She glances down the street, as though she's expecting to see him in the distance, but it's empty.

20

Emilia hands in her edits a week later, and then, as promised, emails the manuscript to Elliot, Trevor, Ottilie, Louise and Jonas, knowing he will let Kristin read it too, although she doesn't know how she feels about this. She can't forget what Louise told her about Kristin's inappropriate questions. She sends it to her father too, after her mum's jibe at the launch. Even Jasmine wants a copy. 'I need to know how you kill off Miranda,' she says defensively, before Emilia can even ask why she wants to read it.

'My books might be a bit dark for you.'

Jasmine had rolled her eyes. 'I'm sixteen in October. You've even let me see an eighteen film,' she said, referring to *American Beauty*, which they'd allowed her to watch one night when Wilfie was in bed, and only because it wasn't overly violent. Jasmine hadn't let her forget it since.

'We'll see.'

'Which means no,' Jasmine had huffed.

Since her launch things have thankfully been quiet. Changing the Alexa passwords has put a stop to further incidents of the skylights opening and the music playing at random, but Emilia has been constantly on edge, expecting the worst every time she goes home. She finds she's hardly left the house all week, except to pick up Wilfie from school.

'I think we need to get away,' Elliot says one evening. 'I know all this is bothering you. You need a change of scene. A break.'

She agrees, so they drive to Cornwall for a week during the school Easter holidays, and as the days progress, with long walks on the beach and mooching around the winding streets, browsing the little boutiques and coffee shops, she finds herself relaxing. By the time they return to London, to find no sinister packages or flowers have been sent in their absence, she's almost managed to convince herself that whoever was behind it has now grown bored.

On Friday, as Emilia is locking up the house to go into town to pick up some dry cleaning, she hears footsteps behind her on the driveway.

She turns quickly, keys still in hand, her heart thumping. A young woman is standing a few feet away from her, at the bottom of the steps.

'I'm so sorry,' she says. 'I didn't mean to startle you. You're Emilia Ward?'

'Who wants to know?' Fear makes Emilia unusually snappy. She descends the steps and appraises the woman: late twenties, with curly red hair, smartly dressed in black trousers and a checked blazer. The sun has come out, reflecting in the puddles on the ground, and the cherry tree has blossomed, its frothy petals already coating the grass surrounding it.

The woman thrusts out a hand. 'I'm Gina Osbourne. I write for the *Mirror* and wondered if you're interested in an interview.'

Emilia stares at her in surprise and doesn't shake her hand. 'Interview me. Why?'

'Because of what's been happening to you. With the strange incidents that are mirroring plots from your books. Love your books by the way – I've read them all.'

'I . . . oh, well, thanks . . . but I'm not sure.' Emilia feels cornered. Sweat pools in her armpits and the wool coat she's wearing suddenly feels suffocating. 'How did you hear about that?'

'Oh, a journalist can never reveal her sources.' She gives a little bark of laughter. She sounds like a Jack Russell. 'It will be great publicity for your new book. I've heard you're going to kill off your main character.'

Her unease intensifies, wondering how she knows this. She's told hardly anyone. She thinks of Ava, her publicist, knowing she'd be encouraging her to do this interview. No publicity is bad publicity and all that. 'I think it's all stopped now anyway.' If she says it out loud it might actually be true.

'What's stopped?' Gina frowns.

'The . . . harassment, I suppose you'd call it. Although I don't even know if you would call it that. It's more nuisance stuff and, like I say, it hasn't happened for a while.'

'Right.' Gina Osbourne looks disappointed. 'The fact it happened to begin with is fascinating and would make a great article. You can tell our readers about your new book too.' She smiles, lifting her pale eyebrows in a silent plea.

'I'm not sure,' she says. The last thing she wants to do is antagonize the person behind it. It might give them a reason to target her again. 'I'll need to check with my publishers.' And the police.

'Okay. Fine. I'll give you my card. Please ring me if you do decide to speak about this. Like I say, it could be great publicity for your new book.'

Emilia takes the card with thanks and pockets it. She waits for the journalist to climb back into her car, then heads into town.

That evening, when Wilfie is tucked up in bed, she expresses her concerns to Elliot. Jasmine is staying the night at Nancy's and it's just the two of them, relaxing with a glass of wine in front of a drama on the TV that they are only half watching. She has already changed into an ivory silk nightdress that she knows is Elliot's favourite, and she has her legs on his lap. He's rubbing her bare calf, making it hard for her to concentrate.

'Do you think I should speak to this journalist?'

'Did you ask your publicist?'

'I spoke to her this morning. She agreed about it being good publicity but said I should only do it if I feel comfortable. But I don't know how I feel. I keep oscillating. My main worry is pissing off the person behind this.'

'It might stop them,' says Elliot, softly, his eyes like liquid chocolate in the half-light. 'They might have the exposure they wanted. *Needed.* Maybe you should say the police are involved and that might scare them – I'm sure they'll be reading any press coverage.'

Emilia takes a large sip of her Chardonnay. Louise had rung her last week and told her she was putting her in touch with a colleague who worked in stalking cases: DC Anthony Haddock. He'd come over to the house yesterday and had sat patiently at her kitchen table while she recounted everything. He was youngish – younger than her anyway – with light brown hair, a freckled, boyish face and very slim wrists. He didn't look like a detective or strong enough to be able to protect anyone. He hadn't seemed particularly worried and told her she was doing all the right things by installing cameras and alarms but to let him know immediately if anything else was to happen. She had rung him earlier to ask his advice about the press interview and he didn't seem to think it would do any harm.

'True,' she says now, to Elliot, swirling her wine around in the glass. 'I'll say whatever I can to scare them.'

He leans forwards and kisses her lightly on the lips. 'Come on, let's have an early night.' He takes her hand and leads her out of the room. She's surprised that he's left the wine glasses on the coffee table and instructs Alexa to turn off the lights.

They've peeled off each other's clothes and are falling into bed when Elliot's phone flashes up.

'Ignore it,' she murmurs, but he sits up. A shaft of moonlight from the slatted blinds falls onto his body, illuminating his muscular shoulders.

'I can't. It's the Ring Cam. There's an alert that someone is on our driveway.'

The desire she'd been feeling only moments before evaporates and a cold sweat breaks out over her body. She sits up too, her heart pounding. Elliot is staring intently at the screen on his phone. Their bedroom window looks out onto the back garden and Elliot jumps out of bed, naked, grabs his dressing gown from the back of the door and pulls it on as he rushes from the room. 'Stay here. I'll go into Jasmine's room and look out of her window.'

She stares after his retreating back, too scared to move. Maybe it's just a neighbouring cat, or some form of wildlife, she tells herself hopefully, but her heart is banging so hard in her chest she's scared she'll have a cardiac arrest. She takes a few deep breaths, but when Elliot doesn't return she can bear it no longer. Picking up her nightdress from where it has been discarded on the floor, she throws it on and creeps out of the bedroom, popping her head around Wilfie's door where he's thankfully fast asleep, and into her daughter's room.

Elliot is standing at the window with the shutters pulled back. The room is dark and his face is in shadow.

'Is anyone there?' she whispers, coming up behind him.

'I'm not sure. I think so . . .'

Her mouth goes dry. 'Shall I call the police?'

'Just wait . . .' He looks down at his phone, then back out of the window. 'Look, can you see? There . . .'

She steps in front of him, her legs trembling, to get a better look. 'I don't know, I . . .' And then her heart pounds even harder. Further down the street there is a figure, dressed in black, standing under a tree and looking towards their house. They are too far away for Emilia to make them out clearly. 'Oh, God, El. Who is that?'

'I don't know,' he whispers. 'I think they must have come onto our driveway. But it was almost like they knew where the camera was because they seemed to avoid it so that only their shoulder was in view.'

'Do you think they can see us?'

'Hopefully,' he says. 'I'm tempted to go down there and confront them myself.'

He goes to move away but she grabs his arm. 'No, El. They could be dangerous.' She's relieved when the figure turns away and walks off down the street, disappearing around the corner.

'They've gone.' Elliot exhales and pulls her into him. She buries her face in his chest. 'Let me look back on the phone,' he says, taking his arm away and scrolling through the screen on his mobile. 'Look, there . . .' He shows her the grainy footage. It's dark and raining, making the picture fuzzy, but she can clearly see a figure walking out of their driveway, then standing in the street, hands in pockets, looking back at the house. Whoever it is wears a dark hooded overcoat. 'Can't see their face. Just their back and shoulder.'

'What about going back further, when they first walked in?' says Emilia. 'We should be able to see the face then.'

'Well, that's the odd thing,' he says, frowning at the screen. 'There is no footage of them walking onto the driveway. Just them leaving. I've rewound right back. So I don't know how they came in . . .' he says as he looks up and her insides turn to ice when she notices his troubled expression '. . . or when.'

21

I spend the next day holed up in my office at the station going through everything I know about the praying-mantis murders and checking my notes from the last time he had struck – that we know of – in February 2005. I was still on the case back then. Belinda Aberdale was found in her bedroom in a Plymouth suburb, similar to the one where Trisha Banks was recently killed. Her husband and kids had gone on holiday and she'd stayed behind, was due to follow them the next day. She never got the chance. Belinda, like the others, had been stabbed, tied up and the insect marking carved into her ankle.

His first victim, Catherine Otis, was killed in November 1997 in exactly the same way. He disappeared for almost sixteen years exactly. Where has he been? Lorraine Butterworth said she couldn't see his face to garner what age he is, but I imagine he must be between forty and sixty. I imagine his minimum age back in 1997 would have been early twenties, so his minimum age now would be somewhere in his forties. But equally he could have been in his thirties or forties then, which would make him fiftyish or even sixty now.

What do we know about him? I look back through the notes I've made, thinking aloud. He stalks his victims first, watching them, sussing out where they live, who they live with and when they are alone. Then he accesses their properties mostly by their skylights, sometimes by breaking in through the window. He's fit, agile, intelligent. And he knows the loopholes, has worked out how to evade capture, leaves no evidence behind. The insect carving is a way to toy with us – and a sign he thinks little of women, that he perhaps blames them for the way his life has turned out.

If he has been in prison for the last sixteen years it would be for something else, not murder. No, he's too clever, too devious, too much of a psychopath to get caught for murder. He likes menthol cigarettes – God knows why: I tried them once years ago and they taste like piss – and he's tall . . .

I'm interrupted by a knock. 'Come in,' I shout, with a hint of annoyance in my voice. Saunders pushes open the door and stands there, touching the tips of his spiky hair, which he does a lot, I've noticed. 'Sorry to disturb you, ma'am, but I wanted to talk to you about the door-to-door calls Doyle and I did last night.'

I indicate the ugly brown chair in front of my desk and he sits down, clutching a takeaway cup. He has a pen behind his ear. I notice a mark on his neck. It looks like a love-bite, and I wonder, idly, who could have given it to him. He places the cup on my desk and pushes up his shirt sleeves.

'Go on,' I say.

'Right. Yes. So, a few neighbours told us they'd seen a man hanging around outside Trisha Banks's flat, wearing dark clothing and a dark hat. He always stood in the shadows, smoking and watching the house. Tall, well-built.'

'Nothing new, then.'

'Most said they didn't think much of it. Hanham Street is a bit . . . well, in a less salubrious part of town. Someone said they thought Trisha Banks was a prostitute.'

I frown. 'Why would they think that?'

'Because they'd seen a few men go up to her place.'

'Lorraine never mentioned that.'

'It doesn't sound like Lorraine was there much of the time, according to neighbours. Her sister's been ill and she's been staying with her a lot.'

'Okay.'

'But a neighbour said Lorraine has a brother who she's certain she's seen in the area the last week or so.'

I think back to my conversation with Lorraine. Did she mention a brother?

Saunders inches closer, his eyes bright with excitement. 'And I did some digging and Lorraine's brother – Martin Butterworth – has just come out of prison. He was banged up for armed robbery.'

'How long was he in for?'

'Well, this is the thing, ma'am. He was in for sixteen years. Banged up back in April 2005. Not long after the murder of Belinda Aberdale.'

I feel a burst of adrenaline. Sixteen years. And then I remember. Lorraine did tell me she had a brother, when we were talking about the menthol cigarettes. She told me her dad and brother used to smoke them.

'We need to interview him,' I say, jumping to my feet. 'Right now.'

22

Last night Emilia hardly slept. Every time she heard the slightest noise she'd wake up in a cold sweat. Elliot, in contrast, was out for the count, gently snoring. In the end she'd snuck into Wilfie's bedroom and got under the dinosaur quilt in his lower bunk while he slept peacefully above. Yet still she couldn't drop off. The house had never felt bigger, or lonelier, and when daylight started to creep in around the slats of the New England–style shutters in Wilfie's room, she'd never been more relieved for a night to end.

'You're going to drive yourself mad if you keep this up,' Elliot says over breakfast when she tells him about it. Wilfie has already disappeared to the den to play Minecraft online with his friends. It had rained last night but now the sun is out, casting light across the parquet and warming the side of Emilia's face through the glass of the bifolds. It feels like a fresh spring day, the kind she loves. Usually she'd be planning a day trip or a walk through Bushy Park but instead she's sitting here, feeling sick with worry. 'You're completely safe,' continues Elliot, opening the paper next to him as he spoons muesli into his mouth. 'We have an alarm now, cameras. The police know what's going on.' He reaches across the table to take her hand. 'I don't like seeing you this way.'

She knows he feels powerless, that Elliot is at his best when he's fixing things, helping in some way, however small. She gets how frustrating this must be for him because he can't do anything to stop it or to make her feel better, despite all the cameras and the security. If anything it's making her feel worse. If they didn't have that app on their phones she would have been blissfully unaware that someone was roaming around their garden last night. But, no, she can't think like that. Better to be prepared. Goose bumps pop up on her arms at the thought of someone outside last night. How long had they been there? Had they been watching them through the shadows in the garden as they snuggled on the sofa, her in her flimsy nightie, her legs draped over her husband? They need to get blinds for those doors. She'll contact some places. She needs to keep busy too.

She pushes aside her toast. Since all this began her once healthy appetite has diminished. She's already lost four pounds – she'd usually be elated at this, but she hates the constant sick sensation in the pit of her stomach. 'It's the thought of someone lurking around outside,' she murmurs.

Elliot pulls his hand away and continues eating. He swallows. 'I know. I think you should tell this detective, what's-his-name . . .'

'Haddock.'

'Yes, let him know. Maybe we could give him the footage. I know it's not very clear, but they might have some special system that will pick up what we've missed.' He shrugs. 'I don't know. It's worth a try.'

'Good idea.' She wonders whether or not to voice her worst fears.

'What is it?'

'I'm worried they'll break in. Hurt me or, worse, the kids.'

His eyes soften. 'I don't think that will happen. They had the opportunity when I was away. And I know they messed around with the skylights but they didn't get in. And now we have the alarms. If someone tries to break in the alarms will alert the security team, who will alert the police.' He gathers up his empty bowl and her plate and takes them to the sink. She watches the muscles in his shoulders that show through his tight jumper as he tips her uneaten toast into the food recycling. He's fit, strong. He'll go to the ends of the earth to protect her. She knows that. This knowledge gives her strength. He stands at the island facing her. 'Whoever's doing this is just enjoying taunting you and messing with your head. Don't let them.'

Is he really that unconcerned or is he downplaying it to make her feel less anxious? She's always felt her superpower is reading people, knowing their moods, how to respond to them based on their personality, but even right from the beginning of their relationship, she's found it hard to read him.

'I'm going to get dressed,' she says, pushing back her chair. She walks out of the room knowing Elliot's eyes are on her.

She's just showered and changed into jeans and a jumper when she gets the phone call. She doesn't recognize the number and wonders if it's Gina Osbourne again. She has already left another message asking about the interview but Emilia hasn't returned her call.

'Is this Mrs Emilia Rathbone?' asks the woman. She has a very posh voice, almost like it's put on. 'Mother of Jasmine Perry?'

Her first thought is that it's the school but then she remembers it's a Saturday and she tenses. 'Speaking.'

'I'm sorry to inform you that your daughter has been involved in a serious accident and is currently in West Middlesex Hospital.'

Horror washes over Emilia. 'What? How?' Jasmine had stayed last night at Nancy's.

'I'm afraid I don't have all the details at present, Mrs Rathbone. But please come to the hospital as soon as you can.'

'Where . . . Which ward?'

'The hospital reception will direct you when you arrive.' The call clicks off and Emilia stands in the middle of her bedroom, frozen for a few seconds, her blood pounding in her ears. Then she rushes down the stairs calling Elliot's name.

'What is it?' He darts into the hallway.

'It's Jas. I've just had a call from a hospital. She's had some kind of accident . . . Oh, God – I can't breathe!' She bends over, gasping, and Elliot has his hands on her back.

'Calm down. We'll go to the hospital now. Wilf,' he calls. Wilfie wanders out of the den, still holding his PS5 controller. 'Get in the car, bud. Your sister has had an accident.'

Wilfie is still in his pyjamas but he does as he's told, his little face crumpled with worry as he puts his controller down on the bench in the hallway and begins pulling on a pair of trainers and a jacket.

Elliot helps Emilia into her coat, then leads her and Wilfie to the car. 'Right. Give Nancy's mum, what's-her-name . . .'

'Marcie.'

'Give Marcie a ring and find out what's going on.'

She clicks on her seatbelt, then picks up her phone from her lap, praying silently over and over again *Please, God, let her be okay. Please let her be okay.* Her hands are trembling as she scrolls to Marcie's number while Elliot reverses out of their driveway and sets off towards the hospital.

Marcie answers the phone, sounding chipper. 'Hey, Em, how are the girls getting on? I hope they haven't kept you up half the night nattering.'

Confusion floods Emilia. 'What do you mean?'

'Nancy and Jas . . . Is something wrong?' There is alarm in her voice now.

'Jas told me she was staying the night at your house. I've just had a phone call from a hospital to say Jasmine's been involved in an accident.'

'What? They weren't here last night. Nancy told me she was staying with you. They're not with you?'

'I'm sorry, they're not. I . . .' Her voice rises in hysteria. 'So they aren't at yours?'

'No. Oh, God. If Jasmine's at the hospital, is Nancy with her?'

'I don't know. I don't understand what's going on.'

'I'll try Nancy's mobile. I'll call you back.'

She ends the call and Emilia takes a deep breath, trying to quell the panic. 'Where have they been all night?' she wails. 'And how has Jas ended up in hospital?'

Elliot grips the steering wheel more tightly. 'Don't worry about that at the moment. Nancy is probably at the hospital too. We just need to hope Jas is okay.'

Emilia takes deep breaths to stop herself hyperventilating.

'Is Jas okay?' pipes up Wilfie in a frightened voice from the back.

'I hope so, sweetheart,' Emilia says faintly.

'I'm sure she's fine, Wilfie. Don't worry,' says Elliot, trying to sound reassuring. To Emilia he says, 'Why don't you ring the hospital and get some more information?'

He takes the turning towards Isleworth slightly too quickly, the phone almost slipping out of Emilia's shaking hands. She presses the number in her call history but it's dead.

'That's odd.'

'What is?'

'I just tried to call the number that rang me earlier but it's not connecting.' She googles the number of the hospital and, after being passed from person to person, gets to speak to someone in Admissions.

'I'm sorry,' the woman is saying on the phone. 'But we haven't had any admissions under the name of Jasmine Perry.'

Emilia feels like she's been doused in cold water. 'But I had a phone call from someone this morning, just ten minutes or so ago, saying my daughter had had an accident so I'm assuming she came through the emergency room?'

There is silence at the other end of the line, just the sound of a keyboard being tapped and a phone ringing in the background. 'No,' the woman says, coming back on the line. 'There are no Jasmine Perrys here. I'm sorry but there has been some mistake.'

Emilia ends the call and swears in frustration.

'What did they say?' asks Elliot.

'What's going on?' asks Wilfie from the back seat.

'I don't know. I don't understand. Jas hasn't been admitted. For fuck's sake, where is she?' She taps on the

Find My Friends app but there is no location for Jasmine, which means her phone must be turned off. All the horrors of what could have befallen her only daughter flash through her mind.

Elliot pulls the car onto double-yellow lines, then swivels in his seat so he's facing Emilia. 'Calm down, you're scaring Wilf. Is the hospital one hundred percent sure that Jasmine hasn't been admitted?'

Emilia nods, panic sitting heavy on her chest so that she can't breathe.

'Then it sounds like a hoax call.' There is relief on Elliot's face.

But Emilia's mind is spinning. 'But if it's a hoax call, where is Jasmine? Because she's not at Nancy's, like she said she would be. Oh, God, Elliot . . .' She can barely bring herself to say it. 'What if whoever is behind all this has done something to Jasmine?'

23

This. All this is her worst fear. Her very worst. She's always kept Jasmine on a tight leash, fully aware that she's more paranoid than a lot of other parents because she writes about such horrific things happening. Her eyes are wide open to the weirdos that lurk among them. After all, she's imagined them for her thrillers: the paedophile hiding behind the respectability of a teacher, the psychopath lurking around children's playgrounds, the men who pretend to be teenagers online in order to groom and violate.

She's always been honest with her children from a reasonably young age about the dangers. Jasmine isn't the kind of kid to lie, to put herself in harm's way. When Emilia lectures her on talking to strangers online she'll roll her eyes and say, in exasperation, 'Do you think I'm stupid? I know it could be some pervy forty-year-old!' Yet she pretended she was sleeping over at Nancy's last night. A story, it was obvious now, that had been concocted between the two of them to hide what they were really up to, whatever that was. And all that would have been bad enough if it hadn't been for the phone call.

Because someone was privy to what they were up to. And had wanted her to know.

She's on the verge of hysteria. It's bubbling up inside her and it takes everything she's got not to lose it because she knows that won't help her daughter. This white-hot blind panic is like nothing she's ever experienced before.

Emilia's at Jonas's house now, the house that used to be hers, where Jasmine took her first steps, said her first words. She'd rung her ex-husband from the car to tell him everything, and Elliot had dropped her there.

'I'll take Wilfie with me,' he'd said, without getting out of the car. 'Just in case she comes home. But let me know immediately if you hear anything, okay?'

She'd nodded tearfully, and when Kristin opened the door, she'd wordlessly pulled Emilia into her arms. She'd been too surprised and upset to reject the hug.

Now Kristin is seated at the small kitchen table, ashen-faced, while Jonas paces the room. Nancy's parents, Marcie and Frank, are with them, standing at the sink. Marcie is silently crying and Frank has his strong, beefy arms around her shoulders.

'I've called around all her friends,' says Frank. 'Nobody seems to have any idea where they are.'

Emilia knows calling their small group of studious friends wouldn't have taken long. Jasmine finds it hard to branch out and make new friends. It's something they've talked about a lot.

'Should we call the police?' says Emilia, even though

she doesn't want to because then this becomes real. And she so doesn't want it to be real, just a figment of her imagination. A plot in one of her books. According to their friends, the girls had been in school yesterday and had left at the normal time of 3.30 p.m. But now it was midday and they'd been gone for nearly twenty hours.

'Won't they just say that the girls are obviously together?' says Frank.

'They've been away all night,' wails Marcie. 'That's not normal for them.'

'I agree,' says Emilia, trying to sound strong, but her hand trembles as she gets out her phone. 'I have a friend in the force. I'm going to speak to her.'

She moves off into the narrow hallway as she dials Louise's number and wants to cry in relief when her friend picks up immediately.

'Hey, lovely,' says Louise, cheerfully.

'Lou . . .' She swallows. Her throat is dry and scratchy, thick with unshed tears. 'Where are you?'

'I'm at home. Why? What's wrong?'

'It's Jasmine. She's missing.' And then she launches into everything that's happened.

'Right. Okay. It sounds like they've just gone off together somewhere so try not to panic. Where are you now? Are you at home?'

'No. I'm at Jonas's house in Twickenham.'

'Okay. Is Elliot with you?'

'No, just me, Jonas, Kristin and Nancy's parents.'

'Right. Okay. I'm coming over now. What's the address?'

Emilia reels it off, and Louise says she'll be over as soon as she can. Emilia is thankful that she lives close by. She tries to fight the guilt that she's asking this favour of her busy friend at the weekend.

'What will she be able to do?' asks Jonas when Emilia joins the rest of them in the kitchen.

'She's a detective in the Met. I can't think of anyone better, can you?'

Nobody speaks. The only sound to be heard is the odd sob coming from Marcie.

Eventually, after what feels like years but is more like half an hour, the doorbell rings and Kristin jumps up to answer it, Emilia following close behind. Louise is in her off-duty clothes of jeans and a sweatshirt with a dog on the front. Her short dark hair looks freshly washed and is still damp. She's wearing no make-up. Kristin steps forwards. 'Hello, again,' she says.

Louise nods curtly and walks into the hallway. The prickly vibe Emilia had picked up between them at her launch is still there. But she hasn't the brain space to think about that now. All she cares about is finding Jasmine.

'This is DC Louise Greene,' says Emilia when they get back to the kitchen, and then she watches, impressed, as her friend switches into detective mode.

'Now,' says Louise, standing by the sink and

addressing them all. They crowd around her, like eager pupils. 'I'm afraid that I can only be here as a friend and in an advisory capacity, but on the way over I called my colleague at your local station and gave the details and this address. Someone will be here shortly. But, in the meantime, can any of you think why Jasmine and Nancy would lie? They're obviously off somewhere together.'

'I'm scared they've been kidnapped.' It's out of Emilia's mouth before she can stop it. She can't help but voice it, this deep-seated fear. But Marcie and Frank look horrified.

'Let's try not to be too melodramatic,' begins Kristin.

But Louise has cut across her, calmly addressing Emilia: 'You have to remember abductions are vanishingly rare. The fact that both girls have lied makes me think they've snuck off somewhere together. Where could they have gone?'

Emilia can't think. She feels inert with panic and anxiety, like a deer that's wandered into the middle of a motorway and doesn't know what to do, except stare at the oncoming cars.

Marcie turns her tear-stained face towards Louise. 'I've rung around their friends. Nobody has seen them since the end of school yesterday. Nancy has started going out with this boy . . .'

Emilia stands up straighter. She remembers Jasmine telling her about him. Jake Someone. It had surprised

Emilia because both girls are shy and feel left out of that whole party scene. She'd told her daughter there was plenty of time for parties, getting drunk and snogging boys. She hadn't done anything like that until she'd gone to university and met Jonas, mainly because she'd been at a single-sex boarding school.

'What's his name?' barks Louise, and even in her red sweatshirt with the Labradoodle on the front, she exudes power.

Marcie wipes a tear from her cheek. 'Jake Radley. He's in their year at school, I think, and runs with the popular crowd. I was surprised when Nance said he liked her.' She suppresses a sob. 'Not because she isn't beautiful. She's my baby girl . . .' Frank hugs his wife harder.

Emilia knows exactly what Marcie is getting at. She's heard of Jake Radley. He's one of the most popular boys in Jasmine's year. She hadn't realized it was that Jake when Jasmine told her Nancy had a boyfriend. He's not the kind to be interested in Nancy, Jasmine and their studious, geeky crowd.

Just then the doorbell rings and Louise runs to answer it. Jonas moves to stand closer to Emilia, takes her hand. 'It will be okay,' he says, but she notices the fear in his blue eyes and feels bonded to him in that moment due to their shared panic. From across the room Kristin clears her throat and Jonas drops Emilia's hand.

Louise returns with a young woman in police uniform, her caramel-highlighted hair pulled back in a sensible low ponytail. 'This is PC Bryan,' she says. 'Can you tell her everything you told me?'

Emilia and Marcie take turns to fill her in. A frown crosses her fine features when Emilia tells her about the hoax phone call from the hospital. She asks for Jake's address and strides out of the room, talking into her mobile. When she's ended the call she comes back into the kitchen and stands beside Louise. 'We'll get to the bottom of this,' she says, and Emilia thinks that this woman can't possibly understand how they're feeling. She doesn't look older than twenty-five. 'Please try not to worry. Now, is anything going on this weekend that the girls wanted to go to? A party, perhaps? Or a concert?'

Emilia's brain is foggy.

After a few seconds Kristin pipes up: 'Actually, yes. Jasmine wanted to go to see that band at the O2 – do you remember?' She starts scrolling through her phone. 'I'm sure it was around this weekend. I remember her saying. Yes, some band called Total Whiplash. Something like that. Wait – here it is. Tonal Whiplash. Not Total. And, according to this, they played last night.' She taps her phone screen triumphantly with a long fingernail.

Emilia recalls it now too. Months ago, Jasmine had asked if she could go with Nancy, but Emilia had said no – she'd felt they were too young to go without an adult.

'She told you I'd said no?' Emilia asks Kristin.

Kristin nods. 'Yes. But we . . .' She sidles up to Jonas so that she's standing between him and Emilia. 'We agreed she was too young.'

Marcie moves forwards, hope in her face. 'Yes! Last year Nancy asked me if she could go. I also said no. Plus it was expensive.'

'Maybe this Jake Radley got them tickets,' adds Frank, folding his beefy arms across his chest.

'But they sold out almost immediately,' says Emilia, frowning.

'Do you think that's where they were last night? But where have they been since?' Marcie rubs at the mascara under her eyes.

'Nancy better not have stayed at this Jake's,' says Frank. 'She's just fifteen. Wait until I get my hands on that bastard.'

Louise throws Frank a warning look. 'We don't know anything yet. But I . . .'

They are interrupted by the buzzing of PC Bryan's mobile phone. She snaps it open. 'Yes,' she says into it. 'Right . . . Okay, that's great. Thanks.' She closes the phone. 'My colleague has spoken to Jake's parents who have confirmed he went to the concert last night. But he's home now. One of our officers has gone over there to speak with them. Jake might be able to shed some light about where they've been.'

Emilia swallows. Please let her have been at the concert, she silently prays. She doesn't care if she and Nancy stayed the night at Jake's, as long as they're safe. It's better than the alternative. She can't stop thinking about the hoax call. Who was it from, and have they done something to Jasmine and Nancy? Her mobile rings. Seeing Elliot's number she quickly answers it.

'She's here. It's Jasmine,' he says jubilantly. 'She's just walked through the door.'

'Thank God.' Her whole body sags with relief and she looks up at the hopeful faces of Marcie and Frank. 'And Nancy?'

24

She was midway through her first term at Exeter University, studying history, when she met Ash.

Daisy was standing in line at the library, staring at her feet clad in her favourite Dr Martens and trying not to look around at all the other students hanging out in their cliquey groups. Daisy didn't like to get too close to people. It was better that way. It protected her fragile heart. As a result, she hadn't so much as kissed anyone. But that was okay. She was happy throwing herself into her university life. And she had people she hung out with, superficial friendships.

She couldn't pinpoint exactly what made Ash stand out from the rest of the students in the library that day. Maybe it was because she recognized another damaged soul when she saw one. Ash was effortlessly cool, with dyed black hair, longer on one side, the other with a shaved undercut, calf-length black coat and black biker boots, standing apart from the others, flicking through a book on French New Wave cinema. Daisy had been transfixed, and instantly wanted to know more. Their eyes met and, for the first time in her life, Daisy's stomach performed a series of gymnastics that made her feel simultaneously sick and turned on. They didn't talk, though. Not then. But after that they kept bumping into each other around campus, acknowledging each other with a shy smile, a tilt of the head, sometimes with a gruff hello.

It was ironically at a party, something she usually tried to avoid, where they got talking. Her flatmate had dragged her along. Ash was standing in the corner, nursing some kind of blue drink and looking around with a neutral expression. When Daisy walked in, their eyes locked, and they held each other's gaze for what seemed like an eternity, until the spell was broken by someone walking between them. She could only watch in horror as a pretty girl with a short skirt and a see-through shirt showing off a lacy bra made her way to Ash, cigarette in one hand and a plastic cup in the other. Daisy couldn't hear what they were saying but, to her delight, Ash ditched the girl and walked over to where she, Daisy, was standing.

'I hate parties. Do you want to get out of here?'

She could only nod, her heart pounding with excitement, the sound of the White Stripes still ringing in her ears.

They talked all night in Daisy's room, slowly revealing

more and more about themselves as the cheap lager flowed. She was surprised when Ash told her about a breakdown and a short stay in a psychiatric ward as a teenager. Daisy was careful not to mention her mother's murder. She'd once made the mistake at primary school of telling some of her friends about it, and the looks of horror and pity they exchanged made her never want to tell anyone again. She felt as if she was tarnished with bad luck and that it might be catching.

They were kindred spirits, Daisy and Ash. Ash and Daisy. Inseparable after that party.

But more than anything, it was down to Fate that they met.

Because if they hadn't, she'd never have found the Doodle Man.

25

According to Elliot, Jasmine and Nancy had walked into the house bedraggled, contrite and bracing themselves for a telling-off.

'I'm sorry to waste your time,' Emilia says, to Louise and P C Bryan, as they file out of Jonas's house, although she knows she doesn't sound very apologetic. She's too ecstatic that her precious daughter is at home where she belongs. That's all she cares about right now. She's euphoric with relief. She could take on the world.

P C Bryan says she's just happy that they've been found safe, then hurries off to her car, but Louise stops in the front garden, the sun catching the red in her short dark hair. 'It was no bother,' she says. 'I'm glad I could help, and I'm just so pleased they're okay. But tell that daughter of yours not to do anything like that again or I'll have to have strict words.' She winks at Emilia and gives her a hug before getting into her little red Fiat 500. Emilia waves her off and turns to the others, who are standing in a patch of sunlight on the pavement outside Jonas and Kristin's house. Kristin has hold of Jonas's hand proprietorially.

'I can't believe they did this,' Kristin says, shivering slightly. There is a chill in the air despite the sun, and she never seems to wear warm enough clothes. 'What were they thinking? They must have known they'd get found out.'

'That's what I want to know,' says Marcie, her chin set determinedly, her tears now forgotten. She turns to Emilia. 'Can we come back to yours?'

Emilia can't feel cross with the girls, not yet. She's too relieved that they're home, that they haven't been kidnapped by her stalker. 'Of course. Elliot's making them something to eat and he'll keep an eye on them until we get back.' She turns to where Jonas is standing with Kristin. 'Maybe you should come too. Show a united front?'

A cloud passes across his face. 'Will Elliot be okay with that?'

'Of course,' she lies. Elliot won't like it one bit, but tough.

Jonas reaches into his jeans for his car keys. Kristin steps forwards too, but Jonas shakes his head at her. 'I think it's best you stay here, darling.'

Kristin's face falls, and Emilia can tell she's inwardly seething but doesn't want to make a scene in front of Marcie and Frank. 'Fine,' she says, white-lipped. 'She's your daughter. Whatever you think is best.' She turns on her heeled boots and marches back into the house before Jonas has a chance to reply. He raises an eyebrow at Emilia but doesn't say anything.

They drive in convoy to Emilia's house. Jasmine and Nancy are sitting at the kitchen island, looking small, with their fingers wrapped around mugs of hot chocolate when they all rush in.

'I'm going to take Wilfie to the park,' says Elliot, tactfully, steering Wilfie away from the others. Despite his feelings towards Jonas, he's polite and shakes his hand as he leaves the room, which Emilia is relieved about.

'Is Jas going to get told off?' she hears her son ask hopefully, as he follows his dad into the hallway.

'Thank God,' cries Marcie, enveloping Nancy in a hug. 'We were so worried.'

Jasmine looks up sheepishly when she notices her parents, and slides off her stool, running into their arms. 'I'm sorry,' she says, bursting into tears as they both embrace her in a group hug. Emilia doesn't ever want to let go. *Thank you, thank you, thank you*, she thinks, inhaling her daughter's familiar scent mixed with something earthy and unwashed.

Jonas is the first to release her. 'What were you thinking?' he says, sternly but gently.

'Yes,' agrees Emilia. 'What the hell happened? We've all been out of our minds with worry. Where have you been?'

Jasmine wipes her nose with the back of her hand and sniffs loudly. 'We're so sorry.' She hangs her head, her dirty-blonde hair falling into her face. 'We really wanted to go to this concert and I'd asked you both last year and you'd said no. And then . . .' She glances nervously at Nancy.

Nancy, a slight girl with a rosebud mouth, curly dark brown hair and wide blue eyes, is actually trembling and Emilia is struck again by how young they really are. They're at that in-between age of no longer little children but not quite adult.

'Let's go and sit down,' Emilia says, leading them all into the family-room end of the kitchen. 'Bring your hot chocolate, girls. You look freezing.'

Jasmine sits solemnly between Jonas and Emilia on one of the sofas, Nancy and her parents a mirror image on the other.

'Where did you sleep?' asks Emilia, rubbing her daughter's back, as though unable to believe she's actually here. She's wearing a hoodie and jeans, which she must have packed and taken to school with her yesterday.

'We stayed at Meghan's house. Not that we got much sleep. It was so cold on the floor.'

Emilia has never heard of Meghan but she doesn't want to ask about that now. She glances at Jasmine's face. Her eyes are downcast. She never thought Jasmine would lie to her like this. She isn't the type to be sneaky. Emilia's always believed they have a very open relationship. She'd kept things from her own parents, of course, but that was because they were emotionally distant. She's tried so hard to make herself approachable to Jasmine. To make her daughter feel loved, not judged, and able to tell her anything.

THE WOMAN WHO LIED

'How did you get tickets?' asks Marcie, her round face pinched with worry.

'Jake gave them to us. He said he'd received them through the post with strict instructions to give them to me and Jas,' replies Nancy, quietly, her fingers tapping on the side of her mug. She has a streak of dirt along her cheekbone.

Emilia's stomach turns. '*What?* Who gave them to him?' This is familiar. *Too* familiar. The room tilts and she has to grab on to the arm of the sofa.

'He doesn't know,' says Nancy, staring into her mug. 'He just said someone had posted them to him with an anonymous letter. And that whoever wrote the letter said he had to give them to us.'

This can't be happening. Concert tickets being sent anonymously to a friend of two teenage girls. Teenage girls who then go missing. It's straight out of her book. Except it's not a past book of hers. It's from the most recent. *Her Last Chapter.* A book that won't be published until later this year.

A book she's sent out to a select few.

26

Jonas is hovering in the kitchen after everyone else has left. Elliot is still at the park with Wilfie, and Jasmine is having a bath. Emilia has made Jonas a cup of coffee and they're sitting next to each other at the kitchen table. He's gazing around the room, at the skylights and the blue-painted units, with its large island and pale parquet floors. 'Wow! This is really stunning, Em. You've done a great job on it. It's a lot tidier than our house used to be when we were married.' He grins to show he's joking. This is the first time he's seen the kitchen since the renovation. He usually hovers in the hallway when he picks Jasmine up.

'Thanks.' She returns his smile, although it's an effort. Her mind has been reeling ever since she realized that the letter and tickets sent to Jasmine and Nancy were like the plot from her unpublished book and that this is all down to someone she knows. It's a far worse thought than it being a stranger. She'd trusted them all, even Kristin who, despite their differences and her odd behaviour lately with Ottilie and Louise, is a great stepmother to Jasmine.

'Are you okay?' he asks, his brow crinkled. 'You've hardly said a word since Nancy and her parents left. Am I outstaying my welcome? You can tell me.' His voice is teasing.

'I'm just a bit in shock, I think,' she says, taking a sip of coffee while stealing a furtive glance at him. He's hurt her in the past, yes, but would he do something as sick, as devious as this? She can't imagine so. Especially as this involves his daughter. Yet she can't imagine *anyone* she knows is capable of this. 'Have you . . . um, read my new book yet by any chance?' She tries to keep her voice light.

'Only the beginning,' he says. 'It's good. Quite dark with all that praying-mantis stuff.'

'So, you wouldn't have reached the bit yet about the two girls disappearing after a concert. They're lured there by a letter. Like what happened with Jas . . .'

His eyes widen in horror. 'No!'

'There's something I need to tell you.' The coffee curdles in her stomach, and she remembers she hasn't eaten anything since breakfast, yet she feels she might be sick. 'I hoped it would all go away but if anything it's escalating. This has been going on for ages . . . God, Jonas. Someone is playing with my fucking head.' And then she tells him everything that's happened so far: the bomb scare, the flowers, the troll, the wreath, the skylights opening by themselves, the man who followed her and Louise. Someone lurking around the house last night. When she's finished, he's staring at her with his mouth hanging open. 'And because they were events that happened in past books, I thought it could be any-one. But now, with this coming from my unpublished manuscript, well, it has to be someone I know.'

'I hope you don't think I'd do this,' he says quickly. Defensively.

'No, of course not.'

'Who have you sent it to?'

She thinks back. It's never very many people at the beginning. 'I have a few early readers, who include my friend Louise . . .'

'The detective from this morning?'

'Yes. And Ottilie. Elliot, obviously, you, Elliot's dad Trevor. My parents . . . with this new one anyway after my mum's spiky comment at my launch.'

'Okay. Who else? I did pass it on to Kristin. I hope that's okay.'

'Fine. I thought you would anyway. Jasmine wants to read it too.'

'And the hoax call? Jesus.' He exhales slowly.

'The hoax call isn't in the book but the other stuff is. I need to see the letter Jake received. It's obviously from the same person who made the hoax call to me.'

'I can't believe someone rang you pretending to be from the hospital. That's just sick.' He stands up. 'I need to get back – Kristin's going to be pissed off with me. Will you be okay? I can stay if you like, until Elliot gets back.'

'Probably not a great idea.'

He grins and thrusts his hands into the pockets of his jeans. With his blond hair and Adidas trainers he resembles the student she'd met all those years ago. 'I'm never going to win him over, am I?'

She laughs. 'Have you ever tried?' She walks with him to the door. 'It doesn't matter anyway. It's not like we're suddenly going to start having cosy foursomes out and about.'

'True.'

She opens the door to the porch. 'How are things anyway? You haven't . . . well, you know . . .'

He shakes his head. 'No. I haven't. I've been a good boy, I promise. I've stayed away from Connie.'

So that's her name. 'I'm glad. And divorce is expensive, you know that.'

'Yes, I bloody well do.' He laughs. He bends down and kisses her briefly on the cheek. 'Say goodbye to Jas for me and tell her she's grounded.'

'Oh, she's definitely grounded.'

She watches him walk down the driveway to where his car is parked behind hers. Then she stands in the porch, next to Elliot's ugly bike, and calls DC Haddock.

An hour later Jasmine is sitting on the sofa, pale and smelling of Emilia's White Company body wash. She's dressed in clean high-waisted jeans and a red hoodie. She looks young without her usual eye make-up, her hair hanging in tendrils over her shoulders. Her bare feet are crossed and she's picking at her fingernails, rather than looking at her mother.

'I'm glad you're safe, but I'm still shocked that you lied to me,' says Emilia.

'I'm really sorry,' she mumbles, her eyes shining with tears. 'We just wanted to be part of the popular group for once.'

'I understand that. I do,' says Emilia, gently. 'But that doesn't mean lying to me or your dad. If you'd explained it all to us we could have come to some sort of arrangement –'

'Like what?' Jasmine sniffs. 'You wouldn't have let me go!'

'Maybe we could have gone too. Been in the vicinity, perhaps, to make sure you were okay.'

'You never said that at the time.'

Emilia pushes down her guilt. 'I know. And I'm sorry. I shouldn't have just said no without hearing you out. But next time, please, explain how you're feeling and then your dad and I will do whatever we can to make it possible. But don't lie to us again.'

'I'm sorry,' she mutters, biting the skin at her fingernail.

'And the tickets?' she presses. 'Jake was definitely sent them in the post? Anonymously?'

She nods. 'Jake and his mates didn't realize you didn't know where we were . . .' She tails off.

'I need to see that note. Can you ask Jake for it?'

'Yes.' She pulls at the sleeve of her hoodie and stares at her mother for a few moments. 'I know something odd has been going on around here and that you and Elliot are trying to keep it from me.'

Emilia stands up. 'It's nothing. Really.'

Jasmine jumps up from the sofa, her expression dark. 'You're always telling me to be honest with you, but you're not with me!'

She sighs. 'Okay, but I don't want you to be overly worried. At the same time just be mindful – and, most importantly, truthful from now on. You have to promise, okay? And not to tell Wilfie. It will only scare him.'

'I promise,' says Jasmine in a small voice. She sits down again, and Emilia tells her everything.

Emilia is emptying the dishwasher and trying to keep herself distracted when Elliot and Wilfie return from the park, all pink cheeks and windblown hair.

'I stopped Dad's goal,' cries Wilfie, excitedly, still clutching a grubby football.

Elliot grins. 'Yeah, you did great, bud.'

Wilfie punches the air and runs back out of the room with the football tucked under his arm. Elliot laughs. 'God, I'm knackered. You do know our eight-year-old runs rings around me?'

Emilia tries to smile in response, but she can't. She feels like she's going to cry.

'What is it?' Elliot comes over to her and pulls her into his arms. He smells of fresh air and his hands are cold as he brushes the hair off her face. 'Jas is home safe and sound. No harm done.'

'I know, and I'm so relieved. It's just . . .'

'What?' His voice is gentle.

She explains about the letter and tickets being sent to Jake. 'It's all things that happen in my book.'

He frowns. 'Which book? I don't recognize that storyline.'

She pulls away from him so he can see her face. 'That's the thing. It's from my new book. The one that hasn't even been published yet.'

His expression changes. 'What?'

'Have you started reading it yet?'

'No, I haven't. I've had this deadline at work. I was going to start tonight.'

'I've told Jas the truth,' she blurts out. 'I want her to be honest with us and felt I owed her the same. I'm worried she's in danger.'

She wants him to pacify her, like he always does. Her glass-half-full husband. But he doesn't. His mouth is set in a grim line, and she notices he hasn't shaved this morning.

She has to tell him what happens in the book. 'I'm sorry for giving it away when you haven't read it yet, but in *Her Last Chapter* Miranda's niece is kidnapped and goes through hell until she's rescued right at the end of the book. It results in Miranda finally discovering the serial killer, but they murder her before they're caught by Miranda's partner.'

He doesn't speak, just stares at her, and she can see the worry etched on his face.

She turns away and continues emptying the dishwasher. 'I've decided I'm going to speak to that journalist, Gina Osbourne.'

'Why?'

'Because it might be a way to stop whoever is behind this.'

'Or,' says Elliot, darkly, 'you could be giving them exactly what they want.'

27

Martin Butterworth is a hulk of a man, with eyes and hair the colour of dirty dishwater and an unhealthy pallor that comes from years inside. Saunders is almost six foot, but this man must be at least three inches taller. The top of the doorway skims his head and his wide shoulders take up the whole space. I don't normally scare easily but I'm suddenly glad I brought Saunders along with me, and I realize, if this is our guy, how terrifying it would have been for his victims to be confronted by this beast.

'Yeah?' He stares at us, his eyes flickering from Saunders to me, then back to Saunders.

I show him my identification and introduce us. 'Can we have a word?'

He scowls and steps back into the grotty hallway. 'Look, I've only been out of the nick a few weeks. I've kept myself out of trouble. I'm still on probation.'

'We won't be long. We just need to ask you a few questions, and surely it's better to do it here rather than down at the station.'

He stares at us in silence, obviously hoping to unnerve us, but I've met his type before. He's clearly a bully and a thug. But a killer? That remains to be seen.

Martin turns and stalks off down the hallway. We take this as an invitation and follow him into a small front room. It's sparsely furnished with a torn leather sofa and an armchair. He plonks himself in the chair and we take the sofa. It's a very similar set-up to where his sister, Lorraine, lives, a few streets away. He doesn't offer us tea or coffee, not that I would take it. The carpet under my shoes feels sticky.

He lights a cigarette without asking if we mind, or if we even want one. I'm disappointed to see they're just the general kind. No menthol cigarettes for him.

'So, what do you want?' He leans back in the chair and lets out a puff of smoke.

'Do you ever smoke any other kind?' I ask him.

He takes the cigarette out of his mouth and stares at it. 'What do you mean? Like a different brand?'

'Like the menthol kind?' Saunders asks.

He shakes his head. 'Nah. My dad did but he's long dead.'

I wonder if he's lying. Lorraine definitely said her father and brother. It's not nearly enough to go on right now.

'We understand your sister, Lorraine, lives in Hanham Street?' I ask.

He nods.

'Have you visited her since you got out of prison?'

He frowns. 'Yeah, just the once.'

'And when was this?'

He sits forward in his seat, his eyes narrowed. The cigarette burns in his hand, the ash falling onto the brown carpet. 'Uh, dunno, probably when I first got out. About three weeks ago. But it didn't go well. She's a judgemental bitch.'

I ignore this. 'And did you meet her upstairs neighbour, Trisha Banks?'

He takes a puff of the cigarette and flicks more ash onto the carpet. 'No, I can't say that I did.'

I turn to Saunders who is watching Martin Butterworth in silence but I can see his mind ticking over. And then he uses the oldest trick in the book. Clearing his throat, he asks Martin if he can use his bathroom.

Martin looks suspicious. 'It's upstairs.'

Once Saunders has left the room, I say, 'Do you live here alone, Martin?'

'No. With a mate.'

'Can I take his name?'

'Shane Long. But he's out at the moment. Working.'

I write this down. 'And are you working at the moment?'

'Bit hard for an ex-con to find a job,' he says, leaning forwards and stubbing out his cigarette on an old newspaper.

'There are organizations that help –'

'I know all that,' he cuts in coldly. 'Where's the other copper? He's been a long time in that toilet.' He stands up, almost filling the small room. I hold my nerve and continue sitting down.

'I'm sure he'll be back in a minute.'

'I need to get on. There's nothing else to say.'

I stand up too, so that I'm facing him. 'Do you know that a woman was murdered in the bedsit above your sister's on Monday?'

His face closes in on itself, his jaw tight. 'No, I didn't. I haven't spoken to my sister since I saw her. You do know I went to prison for armed robbery, right? Not murder?' He folds his arms across his substantial bulk and lifts his chin. His sludge-coloured eyes narrow, challenging me.

'I know. But can I ask where you were on Monday?'

'I was here. All day. And all night.'

'Can anyone vouch for that? Was Shane here with you?'

'Shane was out working during the day and at night he was at his girlfriend's.'

So he has no alibi. We need far more than that, of course. It will be interesting what Forensics and the pathologist come back with. We already have his DNA on the system from his armed-robbery conviction.

'Thank you for your time,' I say, and he looks surprised, as if expecting that I'd arrest him there and then. I can hear Saunders thundering down the stairs and heading into the hallway. The hairs on the back of my neck stand up at the thought of Martin behind me. There is something dark, unsettling about him.

'You took your time, mate,' says Martin, gruffly, as Saunders joins us.

'Sorry,' says Saunders. 'Dodgy kebab last night.'

I try not to smile as Martin hurries us out and shuts the door on us without saying goodbye.

'Well?' I say, as we walk to my Audi.

'I had a bit of a nose about. One bedroom was quite tidy and the other was a bit of a mess. I don't know if it was Martin's but there was a desk shoved up into the corner of the room and on it . . .' He looks back over his shoulder as though Martin might be following us. He reaches into his pocket for his phone. 'I took a photo. But look . . .'

By now we've stopped alongside my car. It's too cold to be standing on the pavement. The February wind whips at my hair and coat. It's not until we're in the car that I take his phone.

It's a photo of a messy desk, but among all the paraphernalia is a penknife . . . and a photograph of a woman with the eyes scratched out.

28

Elliot has bought Emilia a personal alarm from a company that Trevor recommended and has instructed her to have it on her constantly. 'Keep it within touching distance at all times,' he'd said when he presented it to her yesterday, sending chills through her. And it strikes home again how serious this is if even Elliot is forced to admit there's reason to worry. She can feel the weight of the alarm now, tugging down the hem of her denim jacket, as she walks to the café in Kingston where she's arranged to meet Gina Osbourne. It's Tuesday after the hoax call, a gorgeous late-spring day, with the sky so clear it looks like a sheet of glass the colour of forget-me-nots. Next week they're due a heatwave, according to the Meteorological Office.

Emilia takes a deep breath, enjoying the scent of newly bloomed hyacinths, as she makes her way down a residential street full of 1930s houses where she's parked her car. She's relieved to be out. Elliot has been a little short-tempered ever since Saturday. He refuses to go into the office, wanting to work from home. Every time she leaves the house he wants to know where she's going and who she's seeing. It's like being married to a possessive husband and Elliot's never been like that. The only times she sees him irritable or stressed are when he's worrying about something that causes his anxiety to flare up: flying, giving presentations, or having to stay away from home for too long. And she knows all this is getting to him as much as it is to her, because he wants to protect her. To protect all of them.

She'd wanted to charge straight over to Jake Radley's house after finding out about the letter, to demand to see it, to snatch it from him, and to pore over it for clues about who could be behind this, about who could be trying to ruin the life that she was so grateful for, but Jasmine had told her not to, suggesting she call him instead and explain. 'I don't want him to think he's done something wrong,' she'd told Emilia, in a tone that belied her fifteen years and gave Emilia a glimpse of the young woman she was becoming. 'I'll ask him to bring the letter to school.'

When Jasmine got home from school last night she told Emilia that Jake had thrown it away.

First thing yesterday she'd called Lara, her cover editor while Hannah is on maternity leave, and told her what had happened at the weekend and how it appeared in her unpublished manuscript. 'Can you please give me the names of everyone who has read it so far?' she'd asked. 'It's really important.' Lara had sounded shocked but had agreed to compile a list. Her agent agreed to do the same.

When she received both lists later that day she was reassured to see few names on them. Just Hannah and

Lara so far at the publisher's, and Drummond at the agency. 'I was waiting for it to go through copyedits before sending it out to foreign publishers,' he'd explained.

Since then she's contacted all the friends and family to whom she sent the manuscript, asking if they had sent it on to anyone else. Louise never answered so she left a message on her phone. Elliot spoke to his dad, who assured him that he hadn't sent the manuscript to anyone else to read. Ottilie, Kristin, Jonas and her parents all said the same. She tossed and turned last night, her mind going over and over every possibility and always ending up at the same place. It has to be someone she knows.

She's almost at the café when she sees a familiar figure coming out of a Victorian three-storey building. Short pixie cut, a sweatshirt with multiple animals – sheep, perhaps – on the front, turned-up boyfriend jeans. The woman has her head down and is hurrying through the front garden, a rucksack on her back. She almost bumps into Emilia as she rushes through the gate.

'Lou?'

Louise lifts her head, flustered. She pushes her fringe from her face. 'Oh, hi. What are – what are you doing here?' She has dark circles under her eyes.

'I'm meeting someone in Hodges,' Emilia says, pointing in the direction of the café at the end of the small rank of shops. 'How come you're here?'

'I . . .' she says, turning towards the building, then back to Emilia '. . . well, I actually live here. In the basement flat.'

Emilia is taken aback. 'When did you move?' She's never been to Louise's place in Richmond, even though she knew it was only a few streets away from her own house. When Wilfie has play dates with Toby it's always at Frances's house in Teddington.

'Only recently. I loved it in Richmond but, you know . . .' she says and shuffles her feet '. . . the rent went up, so I decided to move.'

'Oh, well, that's great.'

'Anyway, I'd better get on. I'm already running late.'

'Yes, me too. Meeting a journalist.'

Louise's eyes widen. 'Really?'

'Yes.' She quickly fills her in on the anonymous letter and tickets Jake received. 'I rang you to tell you and also to ask if you've given the manuscript to anyone else, but you didn't answer.'

Louise clamps a hand to her forehead. She looks pale. Emilia suspects her friend has been working too hard. 'Sorry, I've been meaning to call back. It's been a manic few days. I think it's a good idea speaking to the press about this. A way of hopefully exposing who's behind it all. You should go on the radio too. The more people who know about this, the better.'

'That's what I'm starting to think. Did the police ever trace the hoax call?'

She shakes her head. 'No, I'm sorry, it was a spoofed number. It's not as easy as they make out on TV.'

Emilia digs her hands into her pockets, her fingers

brushing against the alarm. She pulls it out to show Louise. 'Elliot gave me this. He's really freaked out. It must be someone I know, Lou.'

'Shit . . . I don't know what to say. That's awful.'

'You never showed the book to anyone else, did you?'

'No. Of course not. I wouldn't do that without your consent.' Louise hovers, her hand on the gate, as though she doesn't want to leave Emilia. 'I'm so sorry, but I really have to go – I'm late for work. We need to talk about this properly, though. I'll call you, okay?'

Emilia glances at Louise's jeans and jumper attire. She seems a bit casually dressed for work. 'Sure.' Neither of them moves. 'I'm scared, to be honest,' she blurts out. 'I try to put on a brave face in front of Elliot but the book, the story . . . the whole serial-killer praying-mantis thing, it's dark.'

'I know.'

'I've written that he kills Miranda in the end. And what if –'

'Stop. Em, you can't think like that. God . . .' She reaches for Emilia's hand. 'I'm so sorry you're going through this. I really am.'

'It's not your fault.'

'I know, but –' Louise is interrupted by her phone buzzing. She fishes it out of the back pocket of her jeans. 'Shit. It's the boss. I'm sorry, I really need to go.' She gives Emilia a hug. 'I promise I'll call you later.'

Emilia watches with a heavy heart as Louise rushes

down the street to her little Fiat, her mobile clamped to her ear.

Gina Osbourne is waiting at a table in the corner, her foot tapping impatiently while she scrolls through her phone. She looks up when Emilia walks in.

'I'm so sorry,' says Emilia, pulling out a chair. 'I bumped into a friend.'

'Don't worry.' Gina already has her pen handy and a half-drunk cup of coffee in front of her, a pink lipstick mark on the rim. 'What can I get you?'

'A caramel latte would be fab. Thanks.'

Gina gets up to order at the counter while Emilia shuffles out of her jacket. The alarm clunks noisily against her chair. She's already sick of the bloody thing.

Gina returns with the coffee and passes it to Emilia, then sits down again. 'So, tell me everything. From the beginning,' she says, clicking her pen and magicking a notebook out of thin air.

Emilia takes a deep breath and launches into all of it: lilies, bomb scares, being followed by a shadowy man at night with Louise, the seagull, the troll, the wreath, the open windows, and hacking Alexa, although she decides not to mention Jasmine, the mysterious concert tickets and the hoax call. She'd rather keep her daughter out of the paper. When she's finished, Gina sits back open-mouthed. 'Wow,' she says. 'That's a lot. And all of these things happened in your books?'

'All of them at some point or other, apart from the first bouquet I was sent. The lilies. I can't remember my character, DI Miranda Moody, getting sent those. But she might have. The rest is mostly from my earlier books, the first four.'

Gina presses her pen against her cheek. 'Can you tell me what your new book is going to be called and we'll put in a bit about that too?'

'*Her Last Chapter.*'

'And what's that about?'

'It's about a serial killer who inks his female victims.' She tells her a little about the plot, without giving away any spoilers. 'It's also kind of a revenge thriller.'

'Sounds creepy.'

Emilia laughs. 'Well, I hope so.'

Gina studies Emilia, then adds, 'You really do have a dark mind. Is any of it autobiographical?'

Emilia is thrown for a few seconds. She takes a sip of her latte before answering. 'Well, not really, no.' Heat creeps up her neck. 'My character, Miranda, she's very different from me. Older, stronger. Says what she thinks.'

She's relieved when Gina turns away to continue scribbling in her notebook.

As she's driving home, she gets a call from Jasmine.

'Mum, I'm stressing out. I can't find my PE kit. I thought it was in my locker, but I think I left it at Dad's.' Jasmine only has PE every other week.

'Do you need it today?'

'No, tomorrow. Can you please go and get it?'

'Your dad will be at work.'

'Kristin might be in. Please. I'll get a lunchtime detention if I forget it.' She can hear the anxiety in her daughter's voice.

'Okay. I'll pop over and see if Kristin's in.' The last thing she wants to do is see Kristin, but she doesn't want Jasmine feeling stressed about this with everything else going on.

'Thanks, Mum,' she says, sounding relieved. 'Got to go. Bye.'

Kristin's Mini is parked outside the house and Emilia pulls up behind it. She hopes Kristin can locate the PE kit quickly and she can be on her way. The street is quiet as she gets out of the car, a wood pigeon cooing in the distance. She makes her way down the familiar front path and knocks on the door.

Kristin opens it after the second knock. She looks her usual glamorous self, in a pair of jeans so tight they look like a second skin and a plunging pale-pink V-necked T-shirt. Her dark hair is gathered up in a high ponytail. Her blue eyes narrow when she sees it's Emilia.

'Sorry to drop in like this,' says Emilia, before explaining about Jasmine's PE kit.

'Come in while I go and find it.'

Emilia follows her through to the hallway and into the kitchen. On the table is a clear plastic box of art supplies, and a Stanley knife lies on top of a huge piece of card. Kristin must notice Emilia looking at it as she goes over to it and starts packing it away. 'I was just . . . um, making a card for a friend's birthday.'

Emilia smiles politely.

'Would you like a cup of tea?'

'No, that's fine, thanks, though.'

'Oh, okay. Give me a sec. Let me just check I didn't put it in the wash.' She bends down and rummages through a plastic tub full of clothes. 'It's not here. I'll check her bedroom.'

She leaves the room and Emilia sits at the table. She moves the Stanley knife to the side, wondering if Kristin has read *Her Last Chapter* yet. She remembers what Louise told her about Kristin questioning her about Jonas at her launch. First Ottilie, and now Louise. What is Kristin playing at? It was really inappropriate of her to quiz Louise when they'd never met before. Does Kristin really suspect that she and Jonas are having an affair?

And then her eyes go to the plastic box and her heart stops.

Pressed against the edge, its fake yellow hair spread out like butter, is the familiar face of a troll doll.

29

Daisy,
2005

Daisy had always been a firm believer in Fate, that people came in and out of your life for a reason. And that Christmas it became apparent why she'd had to end up at the same university as Ash.

It was ironic that after she had stopped looking for the Doodle Man, when she had . . . not forgotten exactly, that would never happen, but been distracted by infatuation, he appeared before her, like a mirage, like a gift.

'I'm going to really miss you,' Ash said that fateful day, as they hung out in the student union. 'But you're still okay to come and visit after Christmas? It isn't far from here. You could visit me and then my parents could drop you back here with me for the beginning of term?'

'Absolutely.' She couldn't wait to spend more time with Ash. They had so much in common: music, films, art. Daisy was her happiest when it was just the two of them.

'My parents are going to love you, Daise.'

'I think my dad will love you too. Hopefully next time you can stay with me and meet him.'

Ash had pulled her closer then, a leather-clad arm slung around her shoulders. 'I'd love that.'

The sound of a car pulling up outside made Ash go to the window that looked out over the car park. 'Shit! They're early! Do you want to meet them now? I know you'll see them when you come to stay but –'

'Of course,' she said, getting up from where they'd been lounging on one of the beaten-up sofas.

She grabbed her coat, and Ash's large holdall, and headed outside to where a middle-aged man and a younger woman were getting out of a gorgeous old Jaguar, like the type Inspector Morse drove.

The woman was pretty and blonde, with high cheekbones and eyes that sparkled. She looked a lot younger than Ash's dad, who was fair, broad-shouldered and ruddy-cheeked, as if he enjoyed being outside, preferably with a large Labrador and a hunting rifle. They smiled at her too, introducing themselves as Donald and Stef, shaking her hand and exclaiming how they'd heard all about her from Ash. And all the while a thud of recognition reverberated through her. Where had she seen this man before?

They were still talking and proclaiming and gesturing as Donald lugged Ash's bag into the boot and Stef stood by the passenger door. It was cold, and Stef had a scarf wrapped tightly around her neck almost up to her nose.

'Well, lovely to meet you, Daisy,' said Stef, warmly. She must have been really young when she'd had Ash. 'Looking forward to you coming to stay.'

'Yes,' said Donald, with a wide grin, pumping her hand up and down. 'Hope you have a lovely Christmas.'

And all the while, an air of surrealism surrounded her as she tried to grasp the memories that were disappearing, like a puff of smoke in fresh air.

Ash gave her a brief, almost nonchalant, hug and climbed into the back seat.

And as Daisy watched Donald walk to the driver's side, with a slight left-handed lilt, she was hit with such a vivid memory that she felt dazed.

A double crown, a wide neck like a ham. Tall. Fair.

The back of his head was so familiar, she suddenly knew exactly where she'd seen him before.

Her mother's secret boyfriend.

And her killer.

30

The yellow-haired troll doll. The one that had hung ominously from her tree. The one she'd taken down and thrown away. How has it ended up in Kristin's kitchen? Emilia can't tear her eyes away from it. Panic renders her motionless until she hears Kristin's feet on the stairs. Then she gets up from her chair, a surge of nervous energy pulsing through her.

Kristin walks into the kitchen with a triumphant expression. 'I've found it. It was bundled up under her bed. I'm afraid it needs washing.' She hands the drawstring bag to Emilia. Her smile slips. 'Are you okay? You've gone really pale.'

Emilia takes the bag. 'I, um, I've been having a hard time lately. Has Jonas told you what's been going on?'

Unease passes across Kristin's features. 'He has. I'm sorry you're going through all this. It sounds frightening.'

'Have you read my new book yet?'

'I finished it a while ago. I really enjoyed it.' She folds her arms across her chest.

Emilia indicates the troll doll squashed against the side of the plastic box. 'Where did you get that?'

'That doll thing? I dunno. So much junk ends up in that box. It must have been from when Jas was younger.'

Emilia narrows her eyes at Kristin. 'That one – or one just like it – was found hanging from the tree in my front garden last month.'

Kristin's body stiffens. 'And you think I put it there?'

'I don't know what to think.'

Kristin takes a step back. 'You obviously think I'm capable. It's written all over your face.' When Emilia doesn't speak, Kristin lets out a sharp, sarcastic laugh. 'Oh, I see. I stole your husband so therefore I have no morals and am capable of anything. Is that it? I'm capable of putting my stepdaughter – who I love, by the way – in danger. I'm capable of stalking and obsessing about you. Is that what you want to hear? Because I'm sorry, Emilia, but I don't care that much about you to go to so much trouble to frighten you.'

Pent-up anger and resentment rises within Emilia. She slings the PE kit over her shoulder. 'If you care so little about me, as you say, then why call Ottilie up to question her about me? Why bother Louise at my launch when you'd never even met her before? She told me you were asking about me and Jonas. Do you really think I'm shagging him behind your back? Behind Elliot's?'

Kristin's critical gaze trails over Emilia's body, taking in the jersey dress that shows off her lumps and bumps. 'No, I don't think you're having an affair with *my* husband.'

Emilia knows she needs to leave before she says something she regrets. She stalks out of the kitchen and into the hallway. She can sense Kristin behind her.

'Wait!' Kristin's voice is desperate, and Emilia stops, her hand on the front-door knob.

She spins around. 'What?'

'I *am* sorry,' says Kristin. 'I know we've never talked about it. I tried to ring you so many times after it happened. To explain. But you never wanted to speak to me.'

'Can you blame me?'

'Of course not. My apology seems meaningless now, all these years later. But I am sorry for what happened. I wish we'd been honest with you from the beginning. Jonas was going to tell you about us, and then . . . and then you fell pregnant.'

The truth slaps her in the face. 'You and him . . . it happened before . . . before . . .' She can't bring herself to say it.

Kristin hangs her head but not before Emilia notices a cruel glint in her eye, and she realizes that Kristin wants to feel powerful, to have something over her. Kristin knows Jonas has a wandering eye and she wants to make clear to Emilia that she wins. That she'll *always* win. That Jonas chose her. 'He was going to leave you. Back in 2006. He was going to leave you and then you fell pregnant.'

Her stomach curdles as she remembers their rushed wedding at the local register office with just Ottilie, and

Jonas's best mate, Dan, as witnesses, and Jonas's parents as guests. Her dress that strained across her belly, at that stage of pregnancy when she didn't look like she was carrying a baby but had simply put on too much weight. She didn't even tell her parents about her pregnancy until afterwards.

'You could have had anyone,' says Emilia, sadly. 'Why him?'

Kristin twirls her platinum wedding ring. 'I can't explain it. I just loved him. I still do. You can't choose who you fall in love with. Anyway, you're happy now, with Elliot. Aren't you?'

'Of course I am.' Kristin still doesn't get it. 'It's not about Jonas. I'm not harbouring any feelings for him. But you. What *you* did. You ruined our friendship.'

So many unspoken words float in the silence between them. Things that Emilia will never be able to say, like how much she misses their friendship, their girls' nights out, sitting up to 3 a.m. with Kristin and Ottilie, chatting about everything, laughing until their sides ached. She swallows the lump in her throat. 'I need to go,' she says, her voice thick.

'I promise you, I'm not behind this "campaign of terror" or whatever is happening. I've no reason to do that.'

Emilia stares into Kristin's face, trying to see whether she's telling the truth. The competitive side to Kristin will always show through. If she really thinks Emilia is having an affair with Jonas, who knows what she's

capable of? There is a steel core running through her former friend. There always has been. It's just that Emilia
had never wanted to acknowledge it before.

Without another word, she leaves, closing the front
door firmly behind her.

It's not until she's driven out of the road and around
the corner that she pulls over underneath a big oak tree
and calls DC Haddock, her hands shaking.

'I don't know if it means anything,' she says, as soon as he
answers the phone, 'but my ex-husband's wife, Kristin
Perry, has a troll doll in her possession that matches the one
found on my tree. I thought you should know.'

31

On Thursday morning, as Emilia is standing at the kitchen sink spooning muesli into her mouth, her phone buzzes with a message from Gina Osbourne.

The story is in today's paper.

Emilia puts down the bowl and scans the newspaper's website. Sure enough, there it is. It feels weird to read it in black and white, as though it's happening to someone else. She's still reading it when Elliot storms into the kitchen, his face like thunder.

'What's wrong?' She wonders if he's seen the *Mirror* piece too and is annoyed about it. Although she did tell him she'd spoken to Gina.

'My fucking bike's been stolen.'

She stares at him in surprise. 'What?' Her breakfast curdles in her stomach. 'From the porch?'

'Yes. Did you lock the front door last night?'

'Of course. I always lock it now.'

'Are you sure? There's no sign of a break-in.'

'Have you checked the app?'

'Of course I have.' He shoves his phone under her

nose. 'It looks like it was taken in the early hours of this morning. It's still dark.'

She watches in horror as the grainy footage shows someone dressed head to toe in dark clothes walking down their driveway, between their two parked cars, brazenly opening the front door, stealing the bike and riding it away. 'But . . .' She can't believe what she's seeing. How easy it is. 'What about the alarm? Why didn't it go off? And the door . . . I definitely locked it.'

He runs a hand over his unshaven chin. 'I don't know. I don't understand it. It's like the alarm's been disabled or something. I'll have to ask my dad. But, Em,' he says and glances at her with suspicion in his eyes, 'it doesn't look like the porch was locked.'

She locked it. She knows she did. She would never forget, not after everything that's happened. She tries to keep her panic in check as she asks Elliot to replay the footage again, peering more closely at the screen this time to try to get a better look. 'Here,' she says, pausing the recording, adrenaline pumping, 'the beanie . . . that badge on the front. I recognize it.'

'You do?'

'Yes. It's a Scandinavian brand. I . . .' Her insides turn to ice. 'I've seen someone I know wearing a hat just like it.'

'Who?' Elliot's voice is urgent.

Nausea rises. It could be a coincidence and it's so hard to tell – the person looks taller, but the build is slim. It's impossible to get a clear look at their face. Their head is dipped the whole time, hair hidden by the hat.

'Louise,' she says.

After trying to call Louise five times, Emilia leaves a frustrated message. 'Please call me back. It's really important.'

'I should ring the police,' says Elliot, angrily, pacing the kitchen.

'Louise *is* the police.'

'And yet you think she stole my bike.'

She exhales in frustration. 'I'm not saying it is her, okay? I'm saying she has a beanie like that. But so do lots of other people, I expect. This person looks taller than Louise so I could be wrong. It's – it's hard to tell exactly. We need to give her the benefit of the doubt before we go reporting it to the police. If it is her maybe she needed it for some reason and didn't want to wake us all up.' The argument sounds weak, even to her own ears, but they can't assume it's Louise based on the make of a hat.

'You're right, it could be anyone. And if you forget to lock the door . . .' He lets the implication hang in the air.

Elliot heads back to his garden office, promising not to report it until they've heard back from Louise, and Emilia tries to keep busy by cleaning the bathrooms, still smarting over Elliot's accusation about her forgetting to lock the door. She remembers doing it.

It's not until much later, after she's picked up the kids from school and Elliot is making tea, that she notices a voicemail on her phone from Louise. The call was made at 3.30 p.m. when she was driving to Jasmine's school to pick her up because she doesn't want her to get the bus home.

She wanders away from the cacophony in the kitchen and heads to the front room to listen to it.

'Sorry, mate,' says Louise in a breathless voice. 'It's been a manic day. I've managed to pop home for a bit. But I really need to speak to you. To explain everything. I'd rather do it face to face. Can you come over to my place this evening? It's flat four, Sunnyside Road. Toby's at his dad's so we can have a proper chat. I'm . . .' Emilia is appalled to hear the wobble in her friend's voice '. . . I'm so sorry. I didn't mean for any of it to get this far. Come over as soon as you can. And, Em . . .' she says and sniffs '. . . I really am sorry.'

The message ends and Emilia stares at her phone in alarm. What does Louise mean? Why is she sorry? For the bike? Her heart picks up speed. Is Louise involved in something dodgy? She tries to call her back, but the phone just rings out.

'Damn it,' she mutters to herself.

'Are you okay?' She looks up to see Elliot standing in the doorway. 'Was that Louise?'

She nods, her mind racing. 'A message. She sounded weird. She wants me to go over to hers, now.'

Disapproval radiates from him. 'What? Now? Why? Can't it wait? Dinner will be ready soon.'

'It's not far and I won't be long. I really need to speak to her. I need to find out what's going on.'

He looks doubtful. 'I don't think you should go . . .'

'I'll be okay. I've got my alarm.' She heads back into the hallway and grabs her denim jacket. 'I shouldn't be too long. Save me some fish.' She reaches up and kisses him again but he's still looking at her oddly as she hurries out of the front porch.

It takes her twenty minutes to drive to Louise's. She manages to find a space on the almost deserted street and walks through the communal garden. Louise's flat is in the basement, with iron railings and accessed by steps. It's still light, but the sun is around the back of the building so the front of Louise's flat is in shadow. A Ukrainian flag hangs from the top-floor window but the street is quiet, almost eerie.

She descends the steps, and as she does so, she can see into Louise's kitchen window. It looks empty, with just a wilting plant in the middle of a pine table, but when she reaches the little courtyard at the bottom she sees Louise's door is very slightly ajar. She knocks, but when there is no answer she pushes it open, calling Louise's name, her voice echoing around the empty hallway. She notices Louise's Nike Air trainers by the door. She lives in them so she must be at home. Emilia pokes her head around the kitchen door, feeling like an intruder, but she's not there. She makes her way down the hall to the living room. 'Louise?' she calls again, pushing the living-room door open, and then she gasps.

Her friend is lying face down on the floor, the back of her head matted with blood.

'Oh, my God! Louise!' She rushes over and kneels down, touching her shoulder. 'Lou?' The cold hard feeling of dread presses in on her. 'Lou . . .' she says again, faintly this time, a sob in her throat, because she already knows that she's too late, even as she presses her fingers to her friend's neck to find a pulse. She turns her over, ready to pump her chest, give her mouth-to-mouth, anything that might help. But Louise's skin is too pale, her lips too blue, her body unnaturally cold. She's wearing her llama jumper and the sight of it makes Emilia cry harder. This can't be happening.

Emilia calls an ambulance and sits next to Louise's body, waiting for them to arrive. She holds her friend's hand and talks to her, even though she knows it's fruitless. 'I'm so sorry I didn't get your call in time. I'm so sorry, Louise. Hang in there, the ambulance is on its way.' Her mind is whirring. Her first overriding thought on finding Louise had been to help her friend. But now, like a chink of sunlight struggling through a cloud, her thoughts push through the shock. Before she'd rolled Louise over, she'd noticed a gash to the back of her head, blood matted into her dark hair. If she'd fallen and banged her head she would be on her back, wouldn't she? But she'd been on her front, as though hit from behind.

Emilia looks down at her friend's pale face and gently smoothes away the hair from her forehead. She's like a waxwork figure, no longer like Louise, and another sob escapes her lips. There is a spot of blood on the pale llama. Maybe she shouldn't have moved her. If someone did this to Louise, the police will be looking for evidence. She carefully releases Louise's hand and stands up, pushing down her hysteria. Just being here she could be contaminating the crime scene. She knows this from all the times she's written about it in her books. She'll have to remember to tell the police about the position Louise's body had been in when she found her.

A chill creeps over her body and she breaks out in goose bumps. She feels as if she's in a nightmare and is trying to wake up. This can't be happening. She thinks of little Toby and her heart breaks all over again.

And then she glances down at Louise's bare feet and horror washes over her as she notices something on her ankle. It can't be . . .

She bends down for a closer look. But there's no mistaking it. On Louise's ankle there is a crude marking of an insect's head.

32

I'm hoping to get out early for once. I need to see my father and check on how he's coping, as we have finally persuaded him that it's best for my mother – as well as himself – that she goes into a nursing home. I'm just packing up my stuff and turning off my computer when Saunders bursts into the office without knocking.

I open my mouth to give him a piece of my mind but stop when I notice the look on his face, the mixture of excitement and horror I've come to recognize when he thinks we have a lead on a case that seems unsolvable.

'A call has just come in. It looks like there's been another victim. The praying-mantis murderer's struck again.'

I stare at him in shock. I realize my mouth is hanging open and I close it. It's been over a year now since Trisha Banks was killed and, despite our best efforts, we've never been able to pin down Martin Butterworth for the crimes, even though he remains our prime suspect and we've been watching him like hawks.

'Where?' I say, pulling on my coat.

'Well, that's the weird thing,' he says. 'It's out of our juris-diction. But we've been called in because of the similarity to

past cases.' He reels off an address. It's going to take us three hours to get there, maybe more. And it's already 6 p.m. But we have to go. There's no doubt about that.

'Come on, then,' I say, already getting out my phone to call my sister to ask her to visit Dad instead, and to let my girlfriend, Kim, know I won't be home for a few days.

It's late by the time we reach the quiet, narrow street. We can tell straight away which house it is because of the hubbub outside. Police tape is stretched around the small front garden, and the uniformed officer who is guarding it lifts it up so we can get through. I'm already exhausted, and spending all that time in the car with Saunders has given me a headache but I try to push it aside as we walk down the steps and into the basement flat.

'It's through here, ma'am,' says another officer. Plain clothes, bald with unusually red cheeks. He introduces himself as Detective Sergeant Shawn Watkins from the Metropolitan Police.

A woman is lying on the carpet in the front room. She's youngish, mid-thirties at the most. Slim, around five foot two, with short dark hair.

'How was she killed?' I ask DS Watkins. I turn to see Saunders rushing from the room with a hand clamped over his mouth and frown. That's unlike him. I turn my attention back to Watkins.

'It looks like a blow to the head,' he says. 'So, not your

usual MO of a stab wound. We wouldn't have called you but then we noticed this . . .' He points to the woman's ankle. I crouch to get a better look. It appears to be a drawing of an insect's head. But it isn't the same as the others: this one isn't carved but has been drawn on with what looks like a pen.

This can't be our guy. Yet whoever did this knows about the praying-mantis etchings and only the police have this information.

'Excuse me, are you DI Janine Murray?' Another officer is approaching me. Young with mousy brown hair and a freckled face.

'Yes.'

'I'm DC Anthony Haddock. I came as soon as I heard about this.'

My headache is getting worse as I try to make sense of what's going on. 'Okay?'

'The victim is one of our own, ma'am.'

I look back at the woman on the floor. Her eyes are closed, her face is still, and if her body hadn't been showing signs of rigor mortis she'd look like she was just sleeping. She is wearing a sweatshirt with a llama on the front. 'She's a police officer?'

He nods.

'Right.' My mind is racing, trying to piece together the puzzle. Did she know Martin Butterworth? Maybe she was the officer who put him away seventeen years ago for armed robbery. But, no, that can't be it. She was around thirty-five.

Which means she would have been too young. 'What's her name?'

'DC Louise Greene, ma'am. And the thing is . . .' DC Haddock hops from one foot to the other. 'We're still not sure of all the details but the woman who found her was DC Greene's friend. The crime writer Emilia Ward.'

PART TWO

33

Emilia Ward. I've read some of her books. I've always been impressed with how accurate the police procedural part of her stories is. Now I know why, given she was friends with a detective at the Metropolitan Police.

'Where is Emilia now?'

DC Haddock pushes a lock of hair from his eyes. His face has a greasy sheen. 'I've taken a statement and let her go home. She was in a bit of a state, as you can imagine.'

'You let her drive home on her own? After she'd just found her friend dead?' I shake my head at his insensitivity.

'I offered her a lift but she said she was fine,' he bleats.

Bloody useless. 'She's probably in shock.'

He glances down at his feet like a chastised schoolboy, which is what he resembles in his short-sleeved shirt with an ink stain on the pocket. I'm about to move away from him to talk to his superior when he asks me if he can have a word outside. I nod and follow him to the front garden. I immediately light a fag. I offer the packet to Haddock, and he takes one as we walk around to the back of the building, where it's quieter.

'So?' I begin.

The light from an upstairs window reflects in his pupils. 'The thing is, I've been in contact with Emilia these past few weeks because someone has been targeting her.'

I frown. 'Targeting her?'

'Mirroring the plotlines from her bestselling books to frighten her.' I listen as he tells me about troll dolls found in trees, the broken neck of a ceramic seagull, missing daughters at concerts and hoax calls.

I exhale a plume of smoke that dissipates into the warm night air. 'Right. What's this got to do with DC Louise Greene?'

'That I don't know. But she told me DC Greene had left a message on her phone earlier today, asking to meet. I listened to the message. Louise sounded upset. Contrite and, well, guilty.'

'You got all that from a voice message?'

'Yes. You can listen to it too.'

I need to speak to Emilia Ward as soon as possible.

I stub out my cigarette against the brick wall. 'Do you know what time Louise died?'

'Not one hundred percent yet. But Louise left the message for Emilia at three thirty p.m. Emilia found her at five eighteen p.m.'

So, quite a short window, which should make it easier for the police. 'Does Emilia think that Louise's death is also copied from one of her books?' I think of the doodle on Louise's ankle and how similar it is to the praying-mantis case I've been working on for years.

He angles his body so that he's facing me. 'Well, that's the thing. She said the doodle on Louise's ankle is from her new book. But it hasn't been published yet.'

I stare at him in shock. The doodles might not have been inflicted in the same way but surely they're too similar to be just a coincidence. A similar insect's head, in the same area as the serial killer brands his victims. I need to speak to Emilia Ward pronto to find out what the hell is going on.

34

Emilia doesn't ring Elliot until she's driving home. She'd texted to tell him while she waited for the police to arrive to take her statement, and then she'd called DC Haddock and told him everything, trying not to cry until she'd managed to get all her words out. Then she'd had to wait for him to arrive so he could listen to Louise's message on her mobile.

'Just concentrate on getting home safely,' says Elliot, gently, over the phone. 'I'll see you in a bit.'

Now all her limbs feel like lead and she has a metallic taste at the back of her throat. 'God, I'm so sorry,' Elliot whispers, into her hair, when she staggers into the house at gone 10 p.m. Elliot wraps his arms around her while she cries onto his chest. Her daughter hovers anxiously behind her stepdad, chewing her nails. Thankfully, Wilfie is in bed so she doesn't have to break it to him yet. She thinks of poor Toby, who is maybe still blissfully unaware, and cries harder.

'What is it? What's happened to Louise?' Jasmine's face is white. She hardly knew Louise but Emilia can see how much this has thrown her daughter.

Emilia pulls away from Elliot to wrap her arms around Jasmine. 'I don't know yet, sweetheart,' she says, not wanting to scare her. 'I found her collapsed on the floor.'

'Is she dead?'

'I'm afraid so,' she says, her voice catching in her throat. She doesn't mention murder, instead saying that it might have been an accident. But Jasmine doesn't seem pacified as she eventually trudges up to bed.

'Here, have a glass of wine. It might help,' says Elliot, when they're alone on one of the sofas in the kitchen.

'Isn't it supposed to be brandy? Or whisky?'

'Well, we don't have any, so wine it will have to be,' he says. She notices he has a glass too, and that his hand trembles as he sips. She hasn't even told him yet about the inking on Louise's ankle and how a character in her book – also a police officer who worked with Miranda Moody – died in a similar way while looking for the praying-mantis murderer. Although she doesn't have to tell him that bit. He's read her latest book now. As soon as she mentions the inking, he'll know.

Elliot rests a hand on her thigh, as though he's trying to anchor himself as well as provide comfort for her.

'I can't believe she's dead,' she says again, wiping away tears with the back of her hand. 'I can't stop thinking about Toby, growing up without a mum . . .'

'Don't.' Elliot's face darkens. 'You can't think of that. You'll drive yourself crazy. This isn't your fault.'

'But what if it is?' she cries, moving forward to deposit

her wineglass on the table and dislodging Elliot's hand from her lap. 'I was the one who wrote those *stupid* books. I basically wrote her death!'

'Stop it. You didn't.'

'But I did.' She places her head in her hands and groans. 'You know my book is about a detective looking for a serial killer who draws a praying-mantis head on a victim's ankle after they die to mark them as his. And that's what she had, Elliot! She had that marking on her ankle!'

His eyes narrow and his hand clenches around his glass. 'For fuck's sake. This is ridiculous. What are the police doing about it?' He doesn't have to say it: she knows he's thinking about the ending of her book. The sidekick to Miranda Moody dying in the same way as Louise. And Miranda being killed next.

'You *do* think this is my fault, don't you?'

'Of course not. This is just some nutter –'

'Some nutter who I must know!' she shouts, jumping up from the sofa.

'Calm down,' he hisses, shocking her. 'Sorry, but do you want to disturb the children? You're spiralling. And you can't spiral, Em. You have to keep levelheaded.' He stands up too, and grabs her upper arms. His grip is tight. 'You need to stop blaming yourself. This isn't your fault. You're a writer, that's all. You're not fucking God.'

She hangs her head. He's right, of course he is. This isn't her fault. And yet she can't help the guilt tugging at her insides. And the fear that she may be next.

*

She can't sleep. All she can think about is Louise's dead body sprawled on the carpet of her living room, her still face, her cold skin, the wound at the back of her head. She'd never seen a dead body in real life regardless of how many times she's written about them. She replays Louise's last voicemail over and over in her mind. What had she meant? Why had she kept saying she was sorry? Why did she take Elliot's bike, if indeed it was her?

In despair she gets up. Elliot is fast asleep although he'd taken a while to drop off. They had both lain there, pretending to sleep, until eventually she heard his soft snores. She pads out of the bedroom and hovers on the landing, frozen in indecision. Usually, when unable to sleep, she'd go to the kitchen, make a milky drink and watch a feel-good show that she knows Elliot doesn't like, like *Emily in Paris* or *Selling Sunset*. Now all she can think about is that huge empty kitchen surrounded by glass. She'd feel like a cornered animal, wondering who was out there lurking in her garden, able to see her when she can't see them. Louise's death has shown her that whoever is behind this has been playing with her until Louise's murder. They didn't hurt Jasmine, just orchestrated her disappearance to scare Emilia, like a lion taunting its prey until it goes in for the kill.

She sighs. She can't just stand on the landing in the dark. But she can't go downstairs either. Instead, she decides to head to her office in the attic. Since they changed the passwords on Alexa the skylights have stopped opening so at least she knows she won't have to contend with that. She climbs the steep staircase, panting slightly when she reaches the top. Her grief is pressing down on her chest, threatening to suffocate her. She's gasping by the time she sits at her desk, with the door firmly shut behind her. Straight away she feels comforted by the mess surrounding her, the homely trinkets on the shelves, her beloved paperbacks of authors she admires and looks to for inspiration when she's stuck, a pile of uncorrected proof copies sent to her for an author quote.

With an unsteady hand she pulls out the drawer at the front of her desk. In it is her notebook. She has a new one for every novel she writes. She'd used this one for *Her Last Chapter*: it has a Moomin on the front, with a full moon and an inky black sky in the background. She flicks open the pages, remembering the notes she made before she started writing. Notes about Miranda Moody's new case. A serial killer who likes to ink his victims with the face of an insect. And then the backstory of Daisy and her quest to find her mother's killer, the Doodle Man, how she believes he's the father of her lover, Ash, which culminates in Miranda being stabbed. Tears splash onto the pages as she remembers what she did. And what *Louise* did. And now Louise is dead. How can it not be Emilia's fault?

She shouldn't have written the book because the story, and all the stuff about the praying-mantis murderer, was never her idea.

35

Emilia is asleep on the sofa in the posh living room, a soft cashmere throw keeping her warm, when she's woken by knocking. She bolts upright, her heart racing. Elliot took the kids to school this morning so she could get some rest. She'd been awake all night, crouched over her office desk, only crawling back into bed next to Elliot when the sun rose. She'd got up with Jasmine and Wilfie, made their packed lunches, feeling like a zombie, then crashed onto the sofa when they all left the house.

She glances at the clock on the mantelpiece. Just gone nine thirty.

There is another knock and then the ring of the doorbell. Elliot must have gone straight to his garden office to give her some peace. She reaches for her phone and checks the RingCam App. A woman she doesn't recognize is standing on her doorstep. She's dressed in a black suit with a green shirt and has a neat white bob. Elliot would have been alerted to the doorbell, too, but he might be on a call. Reluctantly she gets up and pulls her dressing gown around her to answer the door.

The woman is standing on the front step looking up at

the house, her brow furrowed in annoyance. She has piercing blue eyes, which she fastens on Emilia as soon as she wrenches open the door.

'Are you Emilia Ward?'

Emilia nods, half hidden by the door so that the street can't see she's still in her dressing gown.

The woman holds up some ID. 'I'm Detective Inspector Janine Murray from Devon and Cornwall Police. Please may I come in?'

Emilia's mind whirls immediately, thinking of Elliot and the children. 'What's this about?'

'I'm investigating the death of a friend of yours, DC Louise Greene.'

'Can I see your ID again, please?' She doesn't want to take any chances. Not after that hoax call from the hospital. What if this isn't a real detective? But the ID looks legitimate, and she hands it back to DI Murray. 'Can I just ask? You say you're from Devon and Cornwall Police. But why? Louise worked for the Met.'

'That's right. We've been investigating, for a number of years now, a serial killer mostly in Plymouth and the surrounding area. We have reason to believe that Louise's death could be linked to that case.'

A serial killer. Like in her book. A shiver runs up her spine and she can't move.

'Can I come in?'

'Yes . . . of course.' Emilia steps back to allow the detective over the threshold, then leads her into the kitchen.

'Sorry I'm not dressed yet. I had a bad night. Would you like tea or coffee?'

'Coffee would be great, thanks.' The detective sits down at the table and gets out a notebook. Emilia uses Elliot's fancy coffee machine to make a cappuccino for herself and DI Murray. The police officer's presence is unnerving her. She doesn't have a friendly face and those cold blue eyes are steely, as though they can see through to her very soul, exposing all her secrets.

She hands her the cappuccino and joins her at the table. The sun streams through the bifold doors, bleaching the area where they sit. Next to this neat, put-together woman, Emilia feels even more of a mess, like she's coming apart at the seams.

'I'm sorry to hear about Louise Greene. By all accounts she was a very well-respected detective.'

Emilia can only nod. She has no idea how respected Louise was by her colleagues. She just knows she's lost a good friend, someone she felt she could rely on. And, more than that, Toby has lost his mum. Her heart twists again.

DI Murray must grasp this as she adds softly, 'I know you lost a good friend yesterday. I understand you were the one who found her.'

'Yes.' Emilia blows on her coffee and takes a sip.

'I can't even imagine what that must have been like for you,' she says, looking intently at Emilia. 'DC Haddock has filled me in on everything that has been happening to you lately. And I've heard the voice message that Louise left you. What concerns me, Emilia, is that Louise's death is very similar to a case I've been working on for a long time. Except the mark on those victims' ankle is a carving of the insect's head, not a drawing like we found on Louise.'

Emilia sits up straighter, her senses suddenly on high alert. 'I don't understand. Are you saying you think this serial killer is responsible for Louise's death?'

DI Murray hesitates, but doesn't answer the question. 'The killer I've been investigating is known as the praying-mantis murderer – that's what we call him in the force.'

The praying-mantis murderer. Emilia's stomach churns.

'The deaths have been made public, of course, throughout the years, but we've never revealed to the press the detail about the insect's head, or the moniker we've given him. Search praying-mantis killer or murderer on the internet and you'll find nothing. So I was interested to learn that you've written a book with a serial killer going by the same name.'

A fresh wave of nausea washes over Emilia. 'But I – I made it up and my book hasn't even been published yet. And mine . . . my killer just draws them on.' Her legs have begun to tremble and she wonders if this detective can tell she's lying.

'Okay. But is there any way someone told you about the praying-mantis murders?' She pauses. 'Louise, perhaps?'

Emilia has to place her hands on her legs to stop them

jiggling. 'Louise never talked about the cases she worked on and she was in the Met Police so she wouldn't have been working on the praying-mantis case, would she?'

DI Murray shakes her head. 'No, she wouldn't. But that doesn't mean she wouldn't have heard about it.'

Fuck. How can this be happening? Emilia digs her nails into the fleece of her dressing-gown. She needs to keep it together. She swallows, not knowing how to answer. She can't tell her the truth. 'I'm . . . not sure. I'll need to think. This has all been such a shock,' she mumbles.

'Okay. But if you think of anything, please call me.' DI Murray slips her notebook into the inner pocket of her blazer. She hands Emilia a card with her name and number on it. Emilia's legs feel weak as she stands up. She can't wait for DI Murray to get out of the house.

Emilia's mind is reeling as she closes the door on the detective. If only she'd answered Louise's call. And now she's totally on her own, picking her way through the darkness, and she doesn't know what to do. How to act.

She screams out into the silent hallway, kicking at the wooden panel of the front-room door, hurting her foot. Stupid, stupid, stupid.

She needs to calm down, get a grip.

'Oh, Louise.' She sighs. What the hell was she up to? Was that what the voicemail message was about? Why she'd said she was sorry? Because she'd known, all along, that the praying-mantis murderer was real?

*

As she's throwing on clothes, she receives a call from DC Haddock. She's not surprised. He tried to interview her properly last night but her mind was all over the place after finding Louise's body. It still is.

'I don't need to spell out how serious things have become,' he says, his voice sombre. She sits on the edge of the bed, half dressed. 'Can you come down to the station? Or I could visit you if you prefer?'

She says she'll come to him. She needs to get out of the house.

When she arrives they sit in a hot room, sweat pouring off Haddock, and he says again how sorry he is about Louise. He looks through the book Jasmine had given her, with the butterflies down the front, where Emilia has written down everything that has happened to her over the last few months. She knows she's already told him some of this, last night, but she needs to make him understand. Louise has been killed and it's because of her book. That etching on her ankle . . . It makes her feel sick to know that someone close to her could have done it. 'My book and Louise's death. It's all linked. It has to be. I just . . . I just don't understand how.'

'And the doll found in Kristin Perry's things?' DC Haddock asks, looking at the list she'd made of all the people who had read her unpublished manuscript. 'Do you think she could be behind this?'

'If you'd asked me a few months ago if any of the people on this list might be capable of all the things that have happened to me lately, I'd have found it hard to believe,' she replies. She sips her water, which tastes of iron. 'But now I just don't know. I can't explain how Kristin came to have that troll doll in her possession but I can't imagine she's a killer. Why would she want to kill Louise?'

He looks up from the list. 'Whoever has been stalking you might not be the same person who killed Louise. We have to keep an open mind. Leave this with me.' His face becomes even more solemn. 'And I don't want to scare you, Emilia, but please be extra vigilant.'

He doesn't need to say it. She's fully aware of just how much danger she and her family are in.

As she leaves the interview room she thinks again about Louise's death and the plot of *Her Last Chapter*, the two things swirling around in her mind. How can there actually be a real serial killer called the praying-mantis murderer? Louise must have known. She feels like she's being pulled deeper into a spider's web, unable to claw her way out. She thinks of Elliot's reaction, her editor's. Her agent's. What would they think? She's lied. To all of them.

And now the truth is coming back to bite her. *Kill her.*

36

As Emilia rushes back to her car she spots herself in a shop window and recoils at how awful she looks, her unkempt hair scraped into a messy bun. She needs to go home, have a shower and get a grip. But all she can think about is Louise's dead body, her bloodied head, the inking on her ankle, the praying-mantis murderer being real, and her part in it all. Louise's last voicemail and what it could mean. The visit from DI Murray. The similarity to a real-life case. She can't breathe. She . . . can't . . . She stops and holds on to the wall of a nearby shop for support.

'Emilia?'

She looks up at the sound of the familiar voice. It's Kristin, looking all summery in a long, floaty dress and gladiator sandals. Has she been following her? 'Are you okay?'

Emilia takes another deep breath, trying to fight off her nausea. 'I'm fine. I . . .' She stands up straighter, still holding the wall for support. She wonders if the police have called Kristin yet to ask about the troll doll. She suspects not. 'Have you heard about Louise?'

Kristin frowns. 'Louise? Louise who?'

She looks genuinely puzzled but Emilia knows Kristin has always been an accomplished liar. 'My friend Louise. The detective. She came over last weekend to help out after Jasmine disappeared.'

'Oh, yes.' Kristin is still frowning.

She has a straw bag over her shoulder with a baguette sticking out. So much for no carbs, thinks Emilia, upset that she can have spiteful thoughts about Kristin even in these circumstances.

'What about her?'

'She's dead. Murdered.'

Emilia watches carefully for Kristin's reaction. She steps back from Emilia and her hands fly to her mouth. 'Oh, my God. That's awful. How? I mean, why? God, I'm so sorry.'

'I don't know why. I found her with a head injury . . .'

'Oh, my God,' she says again. 'That must have been traumatic for you.' She looks genuinely shocked, but she'd acted in that way after Emilia told her she and Jonas were splitting up all those years ago. Before she'd found out it was Kristin he was leaving her for. She swallows, and an expression Emilia can't read passes over Kristin's face. 'When did this happen?'

'Yesterday.'

'Is it in connection to a case she was working on?'

Emilia opens her mouth to tell her about the inking on Louise's ankle but then thinks better of it. If DC

Haddock plans on interviewing Kristin she doesn't want to give her any advantages.

'I don't know. Look . . . I have to go . . .' She stumbles away from Kristin and walks as fast as she can back to her car. She glances over her shoulder once to see Kristin staring after her.

She's relieved when she pulls up on the driveway, until she remembers what might be waiting for her and her heart sinks. She's so tired she can barely think straight, and she needs to be alert, watchful, now more than ever. She approaches the front door with trepidation, terrified of what she might find. But there is no sinister gift waiting for her on the front step and she takes a deep breath before unlocking the door and stepping into the porch. She can hear voices coming from the front room. She reels back in surprise to see her parents sitting on the sofa under the bay window, their golden retriever, Lloyd, at their feet, resting his head on the throw she'd slept with earlier. Elliot is sitting opposite in a high-backed navy blue armchair that was a mistake buy: it's pretty but uncomfortable.

'Here she is,' he says, trying to sound cheerful although his smile is strained. Her husband would not welcome her parents turning up unannounced. The knot of anxiety in her stomach intensifies.

'Hello, darling,' says her mother, crisply, her hands in the lap of her floral dress.

Her father stands up and embraces her. She's so shocked that she can only stand, like a mannequin, for a few seconds, her arms hanging limply at her sides, before hugging her father back. He leads her to the sofa so that she's sitting between her parents, like a child. She bends down to pat Lloyd, marvelling that he's still going. He must be nearly thirteen.

'Hugh and Annabel have come to stay for a few days. Keep you company,' says Elliot, with the same rictus smile. 'Isn't that lovely of them?'

She'd have to make up the spare bedroom. Nobody has slept in it since Ottilie stayed a few weeks ago. 'Sure,' she says, feeling as if she's stumbled into a play, and she's unsure which part she has to perform. She can feel the tension emanating from Elliot. He gets up and claps his hands together, like a bad actor. 'Right, well, I'd better get on. I'll see you all later.' And then he does this weird salute thing that she's never seen him do in the whole time she's known him and leaves the room.

'I'll be right back,' she says to her parents, and she follows Elliot down the hallway to the kitchen. She pushes the door closed. 'What the hell?'

He folds his arms across his chest. 'They just turned up, and with the fucking dog!'

'What? That's unheard of. My parents aren't the popping-in sort. They haven't stayed the night with us since Wilfie was a baby.'

He shrugs. 'They're your parents. I've got to work. I'm

on a deadline,' he says curtly, leaving the house through the utility room.

Her mother is standing at the fireplace, looking at the framed photos, when Emilia walks back into the room. 'What are you doing here?' she asks bluntly.

'Charming,' replies her mother, putting down a wedding photo.

Her father gets up from the sofa, straightening his trousers. He looks well, she thinks. Ex-military, he's always smartly dressed and trim, with a neat little moustache that's darker than his hair. At sixty-five he's still fit. As a kid she was always a little terrified of him. At nearly six foot two he was imposing in his RAF uniform. They moved around a lot, which was why they put her in boarding school so young, so she has never felt truly close to them. She doubts it was the boarding school – her other friends, apart from maybe Ottilie, didn't experience that problem. She suspects it was more that her mother has never been particularly maternal and her father believes in a stiff upper lip.

'I read about your stalker in the paper. Why didn't you tell us?' her father says, folding his arms across his broad chest. 'You didn't mention anything at your launch. I had to read it in yesterday's paper. I called you straight afterwards, on your mobile, but you didn't answer.'

Emilia remembers listening to the message, but she'd never had the chance to get back to him before she'd found Louise's body. 'I'm sorry. It's been . . . an awful time. I have no idea who is doing this and . . .' She falters.

Her dad looks at her expectantly. 'And I didn't tell you because . . . well, I didn't want to worry you,' she lies. She didn't tell them because she hardly sees them and it didn't feel like the kind of conversation she could have at her launch or over the phone.

'Well, we *are* worried,' says her mother, standing up and patting her dyed auburn hair. 'I tried to call you several times this morning but you never answered.'

'I didn't see any missed calls on my mobile from you today.'

She waves her hand dismissively. 'You know I only ever ring your landline.'

Her mother refuses to embrace modern technology, unlike her father. 'Well, then, you can hardly expect me to answer it.' Why did she revert to being a petulant teenager whenever she was with them?

'Do you mind if we stay?' asks her father. He's come to stand next to her mother by the fireplace, his stance wide, his arms behind his back.

She softens. It would actually be a relief to have them here. Extra pairs of eyes and all that. And they can't help the way they are. At least they're here, showing concern, wanting to help in some way. And they did come to her launch. She knows they're trying to be better.

'It would be lovely to have you,' she says.

They want to hear all about it, of course, in minute detail. Emilia is so fed up with going over it and she's so tired that she just wants to crash. But instead they follow her into the kitchen and sit on the linen sofas looking out over the garden. 'You've done wonders with this room,' her mother says, taking a cup of tea with thanks. 'So open plan. That wasn't a thing in my day.'

Emilia has given Lloyd a bowl of water and peeled back the bifold doors so that he can wander into the garden. He's flopped onto the parquet, the slight breeze from outside rippling the back of his fur. From here she can see the side of Elliot's office. The sun is at the back now, high in the sky. There isn't a cloud in sight. Her mother fans herself with a hand.

'So,' says her father. He's perched on the edge of the sofa, next to her mother, ready to jump up at a moment's notice, if need be. She imagines him with a stick under his arm like the captain in *Ghosts*. Every time Jasmine and Wilfie watch that show they laugh that he's like Granddad Hugh. 'Start from the beginning.'

And she does, leaving nothing out. Their eyes widen in shock and her mother gasps from time to time, especially when she gets to the part where she finds Louise's body. 'And now here we are,' Emilia finishes, with a sigh. 'No closer to knowing who is doing all this. But things have changed, can't you see? This isn't just nuisance stuff any more, it's murder.' She swallows a sob but her mother notices and gets up from the sofa to sit beside her.

She pats her knee awkwardly. 'This is awful, darling. What are the police doing about it?'

'They're doing what they can. But now murder is involved they'll step up.'

'I should think so too. How could they have let it get to this stage?'

She sighs. 'Whoever is doing this is clever, Mum. They know how to keep themselves hidden. But they've done something stupid: they've started taking things from my unpublished book. I know I've already asked you, but you're sure you haven't shared the manuscript with anyone else? Friends? Friends of friends?'

Her mother shakes her head, adamant that she hasn't let it out of her sight. 'I've already said we'd never do that.' She sniffs. 'I'm amazed you let anyone read it before it's been properly signed off.'

'Signed off?'

'Yes.' She purses her lips in disapproval. 'It's littered with grammatical errors. I've picked up loads. I've made notes.'

Emilia's heart sinks. 'Mum, that's kind, but I have a copyeditor for that and proofreaders . . .'

'Well, it's better to be safe than sorry.' She rummages around in her handbag, which is by her feet, and pulls out three lined A4 sheets. 'I can go through them with you now, if you like?'

'Er . . . no, that's kind but I'll look at them later.' She takes the notes from her mother and leaves them on the glass-topped coffee table. She can't bring herself to look at that book again. Not now. Every time she thinks of it her stomach plummets.

Her mother stands up, smoothing down her dress, and leaves the room to 'visit the Ladies.'

'I enjoyed the book,' pipes up her father, still literally on the edge of his seat, lowering his coffee cup onto the table. She notices how his hand trembles. 'Very unusual storyline. Where . . . um, where did you get your inspiration for that?'

'Which bit?' She tries to keep her voice even.

'The Doodle Man and all that stuff with the, um, young girl. Daisy.'

Emilia fidgets. 'I don't know. It just . . . well, it just came to me, I suppose, and it grew from there.' The lie lodges in her throat.

'Right. I see.' He clicks his tongue against his mouth. 'It must be hard coming up with new cases for Miranda to solve. Is that why you ended the series?'

'I just wanted to write something else.'

It's on the tip of her tongue to tell him everything, the stoic man she knows would be used to keeping secrets and would probably keep hers.

Yet he's so proud of her for fulfilling his dream when he could not. Her mother told her once that, after he'd retired, he'd tried to publish a novel about life in the RAF but could never find a publisher for it. He'd be so disappointed – she'd shatter their tentative closeness as suddenly as if she'd stamped on a mirror. It was only when she became a bestselling author that her father noticed her.

But now she wishes she'd never written that stupid book.

Because it can't be a coincidence: Louise gave her the idea for *Her Last Chapter*. And if she hadn't, maybe she'd still be alive.

37

It looks as though Louise has tried to personalize her drab flat as much as possible, disguising the worn brown leather sofas with colourful throws and bright cushions with fat-faced animals on them. On the mantelpiece there is a beautiful black-and-white photograph of Louise with a golden-haired toddler on her lap. It must be her son, Toby, and my heart aches for him. I can tell from the other photographs dotted around her living room that he must be eight or nine now. Next to the photos is a clay dog that looks as if it was made by a child, and a framed cross-stitch picture of a hen. I reach out and touch it, wondering if she had made it.

I move away from the photographs. I can't think of the family: it's too emotive, and I need to concentrate on my job. Saunders has already called in sick this morning with apparent food poisoning and is holed up in the hotel. We're supposed to be heading back to Devon tonight, although I'm tempted to stick around for a few more days.

There is still a patch of russet-coloured blood on the carpet in the middle of the room. According to DS Watkins there is no sign of a break-in. Who was this woman and why was she a target? I can't work out whether this is linked to the other murders or if it's just random and copied from Emilia Ward's book. Louise's marking is a drawing rather than a carving.

I nod hello at Watkins, then move into the victim's bedroom. I can't bring myself to look into the single room next to it, knowing it is her son's room when he's not at his dad's. Her bedroom is tidy, the quilt neat. It's sparse, like the living room, with just a wardrobe, a small shelf full of paperbacks and bright scatter cushions on the bed. On her bedside cabinet a document of some kind is printed on A4 paper. I pick it up and read the front page, which has the title Her Last Chapter by Emilia Ward typed in large letters. It doesn't look like Louise had the chance to read it before she died, as the pages are all neat, no dog-eared corners or fingerprints.

I put it down, then wander along the narrow hallway and back into the living room.

'So, what do you think?' Watkins is surveying the room with his hands on his hips. It's just the two of us for the moment. Most of the work was done overnight. He's wearing a tweed jacket with velvet elbow patches that make him look like a college professor. He runs a hand over his bald head. 'Is this the work of your guy?'

'I'm not sure. The past victims have been stabbed. They're usually laid out on a bed. And they were murdered in the early hours of the morning, not late afternoon, and always in the Devon area, mostly Plymouth, except once where a victim was killed in a village about two miles from the city. But, like the other victims, there are no signs of sexual assault.'

'Although we won't know that for definite until the pathologist reports,' he states.

I press my lips together to stop myself saying, 'Obviously,' and instead make a kind of grunting noise. I've never worked with DS Watkins but I can already tell he's one of those men who likes to think he knows more than women, even though I've been in the job at least ten years longer than him and I'm a rank higher.

'There's some paperwork on Louise's bedside table,' I say. 'Do you mind if I take it? There might be something of interest.' I'd like to know how Emilia Ward has written a story that is spookily similar to the case I've been working on for the past seventeen years. I need to read the book to see what else is in there.

'Knock yourself out,' says Watkins, moving away from me and to the little kitchen at the front of the flat to talk to a uniformed officer who has just walked in.

I go back to Louise's bedroom and gather up the manuscript carefully, making sure not to dislodge any pages, and leave the flat without saying goodbye to Watkins, hoping that the clues about the praying-mantis murderer are somewhere within these words.

38

Emilia's parents stay for the weekend and, despite herself, she finds she's enjoying their company. There is something reassuring in their steadfast natures, in her dad's stiff upper lip and her mother's chitchat about the Rotary Club. Since her dad left the RAF, she'd always thought of their lives as so provincial, so mundane, but now she'd swap hers with theirs in a heartbeat. Oh, to live a normal life again, without fear, anxiety and the unease that is now her constant companion. She's lost weight and she feels like she's aged ten years, something her mother has mentioned more than once since she's been here.

Every time she closes her eyes she sees Louise's dead body, her too-pale skin, her slim, bare calves in the cut-off jeans and the branding on her ankle, so she deliberately stays up late with her father, chatting about her books or his time in the RAF. It's the closest she's ever felt to him. Wilfie is delighted that there is a dog in the house and spends most of the weekend playing with Lloyd in the garden, until Lloyd gets too tired and flops down onto the grass and she has to remind her son that he's old.

On Saturday, Elliot asks his dad, Trevor, to arrange to have someone change the locks, murmuring that they can't be too careful now that Louise is dead. Not to mention the concern over Elliot's bike being stolen. She still can't be sure it was Louise, and she didn't see the bike at Louise's flat. Elliot oversees the work, standing with his arms folded in the hallway while some guy in dirty overalls with dark patches under the armpits drills in a new lock. When it's done, Elliot retreats to his office, professing to be bogged down with work, only coming out to eat, but on Sunday he does make them all a huge roast, in his element at the compliments he receives from her parents, even though her mother gives him advice on producing a crisper Yorkshire pudding.

'It's rude that Elliot is spending all weekend working,' says Jasmine as she helps Emilia unload the dishwasher. 'I've not gone out because Granddad and Grandma are here.'

'He hasn't spent *all* weekend working, only yesterday because he has a deadline. And *you* haven't gone out because I want to keep an eye on you,' Emilia reminds her archly. 'And keep your voice down. I don't want them to hear.' She nods in the direction of her parents who are sitting with Wilfie at the family-room end of the kitchen.

Jasmine tuts. 'You can't keep your eye on me for ever.'

'I can until I find out who's doing this.' She still hasn't told Jasmine that Louise was murdered. On one hand she wants to prepare her daughter for what might be out there, but on the other she doesn't want to scare her. She thinks about the visit she had from the female detective on Friday, DI Janine Murray. She wonders if they've questioned Kristin. She tries to visualize Kristin going over to Louise's house, knocking on her door, being let inside, and then grabbing something heavy and hitting her on the back of the head with it. Would Kristin really do something like that? And, if so, why? She visualizes the two of them outside the bookshop at her launch. She can't get over the nagging feeling she'd been interrupting some kind of heated discussion: their body language seemed off, as if they weren't meeting for the first time that night. Louise had said Kristin had been grilling her for information about Jonas, but she can't help wondering if there was more to it. Is that what Louise was going to tell her, on the day she died? Something about Kristin?

She's listened to Louise's voicemail message over and over and over again, hoping she'll hear some clue she missed the first time around, but mainly just to hear her voice, her slight northern accent in the way she pronounced some words. She still can't believe she'll never get to talk to her again.

'Earth to mother.' Jasmine's voice brings her back to the present. 'Are you okay?' Her daughter's pretty face is scrunched in worry.

'I'm fine, sweetheart. Just thinking.' She reaches for her and pulls her in tightly, kissing the top of her head until Jasmine squirms and moves away. She's never loved being hugged.

'It will be okay,' says Jasmine, solemnly, which breaks her heart. She doesn't want her daughter to worry about her and all of this. Now that she's finally starting to make new friends, Emilia has to clip her wings to keep her safe. 'They'll find whoever is doing this soon. I just know it.'

'They will,' agrees Emilia, hoping she sounds more convinced than she feels.

The hot weather breaks on the morning her parents leave, and Emilia tries not to see this as an omen as she waves them off in the rain. And even though they didn't speak about anything deep and meaningful, she's grateful they came. She vows to make more effort to travel down to Guildford to see them in the future.

When she gets home, after dropping Wilfie and then Jasmine at school, Elliot is sitting at the kitchen island.

She places a palm on her chest. 'You scared me. I thought you were in your office.'

He hasn't shaved this morning and runs a hand across his stubble. 'I just came in to make a brew.'

She frowns. The kettle isn't even on. She pushes back her hair, which has got wet after running from the car to the house, and walks behind him to massage his shoulders, which are stiff with tension. He jerks away from her and jumps down from the barstool to switch on the kettle. She tries to push away the hurt. He's usually loving, always holding her hand when out walking – much to the embarrassment of Jasmine – yet now he can't get away from her fast enough.

'Are you okay? I know it wasn't ideal having my parents turning up unannounced this weekend, not after Louise and everything . . .' He has a distracted air about him, as if he's worrying about something, and then her heart twists. 'What is it? What's happened?'

'It's nothing.'

She moves across the kitchen to wrap an arm around his waist.

'I suppose I'm just worried,' he admits. 'Louise's murder has knocked me for six. When you told me about that marking on her ankle being from your book . . .' he says and she feels him shudder '. . . it brings it all closer to home.' He moves so that he's facing her now, holding her at arm's length, his eyes dark with intent. 'And I want you to know that I'd do anything – *anything* – to protect you and the kids.'

'I know you would. But we have to trust the police.'

'Like they were a great help before.'

'It's different now, though. It's not just harassment anymore. It's murder.'

He releases her and they stand in silence, watching the kettle boil. Once it's clicked off Elliot makes tea for them both. 'So, how did you come up with the story? You said that detective who came over . . . what's-her-name . . .'

'Janine Murray.'

'Yes, her. She said it's similar to a real-life case?'

Emilia takes her mug and goes to stand at the doors, looking onto the garden. The rain is coming down so fast it splashes upwards, and puddles are already forming on the sandstone tiles. 'I honestly didn't know that when I started writing it,' she says truthfully. But she feels sick when she remembers the rest. 'It's just a coincidence.'

He wraps his fingers around his mug. 'So you'd never heard of the case?'

'No!' At least she's not lying about that. She turns to him. 'Had you?'

'Of course not. But, then, if the details were kept out of the press . . .'

She hesitates. She needs to tell him. It's been eating her up for days, ever since the visit from DI Murray. Actually, it's been eating her up since long before that. But he wouldn't take too kindly to finding out she'd lied to him. He's always been so honest with her, warts and all. His previous girlfriend had cheated on him, which had devastated him. And, with her experience of a cheating ex, it had been refreshing that Elliot wanted everything out in the open.

But how could she tell him this? He admires her, and she loves the way he looks at her. She knows he puts her on a bit of a pedestal and she wants to be the person she sees reflected back at her through his eyes.

He's staring at her expectantly, as if reading her mind,

waiting for her to confess all. But she doesn't. Instead she turns away from him and goes to the sink, pouring the rest of her tea down the drain. She needs to get away from him so that he can't see the guilt on her face.

'I'd better be off. I'm popping into High Street Ken today to see Ottilie. I'll be back to pick the kids up. I don't want Jasmine catching the bus home, okay?' She can see his reflection in the mirror above the table. His mouth is clamped in a thin disapproving line, his eyes hard. He knows her too well. He knows she's keeping something from him. She hurries out of the room before he can reply and before she admits everything: the truth about her book, about Daisy and Ash, and the whole sorry mess.

39

Despite hating the tube, she decides it's the quickest and safest way to get to High Street Kensington. If she's being followed, if she's next on the killer's list, she'll surround herself with people, with witnesses, and there are plenty of those on the Underground. She'll make sure never to be anywhere alone until the police have caught whoever is behind this. Saying that, the streets are quiet as she makes her way down the hill, probably because of the rain, and more than once she has the unsettling, prickly feeling at the back of her neck that someone is behind her. She has her personal alarm in the pocket of her rain-coat ready to use if anyone so much as looks at her. She thinks again of the man Louise was certain was following them that night. Who was he? And did he kill Louise? Had it definitely been a man? It could have been Kristin: she's tall. But a killer? And what about someone at her publisher's? Not Hannah: she trusts her completely. But someone else there who might have read it. Or a friend or colleague who might have come across it. Someone on the periphery of her life?

The tube is crowded and smells of musty air and fumes.

Despite her bravado she feels nervous every time someone gets too close behind her, and when she's on the escalator, she makes sure to hold on to the handrail tightly. It would take only one push – Stop it, she tells herself sternly. She can't think like that. Even so, she's relieved when she's out of the station and onto the street. She pulls up the hood of her raincoat to hide herself.

Ottilie is standing outside their favourite café with her back to her when Emilia arrives. Her long blonde hair is in a high ponytail and she's wearing a waterproof in a leopard-print pattern. Her phone is clamped to one ear and she holds a see-through umbrella over her head – it looks like it belongs to a child. Emilia can hear her conversation as she approaches. 'No, Trev. I won't. I've said I won't, haven't I? . . . It's fine. She'll . . .' She spins around when she hears Emilia behind her, her face breaking into a grin. 'Yep, Mils is here now, so I'll . . . Yes. Laters.' She ends the call and pulls Emilia into her arms. The spokes of the umbrella tangle in Emilia's hair. 'Oh, Mils, I'm so sorry about your friend. Gosh, you've been through the wringer, haven't you?'

'Was that Trevor?' she asks as she pulls away, detaching herself from the umbrella.

Ottilie looks at the phone in her hand and frowns as though she's shocked to see it. 'What?'

'Was that Elliot's dad?'

'Oh, yes, yes, it was.'

'Since when do you have phone conversations with

Elliot's dad?' Emilia laughs to hide her shock. She pulls back her hood and holds open the door to the café, waiting while Ottilie shakes out her umbrella.

'Oh, me and Trev chat now and again.' She breezes past in a waft of her familiar Tom Ford perfume. 'Where has the heat wave gone? Honestly, this country!' Then she turns back to Emilia, her face falling. 'God, I'm sorry, here's me wittering on ... I can't even imagine what you've been through.'

'No, please. It's good to have a normal conversation.'

They are shown to their table, in the corner by the rain-streaked window. It's busy, and Ottilie pulls a disapproving face. 'Would much rather be sitting outside. We should have met up last week instead when it was hot. But I was in Germany, visiting Dad.'

Emilia's not going to let her friend change the subject. 'So, Trevor,' she begins, as they're handed a menu by a gruff-looking waiter, who disappears into the throng by the bar.

'Hmm . . .' Ottilie is scanning the menu.

'I'm surprised you call each other. He's, well, he's Elliot's dad.'

Ottilie looks up in surprise. 'So? We've always hit it off. He was just ringing me because, it turns out, weird fact, Trevor and my dad used to work together.'

'Really? When?'

'Oh, back in the 1990s.'

'Right.' She remembers Charles from when she used to

stay with Ottilie during the holidays. A tall, handsome man with a thatch of thick blond hair, although she hasn't seen him in years. 'What do you and Trevor talk about?' She can't imagine her father-in-law and her best friend having cosy chats, although she's always been able to tell that Trevor is fond of Ottilie.

'This and that.' She fastens her green eyes on Emilia. 'Why are you being weird about it?' She laughs. 'It's not like I'm shagging the guy.'

'No, I know. It's just . . .' She shrugs. Why does it niggle her? It's not up to her who either of them is friends with. 'I suppose because it's Trevor. I mean, he's Elliot's father, my father-in-law. It sounds like you were talking about me on the phone.'

Ottilie raises her eyes. 'He was just asking me about Louise, that's all, and whether you were okay.' She reaches across and takes Emilia's hand. 'He's worried about you. We all are. God, Mils . . .' She swallows, and Emilia knows that her friend is thinking about Louise. Her eyes smart. She doesn't want to cry, not here in public.

She clears her throat and tries to keep her emotions in check. 'Come on, let's order.'

They choose salmon on sourdough toast and, once the surly waiter has taken their menus, Emilia says, 'It's a shame you never got to meet Louise. I think you'd have liked her. I still can't believe it. I keep forgetting and go to call her . . .' Oh, how she wishes she could call her. She has so many questions that only Louise can answer.

Ottilie places a hand on Emilia's arm. 'Mils, this is some fucked-up shit.'

Anxiety swirls inside her. 'I know. Listen ...' She pauses while the waiter places their drinks on the table and leaves without speaking. 'There's something I haven't told anyone, and I can't keep it in any more. It's about my unpublished book ...'

'Which is great, by the way,' Ottilie interjects, sipping her gin fizz through a straw, then putting the glass down. 'I finished it last week and have been meaning to tell you.'

'Thanks. Well, it turns out that my plot follows very closely a serial-killer case in Devon that has been ongoing for years. He also marks his victims with a praying-mantis head although he carves it into the skin, apparently. A real sicko by the sound of it.'

Ottilie's mouth falls open in horror.

'I know, it's really grim. But when I wrote it I didn't know it was so similar to an actual ongoing case.'

'Well, sure,' murmurs Ottilie. 'How could you have known?'

Emilia fidgets in her seat, running a finger along her glass of elderflower cordial. 'Well, the thing is, the story ...' She doesn't know if she can bring herself to say it. She feels like a terrible person, a terrible writer. 'Oh, God, Ottilie, I was going through a nightmare time. There was Covid and the lockdowns, and Jasmine was having some mental-health issues, and Elliot and I couldn't agree on the best way to handle it all so we weren't getting on, and I knew I wanted to finish this series once and for all but I just had a blank. I couldn't think of anything to write, and I was moaning about it one day to Louise in Marble Hill Park on one of our lockdown power walks last March and . . . and . . .' Ottilie nods encouragingly. 'And I asked her if she had any stories, joking really, but then she told me she had this idea for a book that she'd always wanted to write but knew she never would and, if I wanted, I could use her plot.'

Ottilie's eyes widen but she remains silent.

She continues miserably, 'So she passed on what I thought was a brilliant story, about this girl looking for the man she believes killed her mother, marking her mother's ankle with an insect's head. And I never thought in a million years it was similar to a real ongoing case. She made it sound like it was her idea. That it was fiction. And I was so grateful to her . . .' She blinks back tears.

Ottilie is frowning. 'So what? She gave you an idea and you took it. I'm sure other writers have done similar. It's not like you stole the idea from her. She gave it to you willingly.'

Emilia can't bring herself to admit the rest. This is bad enough. She hates that she has become this person when her natural instinct is to be open and honest, but since last March she's become someone who keeps secrets and tells half-truths. She's so tempted to tell Ottilie everything, to let it spill from her mouth like word vomit until there's nothing left. She gulps and takes another sip of her drink, wishing she'd also ordered a gin fizz. 'What I don't understand is, why? Why did Louise give me the story of a real-life case? And . . .' she says and puts down her glass '. . . is that why she's been killed, and why I've been targeted in this way? Because someone knows she's told me about the serial killer. Possibly the praying-mantis murderer themselves, and they've killed her to shut her up? I've been going over and over it in my head, replaying her last message to me and wondering what it could have meant. She wanted to tell me something important. She kept saying she was sorry. And that she'd explain everything to me. And it has to be something to do with the book and the story she told me. Did she know who was behind it all? Was she trying to warn me about the real killer?'

'But why haven't they tried to kill you too?'

A chill washes over Emilia. 'That's what's terrifying me. I think I'm next.'

40

Daisy,
2005

Daisy couldn't relax that Christmas. She missed Ash with every fibre of her being, but more than that, she couldn't stop thinking about Donald. It consumed her every waking moment, and she dreamed about the morning she'd found her mother dead: the sterile tidiness of the living room, the lingering smell of cigarettes mixed with the metallic smell of blood.

She couldn't bring herself to tell anyone of her suspicions about Donald being the Doodle Man, especially not her father. She needed some kind of proof first, and she was determined to get that when she went to stay with Ash.

It snowed in Yorkshire on the morning she was travelling to Devon. Her father was worried about her as he drove her to the station. 'Let me know if there are any problems. I've checked the weather and down south it's milder. You must bring Ash up to see us next time.' And then he and Shannon waved her off as the train pulled out of the station. She felt a pang of love for them as they stood, arms wrapped around each other, snowflakes falling onto their shoulders and woolly hats. He'd have a fit if he knew she was going to the home of a potential killer.

The journey was long and slow due to the snow. It wasn't until they passed Birmingham that the journey became easier and the snow-topped fields turned green.

She had to change trains at Plymouth to get to the little village station where Ash and Donald were waiting for her. It wasn't the village where she'd spent the first ten years of her life with her mother, but it wasn't far, less than two miles away.

Donald smiled warmly at them as she fell into Ash's arms.

And then she remembered why she was there. As much as she adored Ash – although her feelings were conflicted now – it was Donald she had to concentrate on for the moment.

Donald insisted on carrying her bag and they followed him out of the station to the car park at the back. The sight of his sticky-up hair made her stomach turn. It had been eight years and there were now strands of white in his sandy mop but she was sure it was him, and she wasn't fooled by his helpfulness or his cheery nature.

It was a short drive back to their home, a big old house by the sea. It wasn't until they turned down a lane and pulled into an expansive shingled driveway that she realized this was the only house for miles around.

'Wow, this is remote,' she said as they stepped out of the car. A strong wind smelling of sea salt whipped around her, pulling at her hair and the hem of her coat, like an eager child.

'We love it here,' said Ash, leading her to the pretty front porch with its pointed white roof. 'Secluded, just how we like it.' It should have sounded romantic, but with Donald just yards behind them it made her shiver. She'd had all these plans for confronting him, but how could she do that now they were here, in the middle of nowhere, surrounded by fields and little lanes and sheer cliffs and the sea, which sent spray flying into the air so that she could taste the salt on her lips? Confronting a killer in a place like this wouldn't be wise.

Ash steered her into the house, which was huge and rambling but lived-in and homely, with a farmhouse kitchen that looked out over the cliffs and the sea beyond. Stef stood at the stove, her hair curled around her attractive face. When she saw them, she rubbed her hands on her apron and embraced Daisy in a whiff of Chanel perfume and cake mixture. 'I've just put a Victoria Sponge into the oven,' she said, beaming at them. 'Ash, love, why don't you show Daisy around?'

'Gladly.' Ash twinkled at her and grabbed her hand. God, she already loved the warm, welcoming house, with the lights at the windows, a large Christmas tree in the hallway, and the garland decorated with pretty tartan bows woven around the banister.

And she was about to throw a bomb that would blow it all up.

Perhaps she was mistaken, she thought, hoped, in the days that followed. Perhaps the fact this man had sandy-coloured hair and a double crown was just a coincidence. After all, there couldn't be only one man in Devon fitting this description. And she'd never seen his face. He seemed nice too. Jolly, loving, constantly checking in with her and Ash, making sure they were happy, comfortable. It was hard to believe that Ash had suffered a breakdown as a teenager with a family like this.

The day before she was due to leave for home she'd managed to convince herself that she'd got the wrong guy. Of course it wasn't going to be Ash's dad. She was self-sabotaging. That's what this was. And she very nearly pulled it off, the deception that she'd got the wrong man.

Until she saw the Sunday newspaper on the arm of the chair the day before she was due to leave.

And the doodles in the margins.

41

Emilia can't stop thinking about her conversation with Ottilie. She's sandwiched between two very large men on the packed tube train, and she notices that a guy standing up, holding the railing above, is watching her. He is around her age, maybe a bit younger, with spiky light-brown hair and dressed casually in baggy jeans and a beige Harrington jacket. She can tell he's watching her because every time she looks up from the Wikipedia page on her phone she's pretending to read she catches his eye and his glance slides away.

When the train pulls in at Richmond she hurries out into the open air. It's still raining but has reduced to a light warm drizzle, and by the time she's marched through town and up the hill towards her house, she's sweating. She stops at the brow, peeling off her waterproof coat, not caring if she gets wet, and then she glances at her watch. She's got half an hour before she has to go and pick up Wilfie and Jasmine. It's a forty-five-minute round trip to collect Jasmine too, but she'd drive the length of the UK if it meant making sure her children got home safely.

The streets near her house are empty and she starts moving again.

Then she hears footsteps behind her.

She resists the urge to look around and continues up the hill, picking up her pace despite the stitch in her side. The footsteps are closing in. She can't physically move any faster unless she breaks into a run, and she no longer has easy access to her personal alarm because she's taken her coat off. She tells herself to relax, but Louise's body flashes in her mind and fear grips her. There's nothing for it. She runs, the exertion causing the pain in her side to intensify, but she can't stop: her life depends on it. She's suddenly certain of that. Is it her imagination or is the person behind her running as well? She rounds the corner to her street, relief surging through her that her house is in sight, and doesn't stop until she reaches her driveway. The man who had been watching her on the tube is walking past. His hands are deep in his pockets and he's not looking at her as he crosses the street and turns the corner. Is it a coincidence that he just happens to be walking this way, and so close behind? She takes a few deep breaths, waiting for her heart rate to return to normal, and is just about to head into the house when she hears her name called.

She turns in the direction of the voice and sees Jonas getting out of his car, which is parked further down the street. Her heart sinks as he approaches.

'What are you doing here?'

He looks tired, his hair messy and in need of a cut, and there are dark circles under his eyes. 'Kristin has been taken to the police station for questioning,' he replies.

'What?'

His expression darkens. 'Don't look so shocked, considering it was you who told the police you think she killed *your friend* Louise! I know why you have a vendetta against her,' he says, rubbing a hand over his face wearily. 'But I thought we were over all this. It's been more than a decade.'

Anger bursts from her. 'Do you really think I'd be so petty? The three of us have rocked along together now for years. I saw the troll doll in her possession, and I told the police. I didn't say anything about her killing Louise.'

'Why would she target and hound you? Why? Pretending that Jasmine has gone missing, she knew that would hurt me too, so why would she do it?'

'I don't know,' she spits, her temper flaring. 'Maybe because she thinks you're having an affair.'

He pales. 'But I'm not. What have you told her?'

'I've not told her anything. She mentioned it to Ottilie, and to Louise on the night of my launch. She's not stupid, Jonas. She knows something's going on and I'm worried she thinks it's with me.'

'But I'm not having an affair. And okay, I was attracted to Connie, and I was tempted, but I've not acted on it. I've fucked up once and I'm not going to do it again.'

She stares at him, wondering if he's lying. He looks like he's being sincere, but she stopped trusting Jonas a long time ago. 'Look, I have to go. I need to pick up the kids.'

He deflates in front of her eyes, like all the fight has gone out of him, and he suddenly looks older. 'Can I come and see Jasmine at some point? I suppose you're going to say you don't want her at mine this weekend if you're so sure Kristin is behind this, even though you know what I think. But surely you can't imagine I'd hurt our daughter?'

She feels a stab of guilt. 'Of course not,' she says in a small voice. She wants to cry. She hates this. Hates distrusting those close to her. She just wants whoever is doing this to be caught so that they can go back to how it was before. Louise's laughing face flashes in her mind. Not that anything will ever be the same now that she's dead. 'Why don't you come over this weekend instead?'

'What about Elliot? I know he doesn't want me in the house.'

'It's my house too. I'll talk to him. He'll be fine.'

Jonas nods sadly, then turns on his heel and walks back to his car without saying goodbye. His shoulders droop and she suddenly feels sorry for the man she once loved. But, no: she has to be tough.

Wilfie is subdued when Emilia picks him up from school. 'Toby wasn't in today,' he says mournfully as they walk to the car. She wants to tell him to hurry or they'll be late for Jasmine. But she can see that Wilfie is upset.

'Let's run to the car and you can tell me all about it,' she says, trying to sound jolly, but he drags his feet. In the end she has to grab his hand and practically pull him to the car. She veers away from the kerb as soon as he's clicked on his seatbelt.

'The teacher gave us a talk in class about Toby's mum,' he says from the back seat as she drives. 'They said she was killed because she was a detective.' His bottom lip wobbles. 'I don't want to be a detective anymore.'

'Oh, sweetheart.' She swallows the lump in her throat. 'Toby's mum was a very brave, very brilliant detective but it does come with risks.' She wonders how much the school has told him.

'Toby must be very sad.'

She blinks back tears. She can't bear the thought of it. The guilt and the grief threaten to crush her. 'He must be. She was well loved . . .' A tear rolls down her cheek and she brushes it away. She has to stay strong in front of Wilfie. She asks him to tell her something funny that happened today to take his mind off it and soon he's laughing as he recounts a silly joke his best mate, Freddie, told him while they were queuing for lunch.

She's relieved when they arrive outside Jasmine's school in time for the bell. She knows her daughter is embarrassed by seeing her and her little brother at the school gates, she'd much rather take the school bus home with Nancy, but Emilia can't relax until Jasmine is safely in the car. Ever since she went missing – even though it was only a few hours from when they'd realized she'd gone until she'd walked through the door – it was the most petrified she'd ever felt. Even worse than finding Louise dead.

Jasmine walks out of school with Nancy and a good-looking boy Emilia recognizes as Jake. They stand in a little huddle, their heads bent together, until Jasmine breaks free with an eye-roll in her direction before turning back to wave at her friends.

'Can't you both at least wait around the block?' she hisses when she reaches them. 'It's not exactly cool to be seen being picked up by your mum.'

'It's not for ever,' says Emilia, calmly. She lowers her voice so Wilfie can't hear. 'You know why I have to do this for now.'

Jasmine doesn't say anything but walks slightly ahead to the car, her back hunched. When they get in, she says, 'Jake's found the note, Mum. It was scrunched up under his bed.' She reaches inside the pocket of her blazer, her eyes flashing excitedly. 'He brought it in and, well, here it is.' She hands it to Emilia.

Emilia is amazed. 'Wow. That's brilliant.' She unfolds the note. It's not very big, A5-sized and handwritten in a cursive, slightly messy style. She rests it against the steering wheel, the engine running. Jasmine fiddles with the radio and Wilfie pipes up from the back seat that he's hungry. The note reads:

To Jake

Please find enclosed three tickets to Tonal Whiplash this coming weekend. You are entitled to have the third ticket, or sell it as you wish if you already have one, as long as you give the other two tickets to your girlfriend, Nancy Bradshaw, and her friend Jasmine Perry. It's a surprise for them and something I know they will be very excited to receive. I'm trusting that you will look out for them at the concert and keep them safe.

Kind regards,
M

'Weird, huh?' says Jasmine, leaning back against her seat. She's turned the channel to Kiss FM and some tinny dance tune fills the car, instantly grating on Emilia's frayed nerves. 'Whoever sent it wanted Jake to look after us. They didn't mean to threaten us or hurt us, I don't think. But why do it?'

Emilia studies the letter some more, the flick at the top of the M and the N, the curve of the K. It's done with a fountain pen and a cursive hand. Her mind races and her blood runs cold. Signing it M must be for Miranda Moody. She remembers the phone call, the posh clipped voice. And as for this writing, there is only one person she knows who has flowery handwriting like this.

And that's her very best friend, Ottilie.

42

Elliot is in the middle of making dinner when they get home. He cheerfully informs them he's doing a casserole, but Emilia can hardly take in what he's saying. She dumps her bag in the hall and races straight up the two flights of stairs to her office. Once inside she closes the door and sits at her desk, her heart pumping with exertion and fear. Not Ottilie. It can't be her. She's like family. No, no, no, no, no.

She rummages through her desk for her birthday cards. She usually keeps them for a year, longer if they're from the children or Elliot. She vaguely remembers shoving them into one of the drawers. She pulls them all out and frantically empties them onto the floor, not caring about the mess. And then she finds them, the smaller cards inside the largest. Her hands are trembling as she finds Ottilie's. It has a flamingo on the front in a top hat and dancing shoes, and inside, the most beautiful cursive writing. She fishes the letter out of her pocket and places it next to the card. The writing is very similar. Could Ottilie really have written the note? Could she be behind this – this campaign of terror? Could she have killed

Louise? But why? Her head pounds. Why would Ottilie do this to her?

Ottilie is always telling her how lucky she is to be married to Elliot, and how envious she is of her children and her career. *You've achieved so much, and I've achieved nothing. I can't even keep a relationship longer than five minutes.* Could this all be down to pure old-fashioned jealousy? But she refuses to believe that. Ottilie is amazing. Everyone thinks so. She has no reason to be jealous. And Ottilie isn't vindictive, or nasty. She's not a killer.

She's interrupted by the sound of footsteps on the stairs and Wilfie bursting into the room. 'Daddy said dinner's ready,' he pants, and disappears.

She takes Ottilie's birthday card and the note and slides them into the pocket of her skirt. She needs to ask her about it.

Elliot's dishing up when she gets down to the kitchen. He looks up when she walks in but the smile freezes on his face when he notices her expression. 'Are you okay?'

She tries to look cheerful for the sake of the kids. 'Sure. Just been a busy day.'

'You saw Ottilie for lunch, didn't you? It was all okay?'

Emilia pulls out a chair and sits down. She'd hardly eaten anything with Ottilie and she doesn't feel hungry now. She'd give anything for her old appetite back. 'Yes, it was fine.'

'Only fine,' he teases. He sits down and piles spinach onto his plate. 'Come on, kids, eat up.' He turns to her.

'It's great that you're having some time off before your copyedits are back.'

She's thankful for that as she can't focus on anything right now.

She pushes her chicken casserole around her plate while Wilfie chats about school. Jasmine is also quiet, and every now and again Emilia senses that her daughter is throwing her questioning glances. She tries to pull herself together. Jasmine in particular is so sensitive to a strained atmosphere and must be feeling scared and uncertain because of all this. She concentrates on smiling even though her muscles ache, nodding in encouragement every time one of her children – her precious, precious children – speaks. And all she can think about is that Ottilie was here when Elliot was away. She was here, in the house, with them. She could have been the one to mess up their Alexa. The music started playing while she was staying over. 'Psycho Killer.' An apt song given all that's happened. The only calm amid the storm of her emotions is the note sent with the concert tickets where it sounded like whoever wrote it wanted Jake to look after Nancy and Jasmine. Which means that if Ottilie is behind it all she doesn't want to hurt them, thank God. It's Emilia she's targeting. And poor Louise, who managed to find out something but was killed before she could tell Emilia what it was. Had Ottilie somehow known what Louise had found out? But, as far as she was aware, Louise and Ottilie had never even met. And did she set up Kristin knowing that Emilia already hated her and would gladly point the finger at her former friend? But when? It makes no sense . . . yet the writing . . .

'Em?' Elliot's voice brings her back to the present. 'Are you okay? You seem in another world and you've hardly touched your food.'

She comes to, noticing that Jasmine and Wilfie have left the table and are curled up on the sofa watching TV, their plates emptied and stacked neatly in the dishwasher. Elliot's got them well trained. He's looking at her with concern. His plate is also empty. 'Don't you like it?' He reaches for her hand, then lowers his voice so the kids can't hear. 'I'm worried about you, Em. I'm worried this is all getting on top of you.'

'I found one of my friends dead. Of course it's getting on top of me.'

He squeezes her hand in sympathy and a shadow passes over his face. 'I can't even imagine what that must have been like. I'm so sorry. I'm so sorry this is happening to you at all. You don't deserve it.' His voice catches and she looks up at him in surprise.

'It's not your fault.'

'I just want to protect you. All of you. And it makes me feel so inadequate that I can't stop this.'

She brings his hand up to her mouth and kisses it. 'I wouldn't be able to get through all this without you, El.'

His warm brown eyes shine. 'I'm not going anywhere.'

They sit like that for a while, holding hands, and then he laughs. 'You're not going to eat that, are you?'

'I'm sorry. I've just got too much on my mind.'

'As long as you don't lose too much weight.' He takes her plate as well as his to the island and starts scraping her leftovers into the bin, his chin set and his expression unreadable.

She comes up behind him and wraps her arms around his waist, her cheek pressed against his back. 'I wish all this would go away,' she whispers, the warmth of him making her feel grounded, more in control. She can't tell him about Ottilie. Not yet. Not until she's spoken to her.

He puts the plates down and turns to her, hugging her to him so that her face is against his chest. 'I think now Louise has been murdered the police will be taking it more seriously. It will all be over soon.' He pulls away so that he can look into her eyes. 'I almost forgot, but just after you left to get the kids that policewoman came by again. What's-her-face? Older. Silver hair. Could be a ringer for your fictional DI Moody. I was on a call so couldn't answer the door, but she came up on the RingCam app.'

'DI Janine Murray. So she's still hanging around.'

'What do you mean? Why wouldn't she be?'

She pulls away and switches the kettle on. 'Oh, it's just that she's not from the local force. She's from Devon and Cornwall Police, remember? I'm sure I told you. I thought she was going back after speaking to me on Saturday, that's all.'

He looks uneasy. 'I don't think you mentioned where

she was from. Why do you think she wants to speak to you again?'

'Maybe she's found something out.'

'About this serial killer, do you think? I wonder why a serial killer would murder Louise in Kingston when he targets women in the Plymouth area.' His expression is one of suspicion. 'And you're sure you knew nothing about it?'

She hesitates. Should she just tell him? She can't keep it from him for ever.

He's staring at her, waiting. She has to tell him something. She looks up at him, deliberating, dreading the disappointment she knows she'll see in his face when she confesses. But what choice does she have? She bites her lip.

'Em?'

She sighs and steps away from him. 'Okay. Look, it's a long story . . .'

'Well, we're not going anywhere.' He grabs an apple from the fruit bowl next to the kettle and bites into it with an 'I'm listening' expression.

'I'm sorry I didn't tell you the truth earlier,' she begins, then tells him everything.

Nearly everything.

The tension between them is almost palpable. Without speaking, he throws the barely eaten apple into the bin. Then he stands with his back to the counter, his eyes flashing.

'So, let me get this straight. Louise gave you the idea for this praying-mantis murderer and you just made up a story around it?'

'Yes,' she lies. She can't tell him that the truth is even worse.

'And it just happens to be a real-life serial killer?' His expression darkens. 'How did Louise know about the case?'

'I'm not sure,' she says truthfully. 'Maybe through work. I don't know.'

His eyes narrow as he assesses her and she feels herself blush. 'And now she's been killed with the same marking on her ankle.'

She nods miserably.

'For fuck's sake. Why didn't you tell me this before?'

'I've only recently found out.'

He runs a hand through his hair in frustration. 'I – I don't actually know what to say to you. This is huge and you're only telling me about it now?'

'El . . .' She blinks back tears.

She can see he's trying to suppress his anger.

'I can't talk to you right now.'

'But –'

He storms out of the room before she can say anything else.

She goes to bed early, leaving Elliot brooding in front of the football. She taps out a message to Ottilie asking to meet tomorrow. This isn't a conversation she wants to have over the phone.

Already? Can't get enough of me, I see, Ottilie types back immediately with a winky emoji. The three dots show she's writing another message. Soon enough she adds, *Sure. I'll come to Richmond. Our usual café at 11?*

Emilia replies with a thumbs-up. She can't bring herself to write anything else. Her emotions oscillate from fury to sadness.

When Elliot comes to bed she pretends to be asleep. His voice, when he eventually speaks, shatters the silence, reverberating around their bedroom. 'I know you're really awake.'

'What do you want me to say?' she replies softly, her back to him.

'You know I hate lies.'

She turns to face him and props herself up on her elbow. 'Now you can be disappointed in me. You now know I'm a fraud.'

'Em,' he says, his voice is soft, but it's too dark to read his expression, 'you could never disappoint me and you're not a fraud.'

Her eyes fill with tears but she doesn't say anything. She suddenly feels totally and utterly sad.

He reaches over and gently wipes away a tear. 'I don't want you to feel you can't tell me things because I'm going to judge you in some way.'

She nods, not sure if she believes him.

'And what about the other storyline – the stuff with Daisy and her boyfriend, Ash? Was that all from her too? Or was that yours?'

She doesn't want to lie to him again, so she ignores the question. 'A serial killer who brands his victims has been done before. I'm not the first to write about it.'

'Yes, but this is very specific, isn't it?' He sighs. 'It's odd Louise told you that particular story in the first place, don't you think?'

Yes, yes, yes, she wants to scream. It's all she's been able to think about. Why did Louise tell her this story if it was true? What had been behind her friend's decision to do that?

'We were just bouncing ideas off each other. It was probably somewhere in her subconscious.' She knows she's not being totally honest with him and it's like he can smell it. 'Anyway,' she says and rolls away from him, 'it's getting late.'

He moves closer to her so that he's spooning her. 'Are you sure there's nothing else you want to tell me?' His breath is hot on her ear.

She thinks of Ottilie and the letter. She'll tell him tomorrow after she's spoken to her. She'll make sure not to be alone with her. For once she actually feels afraid of her friend and that, despite meeting when they were just children, she feels she doesn't know her at all.

'I'm sure,' she lies. 'Now goodnight.'

43

It was him. Her instinct had been right. Why had she tried to fight it? But she knew why. Ash. How could they be together now?

After seeing the doodles in the margin of the newspaper, she couldn't get her thoughts in order and sat at the kitchen table in a daze while Ash and Stef buzzed around her. She had to pretend she had a headache so that they would stop asking her why she was being so quiet, which just resulted in Stef rummaging in cupboards until she had found some paracetamol and fussing even more.

She needed to broach it with Donald. She had to get him on his own, away from Ash and Stef, to confront him. The weekend was nearly over, and they were both returning to university tomorrow – she was running out of time. But it was difficult because Ash hardly left her side. On the rare occasions they were apart, Donald was always with his wife. They seemed close and still to be very much in love. Could this man not only be her mother's murderer but also a serial killer? Her dad had told her about the other women killed after her mother. Daisy had looked up serial killers in the local library, and had been shocked to discover some were charming, handsome even, like the one she'd been reading about from the USA called Ted Bundy. Is that who Donald is? she wondered. The UK's version of Ted Bundy? She shuddered right there at the kitchen table despite the heat of the stove.

'Are you okay, Daise?' Ash asked, staring at her with concern. From the kitchen window she could see Donald at the edge of the garden, puffing at a cigarette, hunched against the wind, the smoke blowing out into the cloudy skies. This was her chance to speak to him alone.

She pushed back her chair, which scraped across the terracotta tiles, causing Stef to look around from where she stood dolloping cake mixture into two round tins.

'I just need some fresh air,' Daisy said, unable to bear it any longer. Part of her wanted to run to the safety of her father's house, and never look back. She wished she'd never gone to Exeter. But the other half knew she had to grab this opportunity while she could. For years she'd been dreaming of coming face to face with her mother's killer. It was down to Fate that she was here, eight years after her mother's murder.

'It's really windy outside,' said Ash, getting up. 'I'll come with you.'

'No!' It came out too harshly. 'I'm sorry but I just need

some – some time by myself.' She hurried out into the hallway, grabbing her coat and shoving her feet into her wellies, and almost ran out of the front door. She stood on the path lined with bushes, her heart racing and her throat dry. She imagined it would be idyllic here in the summer even though she knew she wouldn't get the chance to see it. Now she was certain that Ash's dad was the Doodle Man she would have to end things.

She rounded the corner and watched Donald for a while as he stood smoking in his wool coat. The hair at the back of his head had thinned a bit since she'd last seen him but there was no mistaking that double crown. More than that, there was no mistaking those doodles. He'd carved one on her mother's ankle after he'd killed her. Had he done the same to the other women he'd murdered? How could he have hidden it from his family for all these years?

She was staying in the house of a murderer and she knew she had to tread carefully. As soon as she was back at university she'd go straight to the police.

She faltered, suddenly afraid. There was a steep drop at the end of the garden, with a flimsy fence protecting them from the cliff's edge. It would take just one push and she'd be dead. He must have sensed her behind him because he turned around then.

'Hello, Daisy,' he said cheerfully, stubbing out his cigarette on the trunk of a nearby tree and walking towards her. His breath clouded in front of him as he trudged over the grass, his trousers tucked into knee-high boots. 'Are you okay?'

'I . . .' She stepped back against the house, touching the rough brickwork with the tips of her fingers as though it could anchor her. 'I . . . It's strange, but I think I recognize you.'

He laughed. 'Recognize me? What do you mean?'

'I think you were friends with my mother.' *And I think you killed her, you arsehole*, she adds silently, under her breath.

His warm, open expression suddenly snapped shut, his eyes hardening. 'Who was your mother?'

'Jennifer Radcliffe.' She watched as his jaw tightened and a muscle near his jaw spasmed.

And then his mouth turned down and he shook his head. 'No, sorry, that name doesn't ring any bells.'

Of course he was going to deny it. But she was sure she'd noticed the flash of recognition on his face when she mentioned her mother's name. He shoved his hands into the pockets of his coat, smiling benignly again. 'Anyway, better get back in. The wind is picking up.'

'It was about eight years ago.' Her words tumbled out desperately. 'My mum didn't want to introduce him to me. I called him her secret boyfriend. He'd doodle in the margins of the newspaper. He looked like you.'

'Well, I can assure you, it wasn't me. I'm a happily married man.'

'Someone killed her.'

'I'm very sorry, Daisy, I really am, but I never knew your mother.'

The wind picked up then and Donald braced himself against it, leaning closer to her as he did so. He was eight years older now, but still strong, still fit. It was her word against his. How could she ever prove it?

He moved towards her and she shrank back against the wall, her heart racing. 'Daisy,' he said sadly, 'have you said anything about this to Ash?'

She shook her head. She could smell smoke on his breath.

'Good. You should probably keep it that way. I expect lots of people doodle in the margins of newspapers.' His gaze was pitying. 'I'm sure you've realized by now, but Ash is fragile, and if you say anything about this, well . . .' His shoulders rose. 'I don't need you upsetting my family and making accusations.'

She stood there, not sure what to say. He spoke softly, as though he was talking about something as anodyne as the weather, but she could detect the menace in his voice. He was standing even closer to her now, and she felt uncomfortable, pinned as she was against the wall of the house. 'Does Ash know about your mother's murder?'

Daisy shook her head. 'No. Just that she died when I was a kid.'

'I am sorry. But please believe me when I say I didn't know her.' He turned away from her and she watched as he walked back into the house.

44

Emilia stands for a while, staring at Ottilie from a distance. She's sitting on the wall overlooking the river in a white T-shirt and a patterned maxi skirt. Her long blonde hair is in a ponytail, black-rimmed sunglasses pushed back on her head, and she looks fresh and young, her face turned up to the sun. Nearly thirty years of friendship shrinks away so that all they have is this moment. Ottilie has been a constant in her life since they were eleven years old. She'd been family when Emilia was missing her own. She'd been her comrade when Kristin betrayed her. Throughout it all she'd felt Ottilie had her back. She has to broach this carefully, because if she's wrong and she accuses Ottilie, it will ruin everything.

The banks of the river are busy and populated by families or workers out for lunch. Her mouth is dry as she approaches her friend.

'Oh, hello, you,' Ottilie says, looking up at Emilia, shielding her eyes with an elegant hand. 'I got you a Diet Coke. Do you want to go to the café or are you okay staying here?' She hands a can to Emilia, who takes it and sits down. It's ice-cold and fizzes when Emilia opens it. She has to drink some before she can get any words out and takes a large gulp. Ottilie is watching her with a smile. 'You'll burp if you drink it all too fast. Café or here?' she prompts.

Emilia shakes her head. She couldn't possibly eat. 'Here's fine.'

'What a scorcher.' Ottilie turns her face back up to the sun. 'So,' she says, her eyes closed. 'What did you want to see me about?'

Nausea rises in Emilia's throat. She places the can of Coke beside her on the ground. How the hell is she going to broach this? She doesn't know where to start.

Ottilie must sense her hesitation as she turns to look at her. 'What is it, Mils?'

She has to get it out before she chokes on her words. 'Remember I told you about Jasmine going missing and the hoax call and the note with the tickets being sent to Nancy's boyfriend?'

'Yes.' Ottilie frowns and pushes her sunglasses from her hair onto her face.

Emilia wonders if this is deliberate so that she can't read Ottilie's eyes. She reaches into her bag and hands Ottilie the letter. 'This is it.'

Ottilie falls silent as she reads it.

'Do you notice anything about it?' Emilia asks.

'Well . . . only that whoever wrote it didn't intend Jasmine and her friend to come to any harm by the sound of it. It was designed to scare you.' She hands it back to Emilia.

'Anything else?'

'Beautiful handwriting. Someone has taken a calligraphy course . . .' And then she falters, as though it has dawned on her. 'Shit . . . is that what this is about? You think I wrote this?'

'The handwriting is so like yours but I can't . . .' There are tears in her voice now. 'I don't want to believe you wrote it.'

'Of course I didn't write it! For fuck's sake, Mils, how long have we known each other?' She pushes the sunglasses back onto her hair. 'Do you really think I'm capable of all this?'

Emilia shakes her head. 'No. But the writing . . .'

'Don't you think if I was warped enough to be behind this I would have at least tried to disguise my writing? Let me see it again.' She snatches the letter back. She's silent for a few moments while she studies it and then says, 'This here. I don't write my Es like this. Yes, the Ms and Ns are similar, but that's it. Christ.' She shoves the letter back at Emilia, her green eyes flashing.

Emilia looks down at the letter, the words swimming. She didn't bring the birthday card with her so can't compare, but she's known Ottilie long enough to be able to tell her friend is genuinely shocked and pissed off.

Ottilie's expression softens. 'I'm hurt you could think it's me, but I know how fucking awful this must be for you. All I can tell you is that it's not my writing.' She sits up, her face serious. 'I swear to you, Mils, on my mother's grave, I never wrote that letter. I'd never do anything to hurt you. You're my best friend. You're one of my favourite people in the whole world and I hate seeing you like this, distrusting everyone.' She holds up a hand when Emilia starts to speak. 'I know, and I understand why. And I'd love to throttle whoever is behind this, but you can't seriously think it's me, can you?' Her eyes are shining with tears.

'I'm so sorry,' Emilia says, throwing her arms around her friend. 'Of course I believe you.'

She feels as if she's blindfolded, like a child playing Pin the Tail on the Donkey, except she's pinning the blame on her friends at random, without anything concrete.

45

When Emilia gets home she heads straight to her office and retrieves the birthday cards. As soon as she'd clapped eyes on the most recent one Ottilie had sent, and seen for herself how similar the writing was, she hadn't looked at the others. But now she's studying it more closely she realizes what Ottilie means about the letter E. The writing is similar but not identical. She'd jumped to conclusions without thinking it through and is now kicking herself.

She flicks through the rest of the cards until she gets to the last one, right at the back, the biggest, which holds all the smaller cards inside. She opens it and her heart races. It's the same beautifully calligraphic writing as Ottilie's, but with a few differences. Like an E that looks like a backward number three. Her hand trembles and she grabs the letter from her bag, comparing the two. It's the same: there is no doubt about it. Ottilie's had been similar, but this is an exact match, messier and more hurried than Ottilie's.

The writing belongs to Louise.

*

Emilia gets up from her desk and runs downstairs. She needs to speak to Detective Inspector Janine Murray again. She's rummaging through the kitchen drawer, trying to find the contact card she'd given her on Friday, when she feels a presence behind her. She spins around, her heart thumping, but it's just Elliot standing there, watching her with an unreadable expression on his face.

'Are you okay? What's going on?'

'Have you seen the card DI Murray left me with her details on it?' she asks. 'I thought I'd put it in here.'

'You're just messing up the drawer,' he says, coming over to her. 'Make us a cuppa and I'll find it.'

She moves away to put the kettle on, trying to remain calm but inwardly screaming. Louise. It's Louise's writing. Why? Why would her friend have done all this?

'Here it is.' He hands it to her. 'Why do you need to speak to her? Have you found something out?'

She tells him all about the letter and Louise's birthday card. 'So now I think it has to have been Louise behind all this,' she says, pointing to the letter and the card that she'd placed on the kitchen island.

He picks them up and studies them. 'I can't believe it was Louise. She – she helped you, didn't she? When Jas went missing. Why would she do that otherwise?'

'I don't know,' Emilia cries. 'I don't know anything anymore.' Her cheeks are hot and sweat is pooling in her armpits. 'I'm going to show this to DI Murray anyway,' she says, with resolve. 'Don't you think?'

He shrugs. 'Sure, but I don't think it proves anything. It could have been copied so that it looks like Louise sent it to you.'

She feels like they're going around in circles. She watches as Elliot pours them both a mint tea. 'Here, this is supposed to be refreshing. I'd better get back to work.'

'Have you checked the smart cams lately?'

'I have. There's been nothing for weeks. Not since we saw the man ... or woman ... lurking outside that night – apart from whoever stole my bike, that is. Have you told DI Murray about that?'

'Not yet. I will.'

'I check the cameras every day, especially since Louise ... Please don't worry. We're safe here in this house. We've got cameras, alarms, everything. Nobody can get in without us knowing about it.'

Except someone did get in. To steal the bike. She blinks, trying to erase the memory of finding Louise dead in her flat. A place where she should have been safe.

He comes over to her, carrying his mug with Super Dad on the front, and kisses the top of her head. 'It kills me that I can't do more to make you feel safe.'

'El ...'

He smiles sadly at her, then leaves the kitchen.

Janine Murray is at her door within twenty minutes.

'I'm staying at a hotel in Kingston,' she says, by way of explanation, as soon as she sets foot inside Emilia's house.

She's looking around in that way of hers that slightly unnerves Emilia. 'I'm not heading back to Devon for another week.' She has on a smart jacket and a blouse with a bow tied loosely at the neck. Emilia wonders if she's hot. Not that she looks it. She has a calm aura about her, even if she does smell of smoke, which she's tried to disguise with perfume.

DI Murray sits at the oak-topped table and throws her jacket over the back of the chair next to her, while Emilia brings her the glass of water she asked for. DI Murray is rummaging in a large tote bag and retrieves a wedge of papers bound with two elastic bands. 'Actually, I'm glad you rang, as I was aiming to come and see you either today or tomorrow anyway. My partner, Saunders, has come down with some bug so he's been about as much help as a chocolate teapot.' She sighs and snaps off the elastic bands. 'I have your manuscript here.'

Emilia lowers herself onto a chair opposite. 'Where did you get that?'

'It was beside Louise Greene's bed.'

Emilia swallows painfully. 'I emailed it to her to read. She must have printed it out.'

'It's a good story and it makes for very interesting reading. I'm assuming Louise told you about the praying-mantis murderer, being a police officer herself?'

Emilia nods, not trusting herself to speak.

'I thought as much. I wish you'd just admitted it last time I was here. It would have saved me some time.'

A whoosh of heat floods Emilia's face. 'I'm sorry.'

DI Murray continues, 'God only knows how Louise knew so much about it when she's never worked on the case. But then I started considering the rest, and the sub-plot with the character of Daisy interested me.'

Emilia's back breaks into a sweat. 'How so?'

'Because she believes her mother was murdered by the serial killer. But what I really want to know is how you knew the name of one of the real victims.'

'I don't know what you mean,' says Emilia, her stom-ach clenching. She can't believe this is happening to her. This whole sorry nightmare started with that stupid story.

'Well,' DI Murray says and presses her glasses more firmly up her nose, 'how you could possibly have known that a Jennifer Radcliffe was one of the serial killer's victims.'

Emilia swallows. 'I . . . It was just a made-up name.'

'Hmm.' She taps her pen against her teeth. 'Interest-ing, then, that Jennifer Radcliffe was also the name of Louise Greene's mother, wouldn't you say? And that Louise's full name was actually Daisy Louise Greene, Greene being her father's name. She must have dropped the Daisy at some point. Maybe when she moved from Devon to Yorkshire. Or when she joined the police. I wonder whether . . .'

But Emilia can't bear to hear any more. The kitchen spins and she has to rush out of the room to be sick.

46

I patiently sip my water while waiting for Emilia to return. She'd sat there in front of me, going paler and paler until I hit her with my final sucker punch. I'm assuming she's fled to the bathroom to vomit. Maybe it's the same bug that's floored poor old Saunders.

I tap the pen against my teeth, weighing up my next move. There is something very disturbing about this book, about Louise, and especially about how Emilia Ward ended up writing this story. Why would a proficient, successful author with nine novels under her belt resort to stealing someone else's idea? And I'm assuming that's what happened here, because Daisy's story in Her Last Chapter *is too similar to Louise's past. Both having mothers called Jennifer Radcliffe who were killed by the praying-mantis murderer. Come on, this is not a coincidence. I don't know how it all fits together yet, but for the first time in a long while I feel the identity of the serial killer is tantalizingly close.*

I look up as I hear footsteps in the garden. A man is coming out of one of those fancy home offices that popped up over lockdown. He's handsome, with broad shoulders and dark wavy hair, just a smattering of grey around the temples. He looks like he works out – muscular arms protrude from his linen shirt. I watch as he scans the garden, wondering what he's looking for. He reaches up and moves something near the fence. Perhaps it's one of those hidden cameras. I don't blame him for installing them. It's particularly unnerving, what has been happening to Emilia and now this with Louise.

He glances up and spots me, a stranger at his table. And then he quickens his pace as he strides across the lawn towards me, leaving indentations in the still damp grass. The bifolds are already pulled back and he steps into the kitchen, his face open and friendly.

'Hi, you must be DI Murray. Emilia said she was going to call you. I'm her husband, Elliot.' He reaches across the table to shake my hand.

'Nice to meet you,' I say pleasantly. 'I'm sorry about everything that's been happening to your wife.'

His shoulders slump and his face drops. 'Thanks. It's been horrendous.' Then his gaze lands on the manuscript in front of me. 'Is that Em's latest book?'

'Yes. I found it on Louise's bedside table. Although I'm not sure if she'd read it all.'

'She usually checks the police procedural things for my wife.'

I nod noncommittally. His body language is interesting. His expression is open but the way he's standing, arms folded, chin jutting out, there's something defensive about *it. I don't want to tell him anything else until I've spoken to Emilia.*

'Here she is,' he says fondly as Emilia walks back into the kitchen, a bit unsteady on her feet, a sheen to her skin. She flashes him a pale smile and he wraps an arm around her shoulders almost possessively. I can tell he's one of those manly men, who view their wives as someone to look after, to provide for. It's no bad thing, I suppose, although it doesn't float my boat. My ex, Julian, and now my girlfriend, Kim, hopefully see me as tough and independent. Emilia is tiny, though, just about reaching Elliot's shoulder. I can imagine a lot of men would put themselves forwards to protect her. She's like a young Goldie Hawn. She extracts herself from him and sits down again. Elliot doesn't look as if he wants to leave and grips the back of his wife's chair.

'You can go, El. Just boring stuff here.'

Now this is interesting. Emilia obviously doesn't want her husband to hear our conversation.

'Okay, cool. I'll . . . Well, I'll see you later, then.' He sounds unsure now and smiles uncertainly. Then he bids farewell to me and heads back into the garden.

Once he's gone Emilia breathes a long sigh.

'Are you feeling okay?'

She nods, sipping some water. 'I don't think I've eaten enough today. I'm going to make a sandwich. Do you want one?'

I pass, telling her I've already had my lunch, and I watch as she faffs about behind the island retrieving condiments and a loaf of bread. I can see that she wants to keep busy. The island is behind where I sit at the table, so I turn my chair to face her. 'So, go on, then. Tell me how you ended up writing about Louise and her murdered mother.'

Emilia stops what she's doing to throw me a disapproving look. 'I didn't realize I was writing about Louise.'

'Then how did you get the story?'

She continues buttering the bread so vigorously that she tears it. 'You have to understand how hard it is to keep coming up with this kind of plot,' she says. 'And I've been writing about my detective Miranda Moody for nearly ten years. I'd lost inspiration, I suppose, but I was contracted to write this book. And for months all I could do was stare at a blank page . . .' She stops and clutches at her chest. 'It was awful. I told Louise and then she revealed she'd written a short story, almost like a diary, about a girl whose mother had been murdered by a serial killer that would be perfect as a Miranda Moody case, but she didn't want it for herself. She said she didn't have time to write a whole book and that she'd just written it for a bit of fun. And then . . . she offered it to me . . .'

'She gave you the story already written?' I ask in disbelief.

Emilia looks like she wants to burst into tears. Her face reddens. 'Yes. Well, just the Daisy sections. It wouldn't have been enough to fill a whole novel but enough for a side story. I liked it and thought it was interesting, the whole thing about a girl who suspects her boyfriend's dad of killing her mother and of being a serial killer. And she'd promised me that she'd never let anyone else read the short story. She was adamant about that.'

'And you believed her?'

'Yes. She said she'd only just written it. The rest, Miranda Moody's investigation, I added myself, but based on the praying-mantis murderer parts of Daisy's story.'

I leaf through the pages. 'So, the stuff about Miranda's death, her missing niece and Miranda's colleague being murdered – in a very similar way I might add to how Louise was murdered – was all yours?'

She nods. 'Yes. But obviously the idea for all that came after I'd read Louise's story about Daisy and Ash and Daisy's search for her mother's killer. The praying-mantis moniker was Louise's idea and, once I had that and the Daisy sections, the rest just came to me. I know it's not particularly ethical, but Louise didn't mind. As I said, she didn't want it. And I never knew – never dreamed in a million years – it was true, that Daisy was really Louise and it was about her mother and a real praying-mantis killer. I just thought Louise had made it up.'

I can see she's telling the truth. She walks over to the table with her sandwich and I swivel to face her.

'I wonder why Louise wanted you to write this story,' I say, putting my pen down.

She frowns, pulling out a chair and sitting down. She picks at the sandwich but doesn't eat it. 'I don't know. I thought she was trying to help me. But it seems now she had a different motive . . .'

'In your book the way the tattoo is administered is different.'

'From the Daisy sections it sounded like a drawing, so I made the killer murder the others in the same way. Was – was her mother's killer ever caught? Obviously in the book he was.'

'No. If Louise really did believe that the father of a past boyfriend killed her mother, then it was never proven. The fictional ending she came up with might have been how she wished things had turned out. How they should have turned out. Did Louise ever mention a man called Martin Butterworth?'

Emilia shakes her head. 'Not that I can recall. Who is he?'

'Just a person of interest. The murders started up again in February last year after a sixteen-year hiatus. When did Louise give you this information?'

'Last spring. March. I started writing this book not long after, May, I think.'

'Interesting that she gave the story to you when the killer struck again after a sixteen-year break.'

Emilia is silent, staring at me expectantly, like I have all the answers.

A gentle breeze floats in from the doors and I lay my hand on top of the manuscript to stop any of the papers flying away. 'We've been watching Martin Butterworth closely since Trisha Banks was killed last year – we have a witness to say he had been hanging around her address before she died and she lived in the flat above his sister. There are other things, but not enough evidence to bring a conviction right now. As yet there have been no further murders. Until Louise.'

'Do you think this Martin Butterworth killed Louise?'

'I don't know. The branding is different. But he does have a son – who would be in his late thirties now. I'll speak to him to find out if he could be our Ash.'

Emilia takes a bite of her sandwich and sits in silence, chewing. She doesn't look like she's particularly enjoying it. After she swallows she says, 'The reason I called you was because I wanted to show you something.' She gets up from the table and goes to the island. She returns with a birthday card and a note. She explains about the night her daughter disappeared again. 'I think Louise wrote this note. The writing is the same.'

I take the card and the letter and examine both. Now this is interesting.

'And if she was behind this note, it's likely she was responsible for all the other horrible things that have been happening to me. But why?' she asks, and I can see the hurt behind her large blue eyes.

'I don't know,' I say. 'But I intend to find out.'

47

Emilia is glad to see the back of DI Murray. Her whole body is drenched with sweat and she still can't get rid of that sick feeling. It's worse than she'd thought. How can she publish this book now? She'll have to tell her publisher the truth, that unbeknown to her she'd been writing about a true-life crime – an unresolved case. And that parts of the book weren't even written by her but by the daughter of one of the victims. She groans into her hands. Humiliation washes over her and she feels the urge to be sick again. How can she tell them? They'll never trust her again. *Her Last Chapter* is currently with the copyeditor. The book is nearly ready. Early review copies will be going out next month. Oh, God. She can't breathe. She slumps onto the bottom stair. Why did Louise lie to her? Why did she pretend it was a fictional story? Didn't she realize how much trouble this would cause Emilia? Was this what she was going to tell her the night she died? She'd apologized in her voice message. Was she saying sorry for everything she'd put Emilia through? Or was she trying to warn her?

Because if Louise had been behind all of this – if she

was trying to scare her by mirroring her plots – then why? And, if so, who killed her?

She's planning her next move when Elliot comes in from the garden, bringing with him the scent of cut grass. 'Just gave the garden a quick tidy,' he says, kicking off his shoes at the door and placing them neatly on the mat. He has a leaf in his hair. 'I suddenly saw it through DI Murray's eyes.'

'Surely you have better things to do on your lunch-break. But,' she adds, when she sees his face fall, 'I'm grateful.'

He goes to the sink to wash his hands. There are sweat patches under the arms of his T-shirt. 'How did it go with the detective?' She can tell he's trying to appear nonchalant.

Now would be the time to tell him the rest, to admit everything, but she can't. Not yet. She can't face going through it all again. She knows she'll have to admit to him that Louise wrote some of the book, but how was she to know the Daisy sections were true, and were about Louise's past? She'll need to tell her publishers too. Everyone will be so disappointed in her. The book will likely need to be canned, if not severely revised. She brushes his cheek with her lips. 'I'll tell you about it later. I'm just going out.'

Elliot turns off the tap and stands there with his wet hands hanging over the sink. 'What? Where? You should be careful, but you're off gallivanting all over the place.'

'I've got my alarm,' she says, throwing him a tea towel. He catches it and dries his hands, then folds it up and hangs it on the peg. 'And nothing has happened since Louise died, has it?'

'It's only been five days.'

'But if Louise was the one to do all this, which looks likely, judging by the letter, then that's the end of the harassment.'

He sighs and she knows he's thinking the same as her: that Louise's murderer is still out there. 'Em, you really need to be more careful. Just until this has all been sorted out.' He grabs her hand. 'It won't be long now, I expect.'

She pulls away. She needs some space, some air. 'I can't stay here forever. I have to pick up the kids soon anyway.' She wants to call the journalist Gina Osbourne and ask her again who contacted her about the incidents. She thinks she knows the answer, but wants to be sure.

'Suit yourself.'

'I'll be careful, I promise.' She grabs her bag and her jacket, makes her way to the front door and double-locks it behind her. Then she stands on the driveway, unsure where to go. She doesn't want to be totally alone. She gets into her car and heads to Richmond Park. She pulls over in the car park next to a row of other vehicles. There are enough people around for her to feel safe and she'll keep to the main paths.

Gina answers on the first ring. 'Emilia,' she exclaims,

sounding happy to hear from her. Obviously hoping for another story.

'Hi,' Emilia says, walking towards the Isabella Plantation. She used to go there when Jasmine and Wilfie were little, marvelling at the exotic plants. 'I hope it's okay to call out of the blue, but I just wanted to know who tipped you off about me. Back when you first approached me.'

'I told you I can't reveal my sources.'

'Did it come from a police contact?'

'Well,' she says and hesitates, 'yes.'

'And has that police contact recently been murdered?'

'Can I come and see you?'

She bites back her irritation. 'Can you just answer me, please? It's really important. Did DC Louise Greene tell you about it? You know she's dead, so you're not exactly being unethical by telling me now.'

There is silence at the other end of the line. 'Okay, yes. It was Detective Greene. But can I –'

'That's all I wanted to know. Thanks.' She ends the call before Gina can say anything more. She stops next to the little stream, tapping her mobile against her chin. So, Louise wanted what was happening to her to be publicized. Why? So everyone would go out and read Emilia's book? And not just Emilia's book – but Louise's story?

There was only one reason Louise would want to do that. She was trying to smoke someone out.

48

Emilia tries to call her agent, Drummond, to ask his advice about pulling the book, but it goes through to voicemail. And then she remembers he's on holiday in Japan with his family. She just hopes she hasn't tried to call in what is for him the middle of the night. She hangs up without leaving a message.

She follows a young couple walking with their toddler daughter, each holding one of her pudgy hands, the mother pointing out the names of the different azaleas and rhododendrons as they pass. Emilia is impressed. She has never been a keen gardener. She has a pang of nostalgia for when Jasmine, and later Wilfie, was that age. When she could keep them safe, keep an eye on them at all times.

She's at a loss as to what to do next. Perhaps she should call her editor and tell her everything. After all, how can her book be published now she knows the truth? But she can't face it. She'd rather speak to Drummond first, anyway, and get his advice. Maybe all she needs to do is change the name of the killer and Daisy's backstory a little so that it doesn't resemble Louise's and then all will be good. It doesn't have to be career-ending, like she'd first feared. Not if she handles it carefully.

It must have been so easy for Louise when Emilia admitted that she couldn't think of a new story for her last Miranda Moody book. She had handed her friend the opportunity on a plate. She must have been hoping that someone would recognize the praying-mantis murderer – her mother's killer – from the story. Especially if it got enough publicity, which it has. Her story has been picked up by all the nationals and she's been invited on to BBC2 and Times Radio. Oh, how she wishes she could talk to Louise about it! Rage at her, even, especially for the part she'd played in making them all think Jasmine had disappeared.

That hoax call. No wonder Louise had been so eager to play the hero. She knew exactly where Jasmine and Nancy were the whole time. And the troll doll? Had she planted it in Kristin's kitchen when she was around there to take the heat off herself? Kristin would have assumed it was one of Jasmine's old toys and probably not thought much about it. She feels a stab of guilt when she remembers how she'd accused Kristin.

She's so busy thinking about Louise that as she rounds the corner she doesn't notice that everyone else has fallen away, and she is no longer trailing the family with the little girl. Her heart speeds up when she realizes that she's alone.

There are footsteps on the path behind her and she

picks up her pace so that she quickly joins a group of people who are standing by the lake. But she still doesn't feel
safe until she can see her car ahead. She gets the keys out
of her bag as she approaches and holds them between her
fingers, ready. She's nearly at her Nissan when she senses
someone right behind her, so close she can feel their
breath on her neck. She spins around and comes face to
face with a man in his thirties – spiky hair and flinty eyes.
She darts a look past his shoulder. There are people
around. If he tries to hurt her she'll scream.

'I'm sorry, I didn't mean to startle you,' he says in a low
voice.

'You've been following me?' It strikes her that he was
the man on the tube the other day: he had followed her
up the hill towards her house.

She's surprised when he nods. 'My name is Marcus
Saunders. I'm a police officer. I work with DI Janine
Murray.'

She takes a step backwards so that she's nearer to her
car. Is he lying? She can't tell. Why would he be following
her if he's a police officer? He fishes his identification out of
the inner pocket of his Harrington jacket and shows her.
'I'm sorry for all the cloak-and-dagger stuff. I wanted to
talk to you about Louise, but in an unofficial capacity.
You see,' he says as he slides his police warrant card back
into his pocket, 'I'm . . . I mean I was . . .' He clears his
throat, and his cheeks redden.

'Wait.' It suddenly clicks, and she remembers the

conversation she and Louise had on their last night out. Louise had talked about a boyfriend. A colleague. Emilia couldn't remember his name before but now she's sure it was Marcus. 'You were Louise's boyfriend?'

He nods, just once. 'I was the one who told her about Trisha Banks. The last victim of the praying-mantis murderer. Neither of us usually talked about our cases. We wanted to leave them at work. But this killer had resurfaced after sixteen years so I was reeling about it. Louise went pale when I told her. Mumbled something about hoping it was all over. She didn't elaborate even though I pushed it.' Guilt flashes across his face. 'I had no idea until I spoke to my boss a few days ago that her mother had been a victim. I don't think Louise even knew – until I told her – that we'd dubbed him the praying-mantis murderer.'

'And this was last February time?'

'Yes. I gather she told you the story after that. I'm so sorry, but I set all this in motion.'

Emilia's car keys feel sweaty in her hand. 'Does DI Murray know what you did?'

He shakes his head. 'I've been pretending to be holed up in my hotel with a sickness bug all week. Seeing Louise's body . . . not being able to tell anyone what she meant to me . . .'

'Why can't you tell anyone?'

He digs his hands in his pockets. 'The boss wouldn't be too pleased to find out I'd talked about the case, and not only that. Now she's dead they might take me off it. This is a high-profile case. I just wanted you to know, despite everything that's happened, and the boss has filled me in on it all, Louise thought a lot of you, you know. She talked highly of you.'

A lump forms in Emilia's throat. 'Did she say anything about what was happening to me? About a stalker mirroring some of the plots from my books?'

'No, why?'

'I think she was behind it. I think she told me the story to try to reveal who was responsible.'

'So you think she knew the name of the killer? Then why wouldn't she have told the police?' He frowns. 'It seems a convoluted way of going about things.'

'I don't know. Would the police have believed her based on a hunch? Based on perhaps a fleeting glimpse of the back of this man's head when she was a child?'

His shoulders droop. 'No. They'd need more than that. More evidence.'

'Maybe that's why she decided to become a police officer,' she muses. 'She must have thought her mother's killer had got away with it and she wanted to stop it happening to others.'

'She was a brilliant cop,' he says. 'She was studying for her sergeant's exam.'

Emilia sighs. 'What a total mess. I wish she'd just been honest. Told me what she wanted to do. Maybe I could have, I dunno, helped. Instead it was all so underhand.

She could have confessed to you too. Maybe you could have looked into her suspicions. Found out more about this man she believed was her mother's killer.'

'She wouldn't have wanted to put me in an awkward position,' he says, nudging the rain-flattened grass with the toe of his trainer. 'Although . . .' he says before he looks up at her and squints '. . . a few times – earlier this year – I was up in this area, visiting her. And she asked me to go into a florist, pay for some flowers and give them an address, which I've now figured out must have been yours.'

Her mouth falls open. 'So that was you!'

He nods, looking sick.

'And one was a wreath?'

He groans. 'Yes. Shit. I'm sorry. I didn't realize what I was doing. She must have been desperate to have involved me.'

Emilia appraises him. She understands he doesn't want to think badly about the woman he loved. Emilia doesn't either, but it's obvious they've both been used. 'She contacted a journalist to tell them what was happening to me. It was her handwriting on a note that was sent to a boy in my daughter's friendship group that made me realize she was behind it all.' She fills him in on Jasmine and Nancy's disappearance.

His face falls when she's finished talking and he digs his hands further into the pockets of his jacket. 'It still doesn't explain who killed her. And I owe it to her to find out who killed her mother. And who killed her.'

'Do you think the praying-mantis murderer killed Louise as well?'

A muscle throbs in his jaw. 'I don't know. It's a possibility despite the insect markings being administered differently.' He steps back. 'Anyway, I've taken up too much of your time. I'm sorry I scared you. I didn't want to come to your house and make it all official. Thank you for listening.'

He turns and walks away from her before she can say anything else. Full of mixed emotions, she watches his retreating back, trying to make sense of everything. As she gets behind the wheel she thinks again about Louise's motive for telling her the story. Perhaps she was hoping to prod the killer, knowing that he – or someone he knew – would read *Her Last Chapter* and recognize the story. But what then? And why now? Because he had killed again after sixteen years? Or was there another reason?

She slams back in her seat, exhaling in frustration.

What is she missing?

She turns the ignition on, her mind whirling.

And then it hits her.

The reports in the paper. They were about things that were happening to her from her previous books, not from *Her Last Chapter*. Louise had died before she could re-enact those. She must have been planning to do so, for more airtime. But Louise had known not to start with all that because then it would have been obvious to Emilia that she knew the person behind it. And the stuff with Jasmine was obviously meant to emulate her sub-plot about the missing teenagers from *Her Last Chapter*, but Emilia hadn't mentioned it when she talked to Gina.

None of the press coverage had mentioned *Her Last Chapter* and what it was about, apart from a line at the end saying she had a new book coming out later in the year. Louise had contacted Gina Osbourne too soon. She should have waited until she'd orchestrated more of the plotlines from *Her Last Chapter*.

So if the praying-mantis murderer had come looking for Louise, how would he have known that Emilia's new book was about him? Unless it was someone who had actually read *Her Last Chapter*. *And the only people who had read it were her inner circle.*

Horror washes over her as the pieces finally click into place.

Someone she knows is the praying-mantis murderer.

49

Saunders is unusually quiet in the car on the way back to Devon and I wonder if he's still feeling queasy.

'So, you're wondering if Martin Butterworth's son might be Ash from Emilia's book?' he asks when I finish filling him in on Louise Greene and Emilia Ward.

'That's what we're going to find out. Apparently Anthony Butterworth lives in Torquay nowadays and runs a guesthouse. Anthony and Ash. Both begin with an A. Maybe that was deliberate,' I muse as we pull into a side road. I reverse park between two cars, thankful I only have an Audi A3. It was raining when we left London but here the sun is beating down, bouncing off the car hoods. There isn't a cloud in the sky, just a flock of seagulls that screech menacingly as they swoop overhead and descend on a half-eaten sandwich that has been left on a wooden table in the nearby pub garden. I slip out of my raincoat and throw it onto the back seat. Saunders keeps his jacket on.

'It's around here, on the seafront, according to Google Maps,' says Saunders, glancing at his phone and nearly getting knocked over by a cyclist.

'Oi, watch it, mate,' the cyclist calls back over his shoulder.

'He should be careful who he's speaking to,' mutters Saunders, darkly, under his breath. Something is definitely up with him. Maybe he's still feeling ill, but this isn't like him. Normally I can't shut him up. I actually feel a pang of nostalgia for the old Saunders, which I'd never thought I'd experience.

Anthony Butterworth's guesthouse is a powder-blue Victorian building overlooking the bay, with black-painted window frames and a white front door, which is open when we arrive. Saunders glances at me, shrugs and steps over the threshold into the hallway. The red and gold swirly carpet is so loud it would deafen us all at karaoke, and Saunders looks queasy again. 'Wow, this is an assault on the senses,' he says. 'Imagine coming here with a hangover –'

He's interrupted by an inner door opening to reveal a slightly harassed-looking man. He's a few years older than Saunders, I'd say, maybe mid thirties, with a receding hairline and piercing blue eyes. He's still good-looking but I imagine he would have been very handsome in his youth. Is this our Ash?

'Are you looking for a room?' he asks us. 'Or here to check in?'

I explain who we are and show him our identification. He looks resigned, as though he's used to being visited by police. He shows us through an empty dining room into a cosy sitting room. A white Persian cat is curled up in the corner of a navy blue linen sofa, leaving a smattering of hairs on the nearby cushion. He sits on a chair opposite while we take the sofa. 'So, what can I do for you?'

I appraise him. He's tall like his father, but that's where the similarities end.

'I just want to confirm that you're the son of Martin Butterworth,' I begin.

A shadow passes over his face. 'I haven't seen him in years. We lost touch after my mum divorced him.'

'When was this?'

He pulls at the hem of his blue Fred Perry polo shirt. 'Ah . . . years ago. After my dad went to prison. I was probably nineteen.'

I take my notebook out of my pocket and turn the pages, trying to read my scribbled writing. 'I know this is a strange question, but did you know someone at university called Daisy Greene?'

He opens his mouth to speak but we are interrupted by a woman entering the room. She's petite, with long blonde hair and a wide smile. Anthony introduces her as his wife, Sharon, and she asks us if we would like a cup of tea. When we decline she says, 'Anyway, I'll get out of your hair.'

'No. Please, stay,' says Anthony, desperation in his voice. She pulls up a leather pouffe next to his armchair and sits down. She looks a little awkward and I smile at her reassuringly.

'So,' I prompt, 'did you know her?'

Anthony shakes his head, his brow furrowed. 'I don't think so. Why?'

'So you didn't date anyone by that name?'

'No, definitely not. And I didn't go to university either. What's this got to do with my dad?'

I glance at Sharon, who looks like she wants to ask Anthony questions but is politely waiting until we've left.

'Just to reiterate, you have no relationship with your father?'

'Like I said, no.' His pleasant face darkens. 'He's a misogynist and a wife beater.'

Sharon reaches over and places a reassuring hand on his arm. 'He used to hit Ant's mum,' she says softly. 'And Ant when he was a boy.'

Anthony dips his head and I feel a surge of anger towards his father. 'I'm sorry,' I say, biting back my feelings. I hear about this kind of thing too often. 'Do you think he's capable of murder?' I ask.

Out of the corner of my eye I notice Saunders sit forwards, his elbows resting on his thighs.

'It wouldn't surprise me. He's a cold, hard psychopath.' He takes his wife's hand. 'It was a relief, to be honest, when he went to prison. It meant my mum could escape him at last.'

'Thank you for your time,' I say, standing up and handing Anthony a card. Is he lying about knowing Daisy? It's hard to tell, but I'll ask one of the team to check if he's telling the truth about not going to university. 'If you do remember anything at all that might be useful, anything, however small, then please call.'

Saunders stands up too, stretching his legs.

Anthony shows us out and I try not to feel disappointed.

50

Emilia can't stop thinking about the praying-mantis murderer as she heads to Wilfie's school to pick him up. All those old uneasy feelings resurface along with some new ones. Horror that she might know a serial killer. Terror that they might decide she's their next victim. She was going to let Jasmine get the bus home after netball but now she calls her and leaves a message, telling her she'll pick her up.

She has to be honest with Elliot about everything. It's time. And if he loves her, and she believes he does, he'll understand why she used Louise's story. She has to stop trying to be perfect in front of him, worrying that if the façade slips he'll leave her, like Jonas did. She'll tell him tonight.

Emilia is hanging around the school gates waiting for Wilfie to come out when she spots Frances standing alone in the shade of a tree. She's wearing a brown anorak despite the sun, and her usual sensible brown brogues. She reminds Emilia of her old school matron. She hasn't seen her since Louise died, although she sent a card to Toby that Wilfie had made.

'Hi,' she says, approaching her somewhat shyly. She's always been a little intimidated by Frances's prickly personality. She can see why Louise didn't get on with her, both strong women who butted heads. 'Wilfie will be pleased that Toby's back. I hope you're all doing okay in the circumstances . . .'

Frances smiles stiffly at Emilia. 'Yes, it's better for him to be at school with his friends at the moment. It's a good distraction.' She hoists her large handbag over her shoulder. She looks as if she's not going to say anything else and Emilia hovers uncertainly, when Frances suddenly pipes up, 'I didn't think Louise had done the right thing, moving Toby when she did. He was happy at the school in Kingston, but she pulled some strings to get him in here, even though it wasn't local to her, me or his dad. But I have to concede, he's been happy here. I know he thinks a lot of your son.'

'Wilfie thinks a lot of him too.' And then Frances's words hit home. 'I thought Louise was local to the school until recently?'

Frances shakes her head. 'No, she's always lived in Kingston. That was where she lived with my son, and after their divorce, in a flat. The flat . . . well,' she says and clears her throat, 'where she died.'

Emilia's stomach turns when she remembers her last visit and Louise's prostrate body. 'I didn't realize,' she says. 'When I first met Louise, she said she'd recently moved to Richmond and that was why Toby was starting here. And then, a few days before she died, I saw her in Kingston and she said she'd only just moved there.'

Frances folds her arms across her large chest and assesses her with a frown. 'She told me she was enrolling Toby at the school because she already knew you.'

Emilia is taken aback. 'What? No, we didn't know each other before Toby joined. We met for the first time at a coffee morning for the year-two parents.'

'That can't be right. I distinctly remember her talking about you to me and Mike. That was one of the reasons Mike agreed to the change in schools – not that he ever had much choice when Louise made up her mind about something, but there you are. She knew all about you. About Wilfie and your husband. Your friends. Even your father-in-law, Trevor. She said she knew him from when he was in the police force.'

Despite the heat of the summer sun, a chill descends over Emilia. 'Are you sure?'

'Of course. I've got a memory like an elephant. I know I shouldn't speak ill of the dead, and I was fond of Louise in a lot of ways, but she could be . . . obsessive. And I always felt, if I can be so bold as to say it as I know she was your friend, but I always felt she was obsessive about *you*.'

Emilia is lost for words.

Frances shakes back her greying curls. 'Anyway, I know we didn't always get along but I'm sad about Louise. Devastating for Toby, losing his mum. She was a good mum.'

She speaks without emotion, and Emilia opens her mouth to say more but the boys come running out, each holding a sunflower and talking about how they'd planted it at school and they now needed to transfer it to the garden, which will be a surefire way for it to die, being left in Emilia's care. A lump forms in her throat as she watches Toby, his little face alight, as he proudly shows it to Frances. The older woman bends down so she's on his level and Emilia is surprised to see the change in her. Her face, which moments earlier had been so stern and closed, is now open, warm, gentle. It's like watching a different person. It's obvious for anyone to see that she adores her grandson. Frances straightens and ushers Toby away without saying goodbye.

'Can we plant it when we get back?' asks Wilfie as they walk to the car.

'Sure, little man,' she says, but her mind is still mulling over what Frances has told her.

Louise had purposely targeted her.

But why? Just so Emilia could write her story, or was there more to it? Frances had said that Louise knew Trevor. Yet Trevor had left the force years ago, surely before Louise had joined. So how would she have known Trevor?

The house is empty when she arrives home. Wilfie rushes into the garden to show his dad the sunflower, then bursts back through the bifold doors trailing mud into the kitchen, disappointment etched on his still-baby face. The sunflower seems to droop too, as though it can sense his mood. He hands it to her in its little brown pot. 'Dad's not in his office.'

'Are you sure? He didn't say he was going out.'

He shrugs and kicks off his shoes before turning on the TV. She retreats into the kitchen, still ruminating over what Frances had said. She thinks back to her conversation with Louise on their last night out in the restaurant. Had Louise mentioned Elliot or Trevor then? Yes, yes, she had. Now she comes to think of it, she had always seemed interested in him. Emilia had thought it was because he was ex-police, but what if that wasn't the only reason?

She fights back a wave of nausea as it dawns on her. Louise had targeted her. Not just so that she could write her story – she'd moved Toby before that, and before she'd found out that the praying-mantis murderer had struck again – but for another reason.

Oh, God. An awful thought strikes her.

She calls to Wilfie that she'll be in her office and charges up the stairs to her attic room, turning on her computer and opening *Her Last Chapter*. She scrolls down to the Daisy and Ash sections, looking for clues with fresh eyes. Things she hadn't even realized before, when she was typing it up. Exeter University. That was where Ash and Daisy had met. Elliot had gone to Exeter Uni.

And a ham-like neck and sandy hair with a double

crown. Did that sound like Trevor? She's not sure – he's been slowly losing his hair for years and what's left of it is shorn and grey.

A paragraph jumps out at her from 'Daisy' and she reads it with dawning horror.

They talked all night in Daisy's room, slowly revealing more and more about themselves as the cheap lager flowed. She was surprised when Ash revealed a breakdown as a teenager.

It fitted. It all fitted. Elliot had grown up by the sea. He'd gone to Exeter, and he'd suffered anxiety to such an extent he'd missed out on some of his teenage years.

Emilia's blood runs cold.

All this time it's been staring her in the face and she never saw it.

Elliot is Ash.

And so his dad, Trevor, must be . . . she can barely bring herself to think it . . . *the killer.*

51

So many questions sprint through Emilia's mind. Does Elliot know he's Ash? He never mentioned that he might have known Louise at university, but she was called Daisy back then. Yet he must have recognized himself from the description in *Her Last Chapter*. Mustn't he? But maybe not. She hasn't told him yet, about it being Louise who wrote that part of the story. Yet his behaviour lately, the snappiness, the questioning about where the idea for the praying-mantis murderer had come from, not being content when she first told him it was a coincidence. Because he knew. *He already knew.* Maybe he hadn't grasped that the Daisy in the book, whom he'd known at uni, was her friend Louise. After all, they'd never met.

She thinks back to the day Jasmine went missing when she'd called Louise. She'd kept asking then who Emilia was with. Was that because she was trying to avoid meeting Elliot? If she had met him he would have recognized her. And the night of her launch when she saw Louise hanging around outside: Why had she really rushed off? Was it because she realized Elliot was there? Maybe she'd assumed he would stay at home to babysit Wilf.

And what about Trevor? He always reads her novels, sometimes pointing out an inaccuracy that Louise might have missed. He would definitely have recognized the story if it was about him.

She shuts down her computer. Her whole body is shaking and she feels as if she might throw up. Did Trevor kill Louise to shut her up when he realized what was going on? But how would he have known Daisy was Louise? He'd never met Louise . . . or had he? Oh, God. She grips the edge of the desk and levers herself up, her knees buckling. She needs to get a grip. Wilfie is downstairs and she has to leave to pick up Jasmine in ten minutes.

She practically hugs the wall as she descends the stairs, not trusting her own legs. Wilfie is still where she left him in front of *SpongeBob*. Every now and again he erupts in laughter. She blinks back tears. This will devastate him. Destroy the family. His grandfather might be a serial killer, he's –

Emilia jumps when she hears the front door slam, then the clink of keys being dumped in the pot in the hallway. Elliot walks into the kitchen whistling an Oasis song.

'Hey, what's up?' He stops when he sees her. 'You look terrible. Is everything okay?'

She's just about to answer when she hears another voice, equally familiar, from behind him. Elliot steps aside to reveal Trevor, standing there with a sheepish expression and his arm in a sling. 'Dad had an accident at work. I went to pick him up and bring him back here for a few days. That's okay, isn't it?'

She can't answer for a few seconds and just stares at Trevor in shock.

Trevor lifts his sling up and arches a shaggy eyebrow. 'Stupid of me. I fell over chasing a shoplifter.' He has a bruise forming on his cheekbone. Is he telling the truth, or was it the result of an attack he'd made? The smile slips off Trevor's face. 'Are you okay, Em?'

Elliot is frowning at her too.

With momentous effort she concentrates on pulling herself together. She can't let him know anything is wrong until she's spoken to Elliot.

'Yes, of course. It's fine for you to stay, Trevor.' She can hardly say no. 'I need to pick up Jas. Trevor, you sit down and El can make you a brew.'

He smiles uncertainly and joins Wilfie on the sofa.

Elliot turns towards the kettle, switches it on, and lowers his voice: 'It's okay for him to stay, isn't it? I know it's not ideal, but they talked about concussion.'

'I'm going to take Wilf with me to pick up Jas. Give you the chance to . . . er . . . help your dad.'

His eyes widen. 'That's not necessary.'

'It's fine.'

His eyes narrow. 'What's this about?'

'Nothing. Wilf,' she calls. Her son gets up reluctantly, dragging his feet to the door. Elliot looks puzzled as Emilia leads Wilfie into the hallway to put his shoes on.

'Okay. Well, see you in a bit then. Drive carefully.'

Jasmine is full of it on the way home, regaling her with tales of the netball match and how she'd scored three goals. She smells of sweat and body spray.

She's relieved when Jasmine turns up the radio – some dance tune is playing on Radio 1 – and sits beside her with her eyes closed. Wilfie is in the back seat fiddling with a Lego car he'd grabbed on the way out. It takes every ounce of energy Emilia has to act normally.

She doesn't know what to do next. She needs to talk to Elliot, but it will be hard now that Trevor is staying. She could ring DI Murray, but it might be the end of her marriage if she were to rat on her father-in-law without talking to Elliot first.

She pulls onto the driveway, weighed down by dread and indecision, not wanting to step inside the house to confront reality. It's 6 p.m. and still hot. She can hear chattering and glasses clinking from a neighbour's garden, signalling a summer's evening on a Friday night. More than a week since she'd stumbled on the dead body of her friend.

'Are you getting out or are you just going to sit there all night?' Jasmine has already climbed out of the car, her smooth, teenage legs in her skort are brown, toned. Her beautiful, precious daughter, about to inhabit a space with a serial killer. She turns away and takes a deep breath, steeling herself.

'Mum?' Wilfie is already by the front door.

'Coming,' she says. Her body feels like lead as she gets

out of the car, unlocks the front door, and follows her children into the house.

Jasmine dumps her bag in the hall and runs upstairs, saying she's going to jump into the shower. Usually, Emilia would pick up her bag for her – not wanting Elliot to get annoyed – but she doesn't have the energy. Jasmine is nearly sixteen: she should be doing it herself.

Elliot is mixing a salad when she walks into the kitchen. Wilfie flops down next to Trevor in front of the TV and the bifold doors are open, letting in a much-needed breeze.

'What's going on?' Elliot says quietly, when they're on their own at the kitchen end of the room. 'Has something happened?'

'Yes, something has fucking happened,' she snaps, under her breath. 'I think I'm going to go insane if I don't talk to you about it.'

Concern radiates off him. She's rarely spoken to him like that. She darts a glance towards where Trevor and Wilfie sit. 'It's about your dad,' she mouths. She has to repeat it when Elliot steps closer to her, cupping his ear.

'What about him?' he mouths back.

'Can we talk in the other room?'

He turns back towards Trevor and Wilfie but they are oblivious, both laughing at something on the TV.

Elliot follows her into the posh front room. 'What's going on?' he asks as soon as she closes the door behind him.

Oh, God, where to start? She can hardly blurt out that she thinks his dad is a killer. 'Sit down,' she says, and he lowers himself into an armchair, looking puzzled. She perches on the opposite sofa. 'I haven't been completely honest with you still.'

His face instantly falls. 'What do you mean?'

'The Daisy and Ash storyline in my book. It's from Louise too.' She explains how Louise had given her the 'story.' 'When DI Murray was here, she told me that this storyline is true. That Daisy is Louise's real name. And that . . .' she says and gulps, can't look him in the eye '. . . it's all about her real past and her mother's murder.'

A myriad of emotions flash across his face. 'You're kidding?'

She blinks back tears. 'Do I sound like I'm kidding? This is a fucking mess. And I had no idea this was all true. Louise told me she'd made it up and that I could use it as she didn't have time to write a novel.'

'But why would she do that?'

'I think it was her misguided attempt to tell the world who she thought killed her mother.'

'So her mother's murderer is called Donald?' Confusion flits across Elliot's face.

'No. I think that's a made-up name. And so is Ash.' She tells him about her conversation with Frances at pickup. 'She targeted me for a reason and now I'm wondering why. Is it because you're Ash? And could your dad be the Doodle Man?'

He stares at her, his mouth falling open. 'You – you think my dad is this serial killer?'

'I don't know what to think.' She stands up and begins pacing the room. It still smells faintly of Lloyd. 'We've never talked much about our university days, but I know you went to Exeter.'

'Yep. English.'

'Did you date Louise? Or should I say Daisy, as she would have been known back then?'

'I . . .' He frowns. 'I don't know. I mean, I had quite a few girlfriends at uni. Nothing serious. But I don't remember dating anyone called Daisy. I don't . . . I didn't recognize myself in your story, if that's what you mean. Now you've said it there are some similarities, I suppose – I did grow up by the sea and I did go through a bit of a Goth stage, but I never had any girlfriends come back and stay while I was at uni. In fact, I'd left by Christmas 2005. I graduated that summer. I don't think I'm Ash and I'm a hundred percent sure my dad isn't the fucking praying-mantis murderer. Jesus, Emilia, I can't believe this.'

Emilia takes the phone out of her bag and pulls up the news story about Louise. There is a photograph of her, although it's a few years old. Despite everything it still tugs at her heart that her friend is dead. She thrusts it in Elliot's face. 'Do you recognize her? It strikes me that I've never introduced the two of you. She always seemed against coming here, meeting you – any of you. Is this why? Because she knew you'd recognize her?'

He takes the phone from her and studies the photo. Then he looks up at her, his dark eyes huge in his face. 'I can honestly say I don't recognize her.'

She has always found it hard to read Elliot. Would he lie to her?

'It says here that she was thirty-five. I'm nearly thirty-nine, three years older than her,' he says.

She snatches back the phone. 'Yes, Elliot, I'm aware of how old you are. Not everyone goes to university at eighteen.'

He stands up. 'But I did! This is ridiculous. I wouldn't lie to you, despite all the lies you've told me. If I thought I was this Ash I'd say so. Why would I lie about it?'

'To protect your dad.'

He gives a mirthless laugh. 'Sure, yes, why not? I'd protect my dad, the serial killer.' He shakes his head in disbelief. 'If I really thought my dad was behind all those murders I wouldn't let him anywhere near you and the kids. I hope you know that.' He comes towards her and holds out a hand, like she's a dangerous animal and he's not sure if she'll bite. 'Seriously? I know you're looking for answers, but please . . . my dad is a gentle giant. He wouldn't hurt a soul.'

52

Emilia tosses and turns all night thinking about Trevor and Louise. She doesn't know whether to believe her husband. Maybe Louise had looked different at university. It was nearly twenty years ago after all. She believes him when he says he wouldn't protect his father if he thought he was a killer – but the fact is, he might not know. Who wants to believe the person they love is capable of such heinous crimes?

Not for the first time she wishes she could ask Louise.

She needs to speak to DI Murray. She feels like she's betraying her husband, but she needs to voice her suspicions to someone in authority. Maybe they could run checks on Trevor. Find out if Louise had ever made a complaint against him. Surely there would be records about that kind of thing. Louise had told Frances she knew Trevor. How?

'Penny for them,' says Trevor, jolting her out of her thoughts. She looks up from her muesli. All her family are seated at the dining table, staring at her: they must have been talking and she's been in a world of her own.

She notices Elliot flashing her a warning look from across the table.

'Just plot points for the new book,' she lies.

Trevor raises an eyebrow. 'Interesting. Can you reveal what it's about yet? I was sad to read about Miranda Moody's demise in *Her Last Chapter*.'

She glances at him: his expression is unreadable. Why did he mention Miranda's death? Is it some kind of veiled threat? Does he suspect she knows about him?

The muesli turns to sawdust in her mouth. 'Um, not quite yet.' She gets up and takes her bowl to the sink.

Jasmine looks up from her phone. She's still in her pyjamas, her hair unbrushed. 'I've just had a message from Dad,' she announces. 'He says he's coming over this morning.'

Elliot's face darkens but he doesn't say anything. Damn, she'd forgotten she'd told Jonas he could come. 'You shouldn't have your phone at the table,' he mutters instead.

Jasmine ignores him. 'Why is he coming here?' she asks Emilia. 'He never does. Why aren't I going there this weekend?'

'I'll ring Jonas,' she says, relieved to have an excuse to leave the kitchen. She feels like she can't breathe when she's in close proximity to Trevor, like he's sucked all the oxygen from the room.

She goes into the den, a cosy space at the back of the house, behind the posh front room. It consists of a

PlayStation and shelves of kids' books and Legos. Elliot doesn't like to have drawings and magnets on their kitchen fridge so she hangs up Wilfie's pictures here, on little pegs attached to string that snakes around the coving of the room. It reminds her of a primary-school classroom, and she loves it. The kids, like her, need a space where they can be messy.

She dials Jonas's number. He sounds like he's speaking on his car's hands-free when he answers. 'I'm on my way,' he says, without 'hello,' and she knows he's still cross with her.

'I'm so sorry,' she blurts out. 'About Kristin. I was wrong. It wasn't her.'

'I know it wasn't,' he replies, but he sounds relieved.

'I'll apologize to her when I come and pick up Jas tomorrow night.'

'You mean she can stay this weekend?'

'If it's okay with you guys.'

'Of course it's okay. She's always welcome to stay. You know that. Tell her to get her stuff ready. I'll be ten minutes.' He ends the call.

She goes back into the kitchen to let Jasmine know, and her daughter runs upstairs to get ready. Wilfie is debating with Elliot about the pros of having a dog. 'You just don't want one because you think they're messy,' he wails.

'No, bud, that's not it. They're hard work.'

Wilfie pushes back his chair, his lip quivering. 'It's not

fair. All my friends have pets. We don't even have a hamster.'

'You should let Wilf have a pet, son,' says Trevor.

'Right, yeah, thanks, Dad. Like we were surrounded by pets when I was a kid.'

'Only because your mother was allergic. It's nice for kids to grow up with pets.'

Emilia's stomach twists. 'Wilf, go and get dressed,' she instructs from the doorway, and her son hurries from the room, brushing past her, his face like thunder.

'Right, then,' says Trevor, downing his coffee and getting up. 'I think I'll go home today. I don't want to be getting under your feet.' He looks tired.

Elliot gets up too and takes his father's bowl and mug to the dishwasher. 'You're not getting under anyone's feet, is he, Em?'

'No. No, of course not.' The lie sticks in her throat. Was his the last face Louise had seen before she was murdered? The thought sickens her.

Elliot fusses around his father, propping him up with cushions, opening the doors to let the sunshine stream in and switching on the football for him to watch. Then he takes her arm and guides her out of the room into the hallway. 'You have to stop this. My father is an old man.'

'He's sixty-two and fitter than me.'

'He's not a killer,' he hisses. 'How can you think that about him?'

'I don't know what to think.'

They are interrupted by the ring of the doorbell, and it pops up on her app that it's Jonas. Elliot shakes his head in annoyance and goes back into the kitchen, closing the door behind him. Jasmine rushes down the stairs, dressed casually in her usual baggy jeans, with her hair in a jaunty ponytail. Emilia is relieved to get her out of the house for the weekend, away from Trevor.

'Have you got everything?'

'Yep,' she says, wrapping her headphones around her neck, her rucksack on her back.

'Great.' Emilia opens the doors into the porch. It takes her a while to unlock the heavy front door and it enters her mind, not for the first time, how naïve she had been to leave these unlocked, yet she feels nostalgic for the person she was before all this started. Now she's suspicious of everyone she knows.

Jonas is standing at the top of the steps with his hands in the pockets of his shorts. She glances behind her to make sure Jasmine is out of earshot, but she's heading down the hallway towards the kitchen, she presumes to say goodbye to Elliot and Trevor. She turns back to Jonas. 'I'm sorry, again, for what happened with Kristin.'

He studies her through narrowed eyes. 'You've lost a lot of weight, Em. I can see you've been through the wringer so I do understand. And I know Kristin didn't turn out to be a good friend, but she'd never do something like this.'

'I know,' she says, in a small voice.

His brow furrows in concern. 'Is everything okay? Did you find out who it was?'

'It was Louise, if you must know. I found out after she died. It's a long story. I'll tell it to you one day.'

'Your detective friend? Shit.'

'I know. I –'

Jasmine appears at the door. 'Hi, Dad. See you tomorrow, Mum.' She bends down to kiss Emilia's cheek.

Her teenage daughter, who's already way taller than she is. Emilia hugs her fiercely. 'Love you,' she says into her hair.

'Love you too.'

Jonas flashes her a concerned smile and she watches her daughter and her ex-husband head to his BMW parked behind her car on the drive. In that moment she wishes she could gather up Wilfie and go with them.

Wilfie has a sleepover with his friend, Ben, in nearby St Margaret's, and Emilia is thankful to be leaving Elliot and Trevor behind as she drives him over. Wilfie has perked up since his argument with Elliot about pets, and is excited about spending the night with his friend and his two fluffy Cockapoos. Once she's dropped him off and had a chat with Ben's mum, promising to pick him up at 2 p.m. the next day, she gets back into her car and drives to Marble Hill Park.

She's thankful both of her children are safely away

from home. She still doesn't know whether to believe Elliot when he says he isn't Ash. She wants to believe him. Just like she wants to believe that Trevor is innocent. But she can't think clearly. Suspicion and paranoia are clogging her brain. She gets out and wanders through the gardens of Marble Hill House, her mind racing. What should she do?

She decides to call Ottilie.

'Hey, you,' she says, on answering. 'Are you okay?'

'Are you still in London or have you flown off somewhere?'

She chuckles. 'You make my life sound a lot more glamorous than it is. I only ever go to Germany to see my dad. Anyway, I'm in London. Is everything okay?'

She sighs. 'Not really. There's so much to tell you. So much I've found out. God . . . can we meet?'

'I can't today. What about tomorrow?'

'Yes,' she says. 'Yes, let's do lunch.'

'Do you mind if you come to the flat?' she says. 'I'm sitting my friends' cat this weekend, they're away for the bank holiday, and she's quite nervous.'

'No worries. I'll bring some nibbles.'

'Fab. Tell me all then. Looking forward to it.' She blows a kiss down the line and then is gone.

Usually she'd feel pacified after talking to Ottilie, but still the doubt nags at her. She has to tell DI Murray what she knows. Even if she's wrong. She can't leave it another second and have a clear conscience. She stops to dial her number, fingers trembling, then waits. DI Murray answers almost straight away: 'Yep.'

'It's Emilia Ward. I –'

'Oh, Emilia. I'm glad you called.' She sounds like she's by the sea. 'I was just about to ring you. I've had a phone call from one of my colleagues at the Met to say a witness has come forward about Louise Greene's death.'

Her heart speeds up. 'Right.' She stops under the shade of a tree and closes her eyes, leaning against the trunk. Is this it? Did someone see Trevor?

'Someone was seen fleeing on a bicycle around the time of Louise's death.'

'A man?'

'They think so, yes. They had on a hoodie and a dark tracksuit. And my colleagues have found an abandoned bike in the field behind Louise's flat. A bright green one. They're searching the serial number now.'

A bright green bike. *Elliot's.*

'I think the bike belongs to my husband,' she begins. And then tells DI Murray everything.

53

Emilia explains it all to me, everything she's worked out over the past few days. I sit on the wall outside another flat, watching children paddling in the sea in their shorts or swimsuits, making the most of this glorious bank-holiday weekend, unaware of the horrors just a few streets away. My shoulders have started to burn but still I sit, rooted, while Emilia talks. She talks fast, breathlessly, but there is another inflection to her voice, emotion. Her words catch when she speaks about her father-in-law, and I can only imagine the betrayal she must be feeling.

'Louise targeted me on purpose,' she says. 'She found out who I was married to, who my father-in-law is . . . but what I don't understand is, if she believed Trevor was the man she's been looking for all these years, then why didn't she go to the police? Did she . . .' She clears her throat. 'Do you know if she ever made a complaint about Trevor? Is that why he left the force?'

'I'll look into it, but I suspect she didn't have any evidence, so couldn't really go to the police. Why did she tell you the story when she did?' I ask, as it occurs to me that Louise could have done so at any time. Why wait until she had known Emilia for nearly two years?

'Because she'd found out that he'd struck again after a sixteen-year break, and wanted the truth about him out there, I presume. In the public domain. And it coincided with my writer's block. Maybe she thought if I wrote about it, Trevor would think she'd told me and that he'd do something . . .'

'That would have put you in danger, though.'

She sighs and her voice wobbles. 'I think she was so hell bent on revenge, she didn't care whom she hurt. I mean . . . she did all those things to me. Made my life a misery for months and then sat there at the restaurant, while I told her . . . Elliot says he's not Ash. And I want to believe him but . . .'

I frown and push my sunglasses onto my head. 'You can't jump to conclusions, Emilia. Leave the police work to me. But thank you for letting me know, and I'll look into your father-in-law. I'll get back to you as soon as I can.' I end the call. I light a cigarette and sit there, inhaling deeply. When I get back to the station I'll look into Trevor Rathbone but, in the meantime, I need to get back to work.

I hop off the wall, feeling a hundred years old, and head back to the flat where another praying-mantis victim is waiting.

54

Emilia is still thinking about her conversation with DI Murray when she pulls onto the driveway. She feels as if a weight has been taken off her shoulders. She's passed the baton to someone else now, and they can run with it. She knows Elliot will be furious with her, but she had no choice.

She turns off the ignition and sits for a while, her heart heavy, summoning all her strength to go into the house and face Trevor, remembering DI Murray's warning about jumping to conclusions.

She swallows, acid burning the back of her throat. *You can do this*, she tells herself, getting out of the car and heading into the house. She can hear voices coming from the kitchen. The door is open: a man is standing talking to Elliot and Trevor by the island. She vaguely recognizes him, and when he introduces himself as DS Shawn Watkins, she remembers where from. She'd met him the night she found Louise's body.

'I'm here to talk to your husband, Mrs Rathbone, about a bicycle,' he says.

Emilia turns to Elliot but he doesn't say anything. He

continues to stare straight ahead at the detective. Her attention is back on DS Watkins now as he repeats what DI Murray had told her on the phone just half an hour ago.

'We checked the bike's serial number and it's registered to your husband, Mrs Rathbone.' She can tell by the look on Trevor and Elliot's faces that they've just been told this before she walked in and interrupted. DS Watkins is holding something. He steps forwards and passes it to her husband. It's a photograph of a bike in a lurid green. It looks like Elliot's.

'Is this your bicycle, Mr Rathbone?' asks Watkins.

Elliot clears his throat. 'Well, yes. I mean, it looks like it. It's the same colour. But . . .' he says as his eyes flicker towards Emilia for the first time since she arrived '. . . it was stolen. About a week ago, wasn't it, Em? We have evidence. It's on the app.'

Emilia gets out her phone, her fingers feel too big as she fumbles for the right app. She spools back to the night the bike was stolen, remembering how they'd thought the person who took it had been Louise. It was the night before she died. 'Here,' she says, handing it over. 'You can clearly see someone making off with it.'

DS Watkins glances down at the footage. 'It's very grainy,' he says. He looks up at Elliot. 'Why didn't you report it?'

'I told him not to,' says Emilia, taking back the phone from the detective. 'Because I recognized the brand of hat and thought maybe Louise had taken it.'

'DC Greene? And why would she do that?'

Emilia lifts her shoulders. 'I don't know.'

DS Watkins looks grave. 'A witness believes they saw a man on a bike of this description around the time of DC Greene's murder. And now this bike has been dumped not far from her premises.'

A slant of sunshine creates a sheen on the side of Watkins's bald head. 'Would you mind coming down to the station and answering a few questions?' he says to Elliot.

It should be Trevor they're arresting. Maybe it was him who took the bike 'We've just explained that the bike was stolen,' Emilia says. 'You can see the footage for yourself! If Louise did take the bike, it would have been at her flat and the man who killed her would have used it to cycle off. I don't see why you need to take my husband down to the station.'

'It's okay,' says Elliot, to her surprise. 'I'm happy to go with the detective. I have nothing to hide.'

'I agree. It's best just to cooperate, son,' says Trevor, nodding encouragingly and slapping his son on the back, as though he's thanking him for a great meal, and not because Elliot is on the verge of being arrested.

Elliot brushes her cheek with his lips as he passes. 'I'll see you later. Don't worry, it's all just procedure.'

She can't speak. She watches him walk from the room followed by Watkins, leaving her alone in the kitchen – and in the house – with Trevor.

55

They stand there, speechless, for a few moments.

'Emilia . . .' Trevor begins moving towards her, still cradling his bad arm. She backs away, slowly, towards the door. She steels herself. If he threatens her in any way she'll hurt his arm. Or kick him in the groin. She'll –

'Emilia? Are you okay? You look terrified. Don't worry about Elliot. He'll be fine. The fact you can prove the bike was stolen means it could have been anyone using it to get away.'

It doesn't make sense to her. Why have the police asked Elliot to accompany them to the station when they had already explained that the bike was stolen? Did the man fleeing the scene match his description? Would he really kill to protect his dad even if he is lying about being Ash? The questions spin around and around in her mind.

'Maybe it was you who stole it,' she spits. 'You have a key. You know how to deactivate the alarm.' She backs out into the hallway. Not far from the front door.

He stops, his brow creasing. 'What are you talking about?' By now she's at the glass doors. Elliot left them open and she steps backwards into the porch. Trevor moves towards her again.

'I know everything. You've read my book. And so you'll know it too.' She frantically feels for the doorknob, relieved when her fingers find the cool brass handle. She turns it and almost falls over the threshold down the steps onto their driveway. She feels safer outside. She'll scream if he tries anything. Madge and Phil from next door will hear her.

But Trevor is staring at her in confusion. 'What do you mean?'

'The book! It's all true. The serial killer. What happened with Daisy and Ash. It was Louise. It was all Louise. Did you kill Louise to stop her talking?'

He looks like he's been punched and opens his mouth.

'Don't try to deny it, Trevor. It all adds up.'

He shakes his head. 'What has got into you?' His eyes are full of disappointment. 'I know you've been through a lot, but this takes the biscuit, it really does. I think it's best that I leave.'

She stares at him, trying to read him. But he's as inscrutable as her bloody husband.

'I'll get Elliot to drop back the rest of my things. I'll catch the bus.' He steps down onto the driveway and she moves away from him. He shakes his head at her again, and mutters something under his breath. Then he stomps off down the driveway and onto the street, out of sight.

The kitchen still smells of the cigarettes Trevor likes and that linger on his clothes, even though Elliot won't allow him to smoke in the house. She slumps at the kitchen table. Her world feels like it's imploded. It was bad enough when Jonas betrayed her all those years ago – she'd thought she'd never recover. Then she'd got her book deal and started writing about Miranda Moody, and as the character grew stronger, so did she. And then she met Elliot and had Wilfie and her life felt complete. Now a hand grenade has been thrown into her world for a second time, and she doesn't know whether she can cope with this fallout, which is so much worse than the last time. How is she going to explain it all to Jasmine and Wilfie?

It's hot in the kitchen, the sun streaming through the glass of the bifold doors, and she can feel sweat in the small of her back. She wants to cry, to scream. She feels like she's in the middle of a nightmare and she doesn't know what to do. She doesn't want to involve her parents. Louise is dead. She's already put Jonas and Kristin through so much. The only person she has left is Ottilie. She knows she's seeing her tomorrow but she can't wait. She needs to speak to her now.

Ottilie answers on the first ring. 'Hey, Mils.'

Emilia blurts it all out over the phone. Everything. Her suspicions about Trevor being the Doodle Man, Elliot being Ash and his bike being found at the scene. All of it. She can hear Ottilie's stunned silence after she's finished.

'Oh, Mils. Are you sure? I can't imagine Trev being a serial killer. I mean it's all just so . . . utterly hideous. You can't go around accusing people based on something Louise wrote . . . and Elliot told you he wasn't Ash. Don't you believe him?'

'I don't know what to believe,' Emilia snaps. 'I've been going over and over it in my head and there is no other explanation.'

'Where are the kids? Do you want me to come over? Oh, shit, I've got the cat.'

Emilia explains that Jasmine and Wilfie are away for the night.

'Then come here! You need a break, a change of scene. You can stay the night. We can talk it all through.'

'Okay.' She sniffs. 'I'll come over. I'll see you in an hour or so.'

She runs upstairs to her bedroom, her mind full of Elliot, imagining him in some dank interview room, being questioned over and over again.

She throws her pyjamas and underwear into a bag but can't find any socks. It's always cold in Ottilie's flat, even in summer. She turns to where Elliot keeps his socks instead and finds a chunky grey pair in his bedside cabinet. She's just about to close the drawer when something familiar catches her eye. It's a beanie, pushed down among the socks. She pulls it out. She's never seen Elliot wear a beanie. He's not the beanie-wearing kind. He always said it's because he's got too much hair, which made it look as though he had an odd-shaped head. She remembers them laughing about it once when they were in Harrods, not long after they first met, and trying on hats. She'd been doubled over in giggles as he tried to press the hat down over his spongy hair.

But that's not what has caught her attention. It's the badge on the front she recognizes. It's the same Scandinavian brand that the thief who stole Elliot's bike was wearing.

56

Another victim. This time a woman called Suzanne Cham-
bers, a forty-five-year-old who'd moved to Plymouth only a
year ago. That's two now in the last eighteen months, not
including Louise. Because I'm certain DC Greene's death is
something different entirely. It doesn't fit with the rest:
Greene wasn't stabbed, and the etching on her ankle was
drawn rather than carved. Something else about it all is nag-
ging at me too and I can't work out what it is.

'We've got to get this fucking bastard,' mutters Saunders
as we leave the bedsit that afternoon. It's only a few streets
away from where Lorraine Butterworth lives. Is that a
coincidence? 'I hope he's getting sloppier now. Two who live
so close together.'

'I hope so too,' I say, lighting a fag as we head to my car. I
unlock the Audi for him to get in and stand outside to finish
my cigarette.

I think about my call with Emilia Ward earlier and her
fear that the killer is her father-in-law. After our conversa-
tion I'd asked DC Michelle Doyle to run a background
check on Trevor but haven't had the results yet. We're also
working closely with the Met. They've sent someone to find

out where he was last night when the latest victim was killed and if he had an alibi.

I stub out my cigarette and am just about to get into the car when my phone rings. It's a colleague, Matheson. 'We've finally tracked down the supplier we've been after for months,' he says, sounding jubilant. 'Lee Fairbrother was picked up in France on another charge. But we've managed to get him to cooperate on that list we wanted.'

'Of where he's been selling his illegal stashes?'

'Yep.' Including menthol cigarettes.

'Excellent. Can you email it over to me and copy in Saunders?'

'Will do,' he says, and ends the call.

Saunders is already in the passenger seat when I slide behind the wheel. As I strap on my seatbelt I say, 'Just had a call from Matheson. He thinks this Lee Fairbrother has been selling menthol cigarettes to a newsagent near where Butterworth lives. He's made a list of suppliers, and if this newsagent is on it, you can go over and check if he recognizes Butterworth as a customer for these cigarettes, okay?'

Saunders sits up straighter. 'When will we have the list?'

'He's emailing it over now.' I give him the name of the shop and he sits scrolling through the email, then punches the air.

'It's here,' he says.

'Great. I'll drop you there now.' I take a left turn towards the centre of Plymouth. 'Also, I'm looking into whether DC Greene's mother, Jennifer Radcliffe, actually was a victim of *the praying-mantis murderer. In the notes I've been looking through there are a few inconsistencies.'*

Saunders lowers his phone. 'In what way?'

'The house wasn't broken into, like in all the other cases. The door was left open. She lived outside Plymouth in a village, and she wasn't tied up. It's made me wonder if perhaps it was just made to look like she was one of the praying-mantis murderer's victims. If I'm right, well . . .' I say before I turn to him and grin '. . . it changes everything.'

57

Emilia stares down at the beanie in her hands as she sinks to the floor. She pictures her husband creeping out of bed in the early hours of the morning, beanie disguising his hair, deactivating the alarm, tiptoeing out of the back door, around the side of the house, then letting himself in at the front door to 'steal' the bike. She buries her head in her hands and groans, the beanie falling to her lap, devastation ripping through her. She'd so wanted to believe him, but how else can she explain the beanie and what it must mean? She grabs it and shoves it into her bag, a sob escaping her lips. She needs to go to the police but she has to get out of the house first, just in case he comes back.

She picks herself up off the floor, hoists her bag over her shoulder and makes her way outside. Her whole world has imploded and she can't stop the tears rolling down her face. She stands, looking back up at her house: her beautiful, perfectly symmetrical home with the grand pillars either side of the front door and those pretty dormer windows protruding from the roof, like hooded eyes. How excited they'd been when the estate agent had first shown them around. 'It looks like the perfect child's drawing of a house,' Elliot had said, staring in awe at the sash windows and the whitewashed plaster. Her dream home. She'd really thought she had a second chance at happiness, after Jonas, but she's walked into something far, far worse.

She turns and makes her way down the tiled driveway and onto the main street, blinded by tears. She brushes them away as she heads down the hill towards the station. The sun is going down, streaking the sky a beautiful pink and teal blue. She can smell cut grass, sun-soaked pavements, a barbecue: people going about their lives, eating with family, enjoying a night out with friends, basking in the fact that it's a sunny bank-holiday weekend.

Forty minutes later, Ottilie is standing at the threshold of her apartment, enveloping her in a huge hug. Emilia doesn't have much recollection of the journey, or even of getting into the old-fashioned lift in her best friend's building.

'Oh, Mils,' she says, ushering her inside and through to the cosy sitting room. 'Come and sit down. I've made you a brandy.' Emilia sinks gratefully onto the large velvet sofa. She loves this room: inky blue walls, faded pink sofas, lots of gilt-edged photos and pictures on every surface and Persian rugs dotted about the hardwood floors.

A black and white cat with a pink nose mews at her from the rug. He has a tartan collar on and something blooms in the corner of her mind, some memory, but then it's gone and she's taking the amber liquid from Ottilie and downing it, enjoying the burning sensation at the back of her throat, and Ottilie is saying something about the cat, Smudge, and how she's looking after it for friends. She drops the animal onto Emilia, where it settles in the nook of her lap, opening and closing its fluffy paws into the fabric of her dress.

'He's gorgeous,' she says, stroking his soft coat and leaning back against the huge velvet cushions. She's suddenly utterly exhausted. She needs to tell Ottilie about the beanie she found, but she's so tired.

'It's a she. I've made up the spare room,' says Ottilie, fussing around her, tucking a throw either side of her legs, careful not to dislodge Smudge who is now asleep on Emilia's lap. Before long she feels her eyes grow heavy too.

When she opens them the room is dimly lit. She must have dozed off, which she's surprised at, but now she feels groggy, her tongue thick. She can hardly believe she was able to sleep with all the adrenaline that had been coursing around her body. Smudge is no longer on her lap, and Ottilie isn't in the room. It's gone ten. Perhaps she's gone to bed, although that's way too early for Ottilie. She's left a table lamp on in the corner that throws shadows on the opposite wall, but other than that the room is in darkness.

She gets up, no longer tired, anxiety bobbing to the

surface again. She still has on the denim jacket she'd grabbed on the way out of her front door, and reaches into the pocket for her phone. She can see she's had three missed calls. One from Trevor and two from DI Murray. Both have left voicemails. She stands at Ottilie's large bay window and parts the heavy curtains. The moon is up, fat and bright in the sky. She listens to the message from Trevor first, flinching at the desperation in his voice.

Where are you? I came back to the house to check on you and to see if you've heard from Elliot but you weren't there. I hope you're okay. Please call me.

Emilia listens to the other message from DI Murray.

Hi, Emilia. Please call me as soon as you can, it doesn't matter how late. I'll be at the station until stupid o'clock anyway.

Is ten too late? She decides to call anyway. She might have information about Elliot.

'Emilia? Where are you? Are you okay?' She sounds like she's driving.

'I'm staying with a friend tonight.' She closes the curtains and sinks back into the armchair.

She's about to tell DI Murray about Elliot and the beanie but the detective charges on before Emilia can speak. 'Listen, there's been a development here. The praying-mantis murderer struck again last night. A colleague followed up and Trevor's boss confirmed he had a fall at work yesterday. That Elliot came to pick him up. Was Trevor staying with you last night?'

'Yes.'

'Then Trevor can't be our guy.'

She exhales in relief. It feels like a huge weight has been lifted from her shoulders. Trevor can't be involved, so Elliot was telling the truth about not being Ash. There has to be another explanation for the beanie. Maybe he bought it a long time ago and didn't realize he had it in his drawer. It's a popular brand.

'There is a suspect we've had our eye on for over a year now. A Martin Butterworth. I mentioned him to you before.'

Emilia vaguely remembers. 'Right?'

'Anyway, we went to visit his son as we thought he might be Louise's Ash. He isn't. But his wife, Sharon, has just got back in touch with us. It turns out she went to university with Louise when she was known as Daisy. Small world.'

'Okay . . .'

'Except it wasn't at Exeter University. It was Leeds. Apparently Louise *was* at Exeter for a term, but left and took the rest of the year out before starting at Leeds the following year. Anyway, Sharon remembers Louise telling her she'd left Exeter because of an intense female friendship that went wrong. That's all she remembers her saying, but she rang to tell me, wondering if it could be important. So, I interviewed a few of Louise's colleagues and, apparently, she was bisexual. So I'm thinking we may have been looking in the wrong place. Ash could, in fact, be female.'

58

Emilia's head hurts and she feels groggy. 'It's like looking for a needle in a haystack,' she says. 'It could be anyone.'

'It could. But . . .' She hesitates, and Emilia wonders what she's not saying. 'Where are you now?'

'I'm with my friend, Ottilie Bentley-Gordon, in South Kensington.'

'Did you say Bentley-Gordon?'

'Yes. But I'll have to go home tomorrow.' She gathers the throw around her knees. She can't really concentrate. Too many thoughts and questions are crowding her brain and she's still worrying about Elliot's bike and she feels a bit disoriented from her sleep, a headache pressing behind her eyes.

She tries to recall the Daisy sections of *Her Last Chapter*. Apart from a few alterations, she never changed any of Louise's storyline about Daisy and Ash, even sticking to how it was written because she liked that it stood out from her own style. Now she thinks about it, Louise never specified pronouns. It was just Ash. But she'd always assumed Ash was a man.

DI Murray continues, 'I'm also considering that

Louise's mother wasn't killed by the praying-mantis murderer, like Louise thought. Maybe someone made it *look* that way. He had killed two other women at that point. It was very early on. It was just when the police – when I was realizing what kind of killer we were dealing with. No one knew about the carving of the praying-mantis head. Only those working on the case at the time.'

She takes a deep breath. 'Trevor? He was in the police back then. Was it him? Was he working on the case at the time?'

Trevor might not be the praying-mantis murderer, but he could have been having an affair with Louise's mum. Maybe he stabbed her, then made it look like she was murdered by the serial killer. But if that was the case then Elliot *is* Ash. She inwardly groans. She's just going around in circles.

DI Murray's voice breaks into her thoughts. 'No. At that time Trevor was working in Vice on another case.'

'So . . .' she says, confused '. . . what are you saying? Do you think you know who it is?'

'I'm keeping an open mind right now, but think back to your conversations with Louise. I suspect all this is still linked to someone you know. Why did Louise target you in particular?'

Emilia places a hand on her forehead. She feels hot, like she's coming down with something. 'I'm sorry, I can't think straight right now . . .'

'It's late. Just consider what I've said and I'll speak to

THE WOMAN WHO LIED

you tomorrow. Goodnight, Emilia. Try to get some sleep.' The line goes dead. Emilia sighs, clutching her mobile to her chest. She feels even more confused.

'Who was that?'

She looks up. Ottilie is standing in the doorway. She's wearing a long floral kimono with cream silk pyjamas underneath, her blonde hair flowing behind her. She has a mug in her hand, which she places next to Emilia. 'Hot chocolate. I thought you might need it.'

Emilia takes it gratefully, wrapping her hands around the mug. It's not hot, but warm, and she drinks it all. Then she looks up at Ottilie's expectant face. 'It was DI Murray.'

'What did she say?'

Ottilie steps back so that she's standing in the middle of the room. The cat suddenly trots into view and Ottilie bends down to scoop it up. The tartan collar. Emilia's heart drops as a memory surfaces: the photograph on Louise's mobile. She'd pushed it under her nose that night in the restaurant when she talked about getting a cat. She remembers it vividly because she'd been a bit envious, knowing how Elliot feels about pets. The image sharpens in her mind's eye: a photograph of a black cat with a tartan collar and a white bib. The pink nose. Hamish. A boy. And she's suddenly hit with the certainty that the cat Ottilie is holding in her arms is Louise's.

'Where did you get that cat?'

Ottilie looks up in surprise, the moonlight reflecting in her sea-glass eyes. 'What?'

'The cat?'

'It's my friends'. I told you.'

'It looks like Louise's.'

Ottilie frowns and flicks her hair over her shoulder. 'Louise had a cat?'

'Yes.' Emilia places her mug on the table and walks over to where Ottilie stands. 'A male cat. I'd forgotten. But now I think about it, nobody mentioned seeing a cat at Louise's flat at the scene, or afterwards.'

Ottilie shrugs. 'Maybe it ran off.'

'Can I see?' She reaches out to take the cat but Ottilie moves away.

'She's nervous of strangers.'

'I think you'll find that cat is a he, Ottilie.'

Ottilie's body stiffens but she keeps hold of the cat.

How could Emilia not have seen what was staring her in the face for so long? DI Murray's theory was right. A girl not a boy.

'You,' Emilia says, in alarm, as it dawns on her. 'You went to a university in Devon, didn't you? Just for one term. You never said why you left. You had a breakdown back in school. Oh, my God, it's you!' She'd been so blind not to see it before. 'It was you. It was *you* Louise wanted to get close to. That was why she targeted me.'

'What are you talking about?' But there is an edge to Ottilie's voice now.

'You're Ash.'

59

'What do you mean?' says Ottilie. Her expression is in shadow, but Emilia can tell by her body language that she knows exactly what she's talking about.

'Did you know Louise back at university? Daisy Louise Greene was her full name.'

Ottilie lets the cat slip from her arms and it scuttles from the room. 'From the Daisy chapters in your book? It sounds like a love affair. I've never had a love affair with a woman.'

'It could have been one-sided. Louise was bisexual. Maybe she had a crush on you, even if you did just see her as a friend.'

Ottilie folds her arms across her flimsy nightgown. 'I didn't know Louise, or Daisy, or whatever her name was. I've never met her.'

The thing about knowing someone for as long as Emilia has known Ottilie is that she recognizes every little tic, every expression, every body movement. And she knows, without a doubt, that Ottilie is lying.

'Ottilie, please tell me the truth.'

'You just don't want to think your husband is a

killer, do you? That's what all this is about. You'd prefer it was me.'

Emilia takes a step towards Ottilie who is backlit by the
hallway light. 'We have CCTV in the back garden. We have
footage of you stealing Elliot's bike,' she bluffs. 'I found the
beanie in Elliot's drawer.' She leans down and takes it out of
the bag at her feet and holds it up in the air. Her head swims
when she moves and the headache intensifies. 'Here. This is
the type Louise wears. Were you hoping to set up Louise by
making me think it was her who stole the bike? And then
what? Your plans changed to setting up Elliot?' She throws
it at Ottilie, who catches it with one hand.

'I don't know what you mean. I've never seen this
before.' She looks at it in disgust and chucks it onto the
armchair nearest to her.

'I know it was you who stole Elliot's bike. I recognized
you in the footage,' she lies. She hadn't. At the time she'd
thought it was Louise because of the hat.

Ottilie's eyes widen. The look on her face tells Emilia
everything she wants to know.

'Oh, Ottilie . . . why?'

She moves towards Emilia and for the second time in
the last few weeks she feels afraid of her friend. They'd
cuddled under the duvet together in their dormitory
when there had been a storm, consoled each other when
they were lonely, laughed so much in class that Ottilie
had wet herself. Ottilie had been more than a best friend.
She'd been like a sister.

'Daisy knew too much,' she mutters. 'She was a bloody psycho. I'd just gone over there to talk to her. That was all. To tell her I knew it was her behind what was happening to you.'

'She thought your father had killed her mum?'

Ottilie moves from one bare foot to the other, chewing her lip. Emilia can tell her friend is weighing up exactly how honest to be. 'Yes. He cheated on my lovely mum with Daisy's, and when my mum found out it destroyed her and she killed herself.' Her eyes flash, and Emilia shrinks back from her anger.

'You never said . . . You never told me. I mean, I knew she'd killed herself but not why.'

'I didn't want to tell anyone. It hurt too much.' She covers her face. 'This is all such a mess. Such a fucking mess.'

Emilia is rooted to the spot. She's torn between comforting her friend and running from the flat to call the police. She steps around Ottilie but her friend is too quick. Her hand shoots out and grabs Emilia. 'You can't leave, Mils. You'll go straight to the police. You'll put your husband first, like you always do.' She's holding the top of Emilia's arm so tightly it hurts. 'You've always put men first. That vain arsehole Jonas, and now Elliot.'

'He's my husband, Ottilie. He's a good man. You're the one who's murdered someone.'

'Sit down,' Ottilie says, inclining her head towards the sofa. Emilia does as she's told, rubbing the top of her arm, grateful that the fabric of her denim jacket took the brunt of her friend's pincer grasp. Ottilie perches next to her, the light from the lamp casting shadows on her beautiful face. Surely Ottilie wouldn't hurt her. But she killed Louise. The thought hits her like a punch to the stomach.

'Why did you do it?' Emilia asks her softly, her body angled towards her friend. It strikes her as almost funny that, from the outside, they look like they're just having a cosy chat.

Ottilie places her kimono over her knees calmly. Even in this light Emilia can see her friend's eyes are red-rimmed. 'I just wanted to talk to her. That's all. I'm sorry I took Elliot's bike. I suppose, at the time, I thought if you saw the bike was missing, you'd think it was Louise because of the beanie. Like I said, I didn't plan to kill her.'

Emilia stares at her in disbelief. It seems calculated. It's not as though Ottilie lives down the road. She would have had to travel to her house, probably by Uber, at dead of night, and stolen it, knowing that if she wore dark clothing and a hat she could be mistaken for a man. *For her husband, even.* But she nods and lets Ottilie speak.

'She got mad. Started accusing my dad. Said he'd struck again – she really believed he was this praying-mantis murderer. It's absurd, as if my dad would do something like that. I just wanted her to shut up. I tried to reason with her. You have to believe me, Mils.' She reaches over and grabs her hand. A tear slides down her unlined cheek. 'She was obsessed, not in the right frame of mind. She'd orchestrated the whole thing . . . She knew that as soon as I read your book I'd know it was about me. Even though, for the record, she'd embellished the whole romance side of things. She was only ever a friend to me at uni. And then, at your launch, I thought I saw her outside. She didn't come into the bookshop because she must have known I'd be there. But I recognized her even though she tried to hide from me. I nearly went outside to speak to her, to say hello, but she was with Kristin. When Kristin came back into the shop I asked her who she'd been with and she said your friend Louise, and I thought I'd been mistaken, but I had to see for myself. So I found out where she lived and followed her. She's hardly changed. As soon as I saw her I knew. It was Daisy. And everything else slotted into place.'

'Why not just tell me what was going on when you realized Louise was Daisy?'

'Because . . .' she says and chews her lip '. . . because I was worried that you'd start to think my dad was the killer too. And I didn't want you to get involved.'

'Why did she believe your dad was the killer?' Emilia asks gently. 'Because she recognized him when she stayed with you that Christmas?'

'Yes. The part in your book where Daisy stays with Ash that Christmas, that's what we did, except we were just friends. I don't know if she had a crush on me – she makes it sound far more romantic than it actually was. As far as I was concerned, we were just really good, close mates. Intense, I suppose, for that short space of time. I was going through my Emo phase, trying to reinvent myself, you know how it is, and we had so much in common, we just hit it off. And that Christmas, Daisy did visit me at my dad's home in Devon and that was when she recognized him. She confronted him, of course. Typical Daisy. And he denied it. He was on his second wife by then – her name was Stef – and I suppose he didn't want to look bad in front of her. Anyway, as soon as my dad told me what she'd done I ended our friendship and left the university. I hated my course anyway and the only real friend I'd made there was Daisy.'

Something about all this doesn't add up. Ottilie isn't telling her the full story. 'And you knew nothing of Louise's vendetta? That she was writing about your father – until you read my book?'

'No idea. The murderer had recently struck again after years and Daisy – *Louise* – was convinced it was my father. Unfortunately it coincided with my dad coming back to England last February. But he's been away since. My dad isn't a murderer.'

Emilia has only met Ottilie's dad a handful of times. She tries to imagine him in her mind's eye when he'd been younger. He had been handsome back then, with dark-blond hair, but whether or not he had a double crown, Emilia couldn't be sure. She'd never really noticed. He was just her best friend's dad. But now everything she knows shuffles in her mind. Could Louise have been right? Was Ottilie's dad the serial killer? Is that why he's been so hard to track down all these years, because he was living abroad? He was some kind of diplomat apparently who was once in the police force – which was when he must have worked with Trevor – but she doesn't know more than that.

'Daisy thought if everyone read the book someone would realize it was my dad they were looking for. My dad who was the killer. She was so convinced, but she was wrong. Like I say, when I grasped what was going on, I went to see her, to reason with her, to tell her she had to stop this obsession with my dad. To tell her to stop using you to get at me and my father. And it got out of hand. I didn't mean to kill her.'

Emilia's stomach falls. 'Ottilie . . .'

'I'll deny it. If you tell the police, I'll deny everything I've just told you.'

'But Elliot? Because of you, they think it's him!'

'I'm sorry about those things, Mils, I really am. I like Elliot, believe it or not. But I thought if I planted the beanie among Elliot's things . . .' She shakes her head. 'I just wanted it to take the spotlight away from me, that's all. The same with the bike. I didn't think they'd actually arrest him . . . Anyway, they'll let Elliot go. They won't have anything more on him.'

'You say you don't believe your father is the praying-mantis murderer – but do you think he might have killed

Louise's mum and made it look like she was another of the serial killer's victims?'

'Of course not. My dad was a policeman at the time. A commissioner. Very high up. He'd never do that. I think Louise's mum was murdered by that serial killer. Daisy, as a kid, got confused. Thought the man she saw – my father – leaving the house that night came back and killed her mother. She'd put two and two together and come up with five. She was out to get my dad. And he'd done nothing wrong – except cheat on his wife.'

'What about the marking on Louise's ankle?'

Ottilie's eyes narrow. 'After I realized what I'd done, I had to make it look like it was just another incident from your books.'

'But . . .'

'Have you been fucking listening, Mils?'

Emilia flinches.

She's still clasping Emilia's hand and now she grips it a little bit tighter. 'Like I said, I was so angry with her, involving you like she had. I knew what it could do to your reputation as a writer if it got out. You basically stole someone else's story.'

'But she gave it to me, willingly.'

'She's dead, though, isn't she? So she can't tell anyone that. Everyone will assume you've stolen it. Have you told your editor yet? I bet you haven't. Always did like to stick your head in the sand, didn't you? Like the way you refused to see what a bitch Kristin was and how she manipulated you. Or that Jonas is a cheating piece of shit. Or that Daisy was stalking you.'

'There's nothing wrong with trying to think the best of people,' Emilia says quietly.

Ottilie's face softens. 'I know, darling Mils. And I love you for that.' She sighs, still clutching Emilia's hand, which has now started to sweat. 'The problem is I've been fucked up since the age of fourteen.' Ottilie is still talking in a calm voice but there is a manic edge to her tone now. 'Remember when I had the breakdown and I was off school for half a term?'

'Of course.' Ottilie had gone home for the weekend to stay with her dad at his holiday home in Devon, and she'd seemed perfectly fine that Friday night. She'd been looking forward to seeing her dad because she hadn't seen him since Christmas and by then it was February. She hadn't returned on the Monday and was away for the rest of the term. Emilia had written to her, begging her to reply, but she never did. The only information the teachers would give her was that Ottilie wasn't well.

'I do remember. I'd been sick with worry about you.'

'Ah, sweet.'

Emilia tries not to react to Ottilie's obvious sarcasm.

Ottilie hadn't returned to school until after the Easter holidays, acting as though nothing had happened. When Emilia had questioned her about it, she alluded to it as being delayed grief at her mother's death the year before and Emilia had bought it. Had she only seen what she wanted to see?

'I've never told you the truth about what really caused the breakdown.'

Emilia holds her breath.

'That was the weekend I found out that my dad had been banging Daisy's mum for years. While he'd been married to mine. That was the weekend I found all their sordid love letters and he'd admitted it all. It had pushed my amazing mum over the edge.' She laughs bitterly. 'Daisy's mum, this Jennifer, she was our cleaner. Can you believe it? I suppose that day, when I confronted Daisy, well, I saw red because I remembered what her mother did. She was accusing my father of being a killer when he isn't, yet her mother was. Her mother was responsible for my mother's death.'

'Ottilie, you need to go to the police. Tell them all this. It was manslaughter, really, if you think about it.' Emilia isn't quite sure if that's true. She believes it was premeditated. For whatever reason, on that day when Ottilie had stolen Elliot's bike, she'd had one thing on her mind, and that was to kill Louise. And then she'd tried to set up Elliot. How had she even got in that night? Emilia knows she didn't leave the door unlocked. 'Do you have a key?' she asks. 'To my house?'

Ottilie doesn't say anything, just stares at Emilia. Did she get a key cut when she came to stay? She would know the code for the alarm too.

Her head is swimming and she has an unpleasant taste in her mouth. From her peripheral vision she notices

Hamish saunter back into the room and rub himself against Ottilie's leg.

'Why did you take Louise's cat?'

Ottilie glances at the cat beside her feet. But she doesn't release Emilia's hand. 'I couldn't leave the poor thing behind. I'm not a monster!'

Emilia stares at her friend in disbelief. Who is this person who can kill a woman and save an animal at the same time?

'Ottilie,' she presses gently, 'let's call the police. DI Murray is very sympathetic. She'll –'

'No!' Ottilie starts sobbing then, her body shuddering. 'I can't go to prison, Mils. You know that. I wouldn't cope in prison.'

'You might get diminished responsibility. All that pent-up anger and emotion. You could get some help.'

Ottilie squeezes Emilia's hand. 'I don't think so.'

'Please, Ottilie. You can make this right. You need to tell the truth.' She goes to stand up but Ottilie yanks on her hand so hard that she's forced back onto the sofa.

'You know I love you, Mils. You know that, right? It's important you know that.'

'Of course.' Emilia swallows her anxiety. 'Of course I know that.'

'Good.' Ottilie's grip intensifies and one of her hot tears splashes onto the back of Emilia's hand. 'I'm so sorry. I never wanted it to come to this. But I can't let you leave.'

60

We are half an hour away from London when Saunders gets the call. He's sitting beside me in the passenger seat.

'That's brilliant news, thanks, mate. Yes, yes, she's here. I'll tell her.' He ends the call and stares at me, excitement radiating from him like heat. 'Oh, my God, ma'am, we've got him. After all this time, we've got him. They've arrested him. The fucker was trying to flee the country.'

I laugh in relief and jubilation. Prison must have done something to Martin Butterworth's brain because he made a stupid mistake when he killed his latest victim, Suzanne Chambers. A tiny spot of blood that wasn't the victim's was found at the scene, on the hem of her nightdress. Martin Butterworth's DNA is in the database, and it matched. Something as simple as that. He must have cut himself when he was carving the insect's head on Suzanne's ankle. Coupled with the information Saunders has from the newsagent, who confirmed he sold menthol cigarettes to Butterworth, we've nailed the bastard. After all these years and eight victims. But we haven't got him for Louise yet. I'm convinced someone else killed her.

I've guessed that Saunders was in a relationship with

Louise. They'd met on a training day and it started there. I had it confirmed by one of Louise's colleagues, who had also been at the event. That was why he'd run from the crime scene that day, and pretended he had a stomach bug. He'd recognized Louise. And I suspect it was him who told her that the praying-mantis murderer was back, setting in motion the chain of events that has led us here. I'll talk to him about it another time, when we're back in Plymouth and after we've seen Butterworth locked up. But not now. Now I'll let him have his moment.

No lie-ins for us on a Sunday morning. Saunders is already on the train back to Devon to interview Martin Butterworth now an arrest has been made. I will join him later but first I want to speak to Emilia Ward again. And also her friend Ottilie Bentley-Gordon. I recognized the name when I spoke to Emilia last night. Her father, Charles Bentley-Gordon, was my boss twenty-five years ago when the praying-mantis murderer started killing, before he went into diplomatic service abroad. I believe this was the man Louise suspected was having an affair with her mother. His daughter, Ottilie, has to be Ash. I've tried to call Emilia several times and have left messages but there is no answer. I've also been to her house but it's empty. Remembering that she said she was staying with Ottilie last night, I find her address in High Street Kensington – which is under her father's name – and drive over there. I forget how long it takes to travel anywhere in London. I'm

used to the relatively open roads of Devon but here it takes
me nearly an hour to drive a few miles. When I pull up in
a side road and find Ottilie's flat it's nearly 11 a.m.

Ottilie's apartment is in a beautiful white stone-
pillared building with a black front door. There is a
concierge at a desk in the foyer and a lovely old-fashioned
wooden lift in the middle that reminds me of the ones in
old movies. He smiles at me as I enter. I show him my
identification and tell him I'm here to see Ottilie.

'Oh, she left late last night. Or, rather, in the early hours
of this morning, according to the night manager.'

'What time?'

'Around two a.m. She has a friend staying. She's still
there, apparently.'

I push down an uneasy feeling. 'What number is her
apartment?'

'Seven.'

I don't wait for the lift, instead I run up the back stairs,
out of breath by the time I get to Ottilie's apartment on the
second floor. I knock on the door but, as I'd thought, there's
no answer. I'm sure I can hear a cat miaowing behind the
closed door. I rap my knuckles again and call Emilia's name.
An elderly woman from the next flat opens her door, her
face screwed up in annoyance. 'What's all the racket?'

I explain who I am and show her my police ID card. 'I
might have to kick the door down,' I say. 'I'm worried about
the person inside.'

'No, don't do that. Wait.' She disappears back inside the

flat. I can smell something cooking. She emerges again, holding a key. 'We all swapped in case we locked ourselves out.'

'Fine. Thanks. Please, open the door.'

She takes her time about it, and just when I'm about to wrestle the key from her and do it myself the door swings open. She steps aside and I rush in. I can sense the old woman behind me as I hurry through the square hallway into the galley kitchen. It's empty. So are the bedrooms, one of which has all the drawers and wardrobes open, with clothes flung on the bed and floor.

'Emilia,' I call, running now into the living room, pushing open the door. The room is dark, the heavy curtains tightly drawn, but in the corner by the radiator there is a body on the floor.

The old woman turns the overhead light on and gasps.

'Call an ambulance,' I say, rushing over to where Emilia lies fully dressed. She's on her side, her eyes closed, and she would have looked like she'd just fallen asleep if it wasn't for the unnatural pallor. Deathly pale, blue-tinged lips. I kneel down and try to find a pulse, fearing I'm already too late.

61

The first person she sees when she opens her eyes is Elliot, and she wonders if she's dead. Or dreaming. She blinks a few times, his face coming into focus as he looms over her.

'She's awake,' cries a familiar voice and she turns her head to see Wilfie and Jasmine on the other side of the bed. They're all beaming at her but it looks as though both her children have been crying.

'It's all right, love, you're safe,' says Elliot. He's holding her hand, reminding her of her last memory: Ottilie's hand, warm and sweaty in her own.

Her mouth feels dry and she tries to speak. 'Here, have a sip of this,' says Elliot, gently guiding a clear cup of water towards her.

She takes a sip. 'Where am I?'

'You're in the hospital. But you're okay. You're going to be fine.' The relief in his voice is evident and she wonders if there was a point when they didn't know that this would be the case. She tries to sit up but discovers she can't. Elliot pushes a button on the bed and it moves so that she's more upright. 'Is that better?'

She squeezes his hand. 'You're out . . .' she manages.

And that's when she sees the concerned faces of her parents behind her children. She blinks again.

'We were all so worried,' her mother says, patting the regulation hospital blanket over her knees. 'You've been out for nearly twenty-four hours.'

Drugged. Ottilie had drugged the hot chocolate she'd given her. No wonder she'd felt so out of it. That was why her thoughts had been all over the place. Had Ottilie been planning to kill her but hadn't given her enough?

'Where's Ottilie?'

'She's . . . gone, sweetheart,' says Elliot. 'The police are looking for her, but she's probably already left the country.'

Emilia can feel tears on her face. Elliot bends over and kisses her forehead. 'You gave us quite the scare. Thank goodness you're okay.'

She reaches out, her fingers finding Wilfie's soft curls and then Jasmine's hand. 'I'm not going anywhere,' she says.

She has to stay in hospital for a few days to check that she doesn't have organ damage. She can hear the traffic outside, the beep of horns, the blare of sirens, and it's strangely comforting. She still feels woozy from whatever drug Ottilie had given her – the doctors had told her, but it had a long name and Emilia can't remember in her haze, but apparently it's easy to get on prescription.

Elliot has stayed with her while her parents took the children home. She hadn't wanted to let Wilfie or Jasmine out of her sight, but she could see they were tired and, once they'd understood she'd be okay, bored. What if Ottilie came back to finish her off? She expresses this fear to Elliot, who hasn't left her side since she was brought in, so the nurses have told her.

'There is no way she'd risk coming back to London,' he says. 'She'll be far away by now.'

She tells him about the beanie. 'Ottilie planted it in the house. I still can't believe it was her who killed Louise. I knew it couldn't have been you.'

'How could you ever have thought it was me, with my trustworthy face?' he jokes, but she can see the toll the last few days, weeks and months have taken on him. He's aged and she knows she has too. 'I'm just so thankful you're okay.'

Then she remembers the cat. 'Hamish. The cat. Where is he?'

'Don't worry, we've got the cat. DI Murray found him in Ottilie's apartment after you were taken away in the ambulance. I said we'd look after him.'

She stares at Elliot in shock. 'But you hate pets.'

'I don't hate pets.' He laughs. 'And just because I'm a neat freak I don't expect you to be too.' His voice catches. 'It's my issue, Em. Not yours. Or the kids'. It just gives me the feeling of control, I suppose, of safety. It's silly . . .'

She squeezes his hand, remembering the anxiety that

sits beneath his surface, which he tries so hard to control, more even than she'd realized. 'It isn't silly. I get it.' She sighs, picturing Ottilie and their last conversation. A tear slips down her cheek. 'I'm not great at choosing friends, am I?' First Kristin, then Ottilie and Louise. Although Louise, it seems, chose her. She closes her eyes. Her head hurts and, despite everything Ottilie has done, grief sits heavily on her chest. She's grieving for the old Ottilie. The person Emilia had always thought she was.

She must have dozed off because when she wakes up the room is dim and Elliot isn't beside her bed. Instead, a woman sits on the chair, flicking through a magazine. It's DI Murray.

She moves her chair closer. 'Hi, Emilia, how are you feeling?'

'Still a bit groggy. What day is it?'

'Monday. Did Elliot tell you what happened?'

'That you found me? Yes, he did. I can't thank you enough. You probably saved my life.'

DI Murray grins. It softens her. 'I'm sorry about Ottilie. And I'm sorry it took me a while to realize what was going on.'

'I'm relieved that you did, and that Elliot was released. And poor Trevor. I owe him an apology.'

'I'm sure he'll understand. I can see why you thought it would be him. I did too for a bit. We've caught the praying-mantis murderer. A man named Martin Butterworth.'

She remembers DI Murray mentioning him before. 'So it was him who killed Louise's mum?'

DI Murray hesitates. 'Ottilie's father did have an affair with Louise's mother. That much is true. We've spoken to him and he's admitted it. He left the force not long after Jennifer Radcliffe was murdered. Took up a post abroad when Ottilie recovered from her breakdown and went back to boarding school, only returning to the UK now and again, staying in his Devon house or in London when he did. Louise wasn't wrong about seeing him with her mother. But in terms of the murder, it bothered us that Jennifer wasn't tied up or that her house hadn't been broken into, despite other aspects matching the serial killer. For a while I wondered if it had been the work of someone else, just trying to make it look like she was a victim of the serial killer. But now I'm not so sure. It's a possibility, of course, but I think what probably happened is that Charles left Jennifer that night, maybe not locking the door behind him, and Martin Butterworth was watching the house, let himself in and killed her while poor Louise was upstairs asleep. That's why there was no sign of a break-in, like with the other cases. Maybe he didn't have time to tie her up. I don't know. Anyway, Butterworth is denying all of it but we have proof of the latest murder, at least, thanks to his DNA found at the scene. But the markings tie all of the crimes together, so we hope it stands up in front of a jury.'

'So all those years Louise wrongly believed Charles

was the killer, not only of her mother but of the other women too?'

'Yes. But he was untouchable. Living abroad. She tracked down Ottilie instead, and when she found out she was a friend of yours she inveigled her way into your life.'

'I wonder if she always planned to get me to write about it. Or whether that was just luck.'

DI Murray shifts in her chair. 'I think she used you to get to Ottilie at first, and then, when she learned the murderer had struck again – thanks to Saunders telling her about it – she thought she needed to act. And luckily that coincided with you having a dry patch creatively. But there's something else that the post-mortem threw up. Louise was gravely ill.'

Emilia's heart twists. 'What was wrong with her?'

'She was diagnosed with an inoperable brain tumour, six months ago. She knew she didn't have much time. Which might explain why she chose to harass you like she did, to escalate matters, to get your new book national press coverage, to try to discover her mother's killer as soon as she could. I'm not saying it was an excuse for what she did, but her illness wouldn't have helped her think rationally.'

Tears press against Emilia's eyelids. She gathers the blanket in her hands. 'I had no idea.' She remembers the last time she saw Louise. How tired and pale she looked. How she said she was going to work but was wearing casual clothes.

'Nobody did. Not even Saunders.'

'And Ottilie? Will they catch her, do you think?'

DI Murray lets out a long sigh. 'I don't know. I hope so. But it depends where she's gone. She had a whole ten hours' head start to get away before you were discovered.' She stands up. 'Anyway, Emilia, I have to go, but keep writing, won't you? I enjoy your books, but please be careful what you write about next time.'

Emilia can't help but laugh. She's got a lot of explaining to do to her editor and agent. But she can't think about that now. She has to concentrate on getting better so she can return home and be with her family.

Epilogue

Three months later

It's a Saturday morning at the beginning of September when a brown A5 envelope lands on the doormat. At first Emilia thinks it's a bill of some kind. Or from HMRC, one of her bugbears. Elliot is in the kitchen, singing along to Radio X while making pancakes, Jasmine is lounging on the sofa with Hamish curled up in her lap, and Wilfie is kicking a ball about in the garden with their new puppy. It's a typical Saturday, something Emilia appreciates more than ever after the turmoil of the last year.

After she was discharged from hospital it took a few weeks to get her health – mental and physical – back to where it had been. She was honest with her editor and Drummond about *Her Last Chapter*, and they have given her extra time to rewrite Daisy and Ash's sub-plot and to change the specifics of the serial killer storyline so that it no longer resembles the praying-mantis murders. Martin Butterworth pleaded not guilty to all charges, and she didn't want to do anything that could jeopardize the trial that was due early next year. It's taken a while to get her relationship with Jonas and Kristin back on track. Kristin admitted that she'd suspected Louise was ill after seeing her nearly collapse when they were standing outside the bookshop on the night of her launch. That was what their heated discussion had been about. Kristin, in her tipsy state, had been trying to persuade Louise to tell Emilia, but Louise had denied she was unwell.

Emilia also had some serious making up to do with Trevor, but she feels now that they're moving forward.

She is closer to Elliot than ever before. He was hurt that she hadn't been honest with him about Louise and the story from the start, and she admitted that she felt she couldn't be less than perfect in his eyes, or he might leave her. He assured her he didn't care about that stuff. The kids' drawings from the den had moved to the fridge, and she let herself relax for the first time since she'd met him. They even got a golden retriever puppy called Brambles, much to Wilfie's delight, and Emilia appreciated how Elliot tried not to wince when the dog got muddy paw prints on their parquet floors or chewed up his favourite pair of trainers. Hamish is learning to love Brambles too.

Despite everything, she grieved for Ottilie after she did her moonlight flit. A large part of her hates her for what she has done, but it's hard to forget all those years when she was the closest person to Emilia. She had loved her fiercely and she has mourned her as if she has died. And the Ottilie she thought she knew is dead.

During the last few months she has replayed their final conversation over and over in her mind, like a well-worn tape. Ottilie had told her she only sees what she wants to see, and she wonders if that's true.

If only Emilia had seen what was really going on she might have been able to prevent it all. Louise was desperate, ill, wanting to do whatever she could to find out who had killed her mother before it was too late. Emilia can't forgive Louise for what she did, but she can understand it, empathize even, now that it's all behind her. Now that she's safe.

Emilia picks up the envelope and rips it open without thinking, surprised when she sees a slip of A4 paper folded in two, typed out like a manuscript. And she realizes that it's a story, not a letter, as she'd first thought. She slumps onto the bottom stair, still in her dressing gown, and begins to read.

> *Let me tell you a story. Except this one is true. It's about a woman who lied. And a woman who loved. It's about betrayal and revenge. It's about a young girl – let's call her Liza – who went home for the weekend, aged just fourteen, and found out that the father she had adored had cheated on the mother she had adored. She found out that the mother was so distraught by this betrayal that she stood on a railway line and waited until a train came. She found out that everything she'd believed in, everything she had loved, had been destroyed and that one woman was to*

THE WOMAN WHO LIED

blame. A woman who came into the family home on the pretence of cleaning but really to steal another woman's husband. So Liza took her own revenge. She walked the half-mile to the thieving woman's home, that cold February night – Valentine's Day, would you believe? – in the wind and rain and she confronted her. And then, in a fit of anger, she took a knife from the butcher's block on the worktop and stabbed her, just once but in the wrong place. In a fatal place. Her father came and he helped the young Liza but he was conflicted because he loved his only child and he wanted to protect her. So he carefully carved the woman's flesh to match that of a killer he knew was terrorizing the locals and everyone thought the thieving woman was just another victim. And Liza, poor Liza, was taken to an institution to get better. But she was never better because this massive secret, this 'bad thing', festered inside her until she met the daughter, years later, except they couldn't be friends because of who their parents had been. So the resentment grew and grew, like a disease, making her even more rotten. But one thing made Liza less unhappy, less rotten and that was you. She loved you, you see. Like a sister. She'll think of you often and hope that you're happy. And she wants to say how sorry she is. For all of it. And that she will miss you for the rest of her life.

Some stories deserve to be told. Does this one?

A shiver runs down Emilia's spine and she reads it through again. She checks the envelope for the postage.

Somewhere in Central America by the look of it. Her hand trembles. This is basically a confession. She could take it to the police. Or she could destroy it.

She hears Elliot in the kitchen singing along to Oasis, every now and again breaking off from 'Champagne Supernova' to call a word of encouragement to Wilfie in the garden. Brambles barks playfully, and she imagines the puppy lolloping across the grass with his uncoordinated legs, joining in. She knows Jasmine is on the sofa with the cat on her lap, probably watching them with an amused expression while simultaneously texting Nancy, her best friend.

Her best friend.

Ottilie had drugged her and left her to die, that was the commonly held belief. Yet the doctors had told her the amount of the drug in her body was only enough to knock her out, not to kill her.

Some stories deserve to be told. Does this one?

Emilia sighs, tearing Ottilie's story into tiny shreds, then goes to join her family in the kitchen.

Acknowledgments

This has been a very special year for me professionally, and I owe it all to the wonderful team at Penguin Michael Joseph, who really have gone above and beyond. A HUGE thank you to the wonderful Maxine Hitchcock and Clare Bowron, who make my books so much better than they would have been, and whose edits, comments, notes and encouragement on *The Woman Who Lied* have been invaluable. Also to the rest of the amazing team: Emma Plater, Ellie Morley, Vicky Photiou, Ella Watkins, Beatrix McIntyre, Deirdre O'Connell, Hannah Padgham and Katie Corcoran. To Lee Motley, for the beautiful and striking book jackets, to Stella Newing and the audio team, who do such a fantastic job on the audio books, and to Hazel Orme, for her meticulous copy-edits as well as her enthusiasm and kind words. I'm so grateful to you all.

To Juliet Mushens, the most talented, hardworking, kind and supportive agent in the world. It's been ten years now that we've worked together and she has taken my career from strength to strength. She really is the agent of dreams! I'm also indebted to Liza DeBlock,

ACKNOWLEDGMENTS

Kiya Evans, Rachel Neely and Catriona Fida—the rest of the brilliant team at Mushens Entertainment.

To my foreign publishers, in particular to Eva Schubert and Duygu Maus at Penguin Verlag in Germany and Sarah Stein at Harper US and HarperCollins Canada.

To my West Country pals, Tim Weaver, Gilly Macmillan, C. L. Taylor and Cate Ray for all the laughs, support, texts and lunches. I couldn't be without you, guys! And to the lovely L. V. Matthews and Kate Gray for all the word races and encouragement.

To all the authors who have given their time so generously to read and quote for my books over the years.

To the booksellers and librarians for getting my books into readers' hands, and to book bloggers for the reviews, cover reveals, and so much more. I'm so grateful.

To the readers who have bought copies of my books, for the kind messages and reviews. I couldn't do this job without you!

Thank you as always to my mum, dad and sister, Samantha, and to my in-laws and step-family.

To my children, Claudia and Isaac, who make me so proud every day.

And to my husband, Ty, on our twentieth year married. This book is for you.

About the Author

Claire Douglas is the *Sunday Times* number-one best-selling author of eight stand-alone novels: *The Sisters, Local Girl Missing, Last Seen Alive, Do Not Disturb, Then She Vanishes, Just Like the Other Girls, The Couple at Number 9*, and *The Girls Who Disappeared*. Her books have sold more than a million copies in the United Kingdom and have been published worldwide.

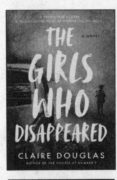
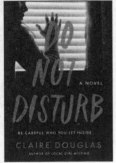